They Forged
The Signature of God

by
Viriato Sención

translated by
Asa Zatz

Curbstone Press

Printed in the U.S. on acid-free paper by BookCrafters
Cover design: Les Kanturek

Curbstone Press is a 501(c)(3) nonprofit publishing house whose operations are supported in part by private donations and by grants from ADCO Foundation, J. Walton Bissell Foundation, Inc., Witter Bynner Foundation for Poetry, Inc., Connecticut Commission on the Arts, Connecticut Arts Endowment Fund, The Ford Foundation, The Greater Hartford Arts Council, Lannan Foundation, LEF Foundation, Lila Wallace-Reader's Digest Literary Publishers Marketing Development Program, administered by the Council of Literary Magazines and Presses, The Andrew W. Mellon Foundation, National Endowment for the Arts-Literature, National Endowment for the Arts-International Projects Initiative and The Plumsock Fund.

Library of Congress Cataloging-in-Publication Data

Sención, Viriato, 1941-
    [Los que falsificaron la firma de Dios. English]
    They forged the signature of God / by Viriato Sención : translated by Asa Zatz. — 1st ed.
        p.   cm.
    ISBN 1-880684-33-0
    1. Zatz, Asa.   II. Title.
PQ7409.2.S38L613   1995
863—dc20   95-41604

published by
CURBSTONE PRESS   321 Jackson Street   Willimantic, CT 06226

They Forged the Signature of God

CURBSTONE PRESS, INC.

is a non-profit publishing house dedicated to literature that reflects a commitment to social change, with an emphasis on contemporary writing from Latin America and Latino communities in the United States. Curbstone presents writers who give voice to the unheard in a language that goes beyond denunciation to celebrate, honor and teach. Curbstone builds bridges between its writers and the public – from inner-city to rural areas, colleges to community centers, children to adults. Curbstone seeks out the highest aesthetic expression of the dedication to human rights and intercultural understanding: poetry, fiction, testimonies, photography.

This mission requires more than just producing books. It requires ensuring that as many people as possible know about these books and read them. To achieve this, a large portion of Curbstone's schedule is dedicated to arranging tours and programs for its authors, working with public school and university teachers to enrich curricula, reaching out to underserved audiences by donating books and conducting readings and community programs, and promoting discussion in the media. It is only through these combined efforts that literature can truly make a difference.

Curbstone Press, like all non-profit presses, depends on the support of individuals, foundations, and government agencies to bring you, the reader, works of literary merit and social significance which might not find a place in profit-driven publishing channels. Our sincere thanks to the many individuals who support this endeavor and to the following foundations and government agencies: ADCO Foundation, J. Walton Bissell Foundation, Inc., Witter Bynner Foundation for Poetry, Inc., Connecticut Commission on the Arts, Connecticut Arts Endowment Fund, Ford Foundation, Lannan Foundation, LEF Foundation, Lila Wallace-Reader's Digest Fund, The Andrew W. Mellon Foundation, National Endowment for the Arts, and The Plumsock Fund.

Please support Curbstone's efforts to present the diverse voices and views that make our culture richer. Tax-deductible donations can be made to Curbstone Press, 321 Jackson Street, Willimantic, Connecticut 06226. Telephone: (203) 423-5110.

PART ONE

And God saw the light,
that it was good; and God
divided the light from the
darkness.
Genesis

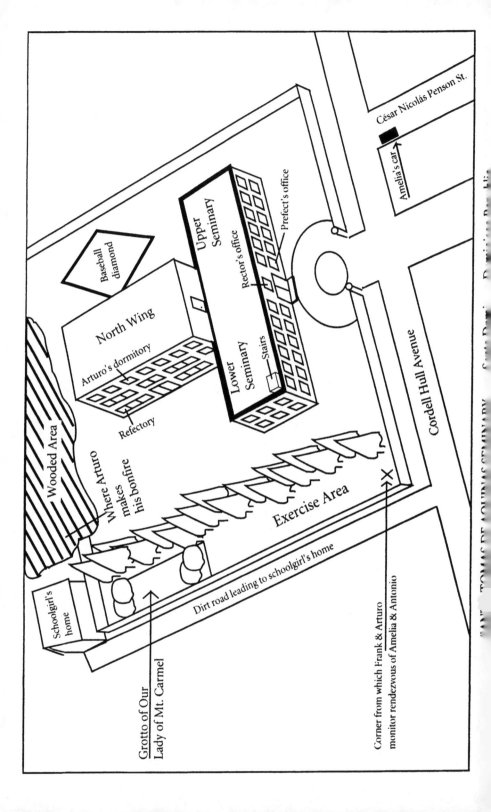

CANT. TOMÁS DE AQUINAS SEMINARY   Santo Domingo   Dominican Republic

I

The walls of the government building were sweating molten lead as a baby-faced youth, Antonio Bell, barely fourteen years old, huddled in a black cassock, sat sweltering and cracking his knuckles incessantly. He had been thrown into prison a month before and had no idea why he should now have been taken out of his cell and brought to the Presidential Palace. He was told: "Put this cassock on, you Communist piece of shit, sit down there and don't move, you haven't got much longer to live."

A pair of bull-necked policemen with rifles menaced him, their eyes like hot coals. Blinded by the stream of sweat running down his forehead, by the hellish August sun pouring through the sealed windows, by the brutal glare of a light bulb hanging from the ceiling, Antonio had been in that room for well over an hour. It was completely empty except for the chair of which he seemed a hinged part.

"What do you people have to say about this enemy of my government who has been taught by priests at your seminary how to make bombs and carry out acts of sabotage for sowing terror throughout the nation?"

There were other people in the room now. Clustered together in a corner like chickens confronted by a weasel stood the bishop, the Papal Nuncio, the Rector of the Seminary and two other priests, one of them the Seminary Prefect. In the center, Tirano, accompanied as usual by a short, flabby individual whose eyes wore a studied expression of weariness as he surveyed the scene through expensive eyeglasses that lent authenticity to his highly regarded intellectual powers. This was the well-known Dr. Mario Ramos, a mournful looking functionary who gave an impression of timid foolishness.

The clerics had been shunted into the room a few minutes before by the same police who had brought Antonio there. "Stay in here and wait," they ordered in gruff, aggressive tones as they went out. The boy felt in a way relieved to see the priests and for the first time able to summon the necessary will power to stand up, but when he tried to address them they glared at him with hostility so intense that he was flung back into his chair. Antonio sat down with such a crash that the guards outside opened the door, looked in, and upon seeing nothing amiss shut it again. The priests turned their backs on him, standing paralyzed in total silence.

It was at this point that Tirano had made his entrance in one swoop to the center of the room, stiff, arrogant, dazzling in full-dress Generalissimo uniform, his chest covered with medals.

The reverend fathers answered as though they had rehearsed their replies from the moment they had received Dr. Mario Ramos's notification to appear at the Presidential Palace. In response to Tirano's venomous questioning they chorused that they had not the slightest hint of such a thing; that, bless their souls, how could His Excellency have the slightest doubt as to the Church's support of his government's great achievements, and adding that the poor devil, who had been under the seminary's benevolent care for some time, was simply crazy, yes, literally a lunatic suffering from hallucinations. Blurting out the same words, they kept insisting that he was a lunatic and were apparently prepared to keep repeating it indefinitely had Tirano not cut them short, brandishing a finger thick as a cudgel at them, and shouting. "Get him out of here. He is forbidden ever to set foot outside the Seminary grounds till he is ordained. You will all be held responsible for carrying out that order." And, pointing to his companion, he added, "Dr. Ramos will keep me informed on a regular basis."

Satisfied that the priests had followed his advice—to "declare the boy insane before the Generalissimo and be ready to prove it in due course"—Dr. Ramos turned slowly towards the expectant priests and, exaggerating his fool's expression, indicated with an almost imperceptible movement of his right hand that they should remove the boy. Tirano continued to hear the interminable litany of "Yes, Your Excellency..." even after he had moved some distance down the hall. Meanwhile, Antonio Bell, in utter despair, interpreted the expressions on the faces of his new keepers in the most foreboding way, as if they had already said to him, "You just wait, you'll be getting yours from now on."

Tirano entered his office, Dr. Mario Ramos at his heels. He sat down but Dr. Ramos remained standing, hands clasped over his abdomen, head tilted slightly to the right.

"Have a seat, Dr. Ramos," Tirano ordered, his voice oozing satisfaction. "I believe your advice was most apt, the best thing that could have been done. But saying that the terrorist was crazy...! Hey, that was really good! They're crazy themselves. What remains to be seen is how those ingrates will settle accounts with their lunatic. Did you see the look on their faces, Doctor? As though I was turning them over to the very devil."

Dr. Ramos crossed and uncrossed his legs and finally muttered darkly, the words slowly fighting their way out of his almost closed mouth, "They're dangerous, Boss, dangerous. They must be handled with great tact."

Lips curled in a disdainful smirk, Tirano observed Dr. Ramos at some length. In anyone else's presence, he would at the same moment certainly have grabbed his testicles with both hands to indicate that only he was dangerous. However, Tirano maintained a certain reserve before the enigmatic Dr. Ramos. After discussing other matters, when the Doctor considered the Boss's agenda to have been covered, he rose, asked to be excused, and took leave with a prolonged bow.

Tirano followed him with his eyes, observing the tired puppet steps, always slow and unvarying regardless of circumstances. His thoughts accompanied him out, picturing him as he crossed the reception room, making his way through the long hallways... He knew for certain that he would not stop before he reached his office located on the same floor, perhaps nodding a cold, indifferent greeting on his way... He had served him for twenty-eight years and never for a moment during that time had Tirano doubted his loyalty. He was highly effective—no question about it— his soundest adviser. Furthermore, he had risen through the ranks to his present position, clashing with no one, proceeding with the tenacity and adaptability of a shadow. He was a solitary being. This suited Tirano. No third parties were involved, no one whose ambition might sway him to commit a disloyal act. Yet, something in the man eluded him...a mystery of some sort he was unable to fathom. He had no known friends. Even he, the Boss, could not consider himself one. Nor had they ever shared a moment's intimacy, a hiatus unrelated to official matters. What a strange character! Finally, he imagined him at his desk organizing the day's work with his same unfailing punctiliousness.

Dr. Ramos was detained very briefly in the hallway by a sergeant who handed him a note requesting a letter of recommendation that he slipped into his pocket as he continued on to his office. A little cat, his inseparable companion, met him at the door. He picked her up, absently stroked her head with his finger tips, meditating, his thoughts off at some bend of the future. He tried to smile at his secretary but produced only a grimace.

Antonio Bell had entered the Seminary two months before his thirteenth birthday. He was still wet behind the ears when he was received by Father Sáez, the provost disciplinarian, who was welcoming the novices that afternoon. His mother and only sister, Aurimaría, had with deep emotion, delivered him over, firm in their conviction that they were carrying out a holy mission. As this sacred transmittal was being consummated, the mother stood before her son, taking his two hands into hers and looking ecstatically into his eyes while Aurimaría wove her fingers in and out of his hair that fell in a cascade over his eyebrows. At the very moment his mother was turning him over to the Prefect, a thought entered her mind that could not be blocked out and she stammered, "Dammit, Antonio, lose if you want to!" The phrase emerged automatically from her lips like something that had welled up from inside without her willing it. She regretted it immediately because those words were associated with a mysterious, bloody deed and with Antonio's grandfather, a bullheaded old man who all his life would never have anything to do with the church.

The saying "Lose if you want to!" originated in the village cockpit, uttered by that same grandfather one terrible Sunday. It remained afloat in the minds of all who heard it and was subsequently incorporated into the town's collective consciousness where it remained embedded.

But Alfonsina Reyes, Antonio's mother—Doña Fonsa to all—retracted her initial repentance and repeated the words "Antonio, lose if you want to!"—this time for all to hear. And the provost stared at her with his lizard's eyes as the boy's hands slipped from his mother's hands in farewell.

The grandfather, Santiago de la Caridad Bell, remained in town that day. He had said good-bye in the early morning to his grandson, son of his dead son, following the same ritual with which he tossed the bird into the cockpit seven years before. Doña Fonsa had trod close on his heels since the night before, not giving him a chance to be alone with Antonio. The old man had been in bad humor those last few days at his grandson's going off to become a priest, and Doña Fonsa feared that he might make one of his senseless remarks to him at any moment. She stood by watchfully while he was saying good-bye to the boy, but the grandfather, mute, did no more than stroke his hair, kiss him on the forehead, and, finally, throw his arms around him and hug him tight to his breast.

They drove to the capital in a jitney and the only thing that disturbed Doña Fonsa during the trip was the thought of her father-in-law's wordless leave-taking. She had expected him to come out with his notorious cockpit remark which, though it brought back discordant memories, would have been preferable to an outright condemnation of Antonio's entering the seminary, such as, "Oh, Antonio, if only you realized how they're screwing up your life with this business of sending you off to be a priest."

Arturo Gonzalo entered the gate house with the assurance of a veteran. He would be taking third-year Latin. Seeing the new boys brought on an irrepressible surge of nostalgia that aroused a sensation of longing mixed with sadness at the thought of the innocence of those near-children who were approaching the edge of a mirage so trustingly or timorously, and who as he looked at them, became transformed into a reflection of his own former state of innocence. "I'm not like that anymore," he thought. "So many things have changed. The same will happen to them. It's inevitable. It happens to us all sooner or later."

The hall was crowded with mothers, aunts, sisters, and parish priests who had accompanied the novices from the provinces or the capital. They were supportive, a stimulus that provided a final lift for the boys' morale in the face of the grave decision they had taken or been induced to take. The older students arrived alone, carting their valises, and went into a classroom where *maestrillos* held the lists of the wings, dormitories, and bell codes to which each had been assigned. They then took off to settle in and could be seen soon after, in the halls and the yard by themselves, or chatting quietly in pairs or groups of three and four. As the hours went by, they would be catching up bit by bit on the most intriguing aspect of the new term: which of the students would not be coming back from vacation. Names were fearfully whispered but never the possible motives, which remained in the dark. They would, of course, have liked to snoop into the details but mutual trust was wanting and prevented any real comradeship from developing among them. The Seminary authorities discouraged intimacy and whenever any manifestation of the kind was noted the most drastic disciplinary measures were taken to throttle it. How, then, to reach inside one another to tap into the words, the true reactions, the feelings they zealously kept to themselves?

The school year was beginning and worldly contamination had to be exorcised from the seminarians. The dawn of the following day ushered in a week of retreat: Strict silence, sermons, penitential fasting, deep meditation to find God's immanence in the depths of one's consciousness. By the time the retreat period was over, most first-year students, many of second, some of third, one or two of fourth and, perhaps, fifth were atoning for sins committed by their great-grandparents. Their gait and demeanor had taken on such an air of sanctity, eyes closed, words mouthed with fingers interlaced over the abdomen, head lowered—each an agonizing Jesus on the cross—that they looked like divinities of smoke floating upon a platform, acting out life's deception. Repentance reached such a pitch that they recriminated one another as if they bore the guilt of having been the outcome of their progenitors' carnal relations. In expiation of their sinful past they mortified the flesh and scarcely took nourishment. However, this state of ecstasy was short-lived, and after a few days, human nature was back on course and they were themselves again.

Seen from above, from the planes that skimmed continually over the imposing silence of the buildings during class hours until their wheels touched down at General Andrews Airport, the Seminary building resembled a cross laid out on the ground. The Upper Seminary, for philosophy and theology, with students ranging from eighteen to twenty-five years old, formed the left arm; the Lower Seminary, together with the third floor of the center, made up the right arm. The latter housed the bulk of the student body which consisted of boys twelve years old to youths of seventeen whose studies went as far as fifth-year Latin. The ground floor was given over to chapels, classrooms, mess halls, and the offices of the Prefect and the Spiritual Father, and the second and third floors were taken up by dormitories. The office of the Rector, the head of the Seminary, was on the second floor, facing the front gardens. Unauthorized crossing of the border between the Upper and Lower Seminaries was a punishable offense. Under no circumstances were direct relations between the two tolerated by the authorities. One had to resort to imagination to interpret regulations never explained. On Sundays, however, everybody gathered in the Upper Seminary chapel to hear high mass. It was the activity most eagerly looked forward to—a well-kept secret among the student body—because this mass was attended by several beautiful neighborhood girls, accompanied by their parents. A lascivious aura then pervaded the atmosphere in the chapel, which gave rise to a murky tingling of erotic seminarian nerves.

Bordered with shade trees, the yard covered a considerable area, the playing fields on two sides and, beyond, boundless, mysterious scrub. To the south, where the Lower Seminary was located, lay the wooded sector now invaded by the first dwelling to have been built there. The occupants bumped their car along a dirt road that ran from Cordell Hull Avenue to their house. This stretch ran parallel to a long cement wall that reached as far as its gate. Pine trees extended in an unbroken fringe along the compound beyond which a splendid view could be had from the Seminary roof. El Embajador hotel rose up against the background of the Caribbean Sea like a dawn-age monster, behind it the tall buildings of La Feria sector. Scattered among the trees of the Seminary yard were little grottos of saints, male and female. The favorite among them, perhaps because of its seclusion, was the shrine of Our Lady of Mt. Carmel, which had a number of small benches around it.

September was drawing to a close but August torpor was still palpable in the drooping trees. Arturo Gonzalo, at four o'clock recess, was out of sorts. He didn't feel like running on the track, tossing a ball or, sweating in general, and so he decided to take a shower, cool off, and then go down among the pine trees. A short time later, refreshed by his bath, he stood in that pleasant corridor of perpetual shade. He stopped to press himself up against the wall. Noting that it was no higher than his chin, he smiled, pleased to be taller than the year before. He frequented that spot to avoid, insofar as possible, the harsh reality of Seminary life. He imagined his home town and began to poke at the ashes of recollection. His thoughts were far afield when unexpectedly he felt a presence, a sensation of something from another world floating nearby. It reached him by scent and, in the act of sniffing, he noted a difference from the accustomed odors of those surroundings; then, he was to sense it again in the subtle elegance of a stride. Drawn by a strange spell, he raised his head above the wall and remained there, transfixed. He had discovered on the other side the most beautiful girl in creation. She was wearing the familiar Santo Domingo schoolgirl's uniform and moved with an air of forthrightness and a firm, self-assured tread characteristic of upper-class young ladies. The fullness of the blouse was unable to shroud the budding little breasts. Her profile was perfection and a pair of very black braids danced around her neck. Arturo stood on tiptoe, straining to make himself taller. Finding this unsatisfactory, he picked up a dumbbell that lay nearby, set it against the wall, and standing upon it made himself taller by a span. A full view of the supreme temptation was now his, to be gazed upon to his heart's content. Eyes wide, he watched the beautiful creature until she disappeared into the house. Entranced, he remained there for a long time, his glance lost at world's end until, finally, fearful that he might be seen, he stepped down to peer anxiously in all directions.

The following afternoon, Arturo was at the same spot, his eyes glued to the roadway. Could she have been an illusion? In any case, it was Saturday and she wouldn't be returning from school. He then decided to walk on hugging the wall with the intention of approaching the house close enough to, at least, catch an aroma or some manifestation of the being that had held him enraptured since the day before, but he was obliged to turn back for he had moved far beyond the areas designated for student recreation. At any rate, it was going to be impossible for him to get a glimpse inside the house since a newly built wall reaching to the sky obstructed the view from that part of the Seminary yard. In frustration, he walked about in aimless circles until, finally, needing a place to sit down and be alone, he decided to go to Our Lady of Mt. Carmel's grotto since the yard was now beginning to fill up. But somebody was already there in that secluded spot, standing piously before the image. It was one of the first-year boys. Three weeks had passed since the spiritual retreat and the novices were still going about in bewilderment. Arturo observed the youth from a prudent distance, his attitude one of sympathy tinged with curiosity. He had seen him around a number of times but hadn't yet spoken to him and didn't even know his name. Arturo watched discreetly not wanting to startle the boy or cause him to feel ill at ease. Moments before, he would have preferred to be by himself, but for some inexplicable reason, he now wanted to talk to this novice. Arturo, a third-year boy, was seasoned enough to sense that this youngster might be going through conflicts that are never viewed sympathetically or given serious consideration by the Seminary. Observing him, he had the impression that he was communing not with the saint but with memories or things left behind in his home town. He could very well be suffering from neophyte's syndrome: nostalgia-induced heart pangs.

"Hello there, my name is Arturo Gonzalo," he said, approaching cautiously. "What's yours?"

"Antonio Bell," the boy replied, a timid smile flitting over his lips.

Birds playing in the branches above them could be heard chirping sweetly.

"Where are you from?" Arturo inquired, returning the smile with another broader one.

"Jarabacoa," replied the youngster, turning away from the image.

"Tell me something, how do you feel about being here in the Seminary?" he inquired in a friendly tone.

One of the tiny birds lit on the tip of the Virgin's nose, hopped onto her shoulder, and flew off to the tree top.

Antonio's answer was limited to a fleeting smile followed by a brief lift of the shoulders, then a slight head movement to the right. Just then, other seminarians began to arrive, and Arturo said good-bye with the suggestion that they have a talk another day.

"I'm always over by the exercise bars at four-o'clock recess, there under the pine trees," he said, pointing in that direction.

In time, a close friendship developed out of this initial encounter. Such a thing was little short of miraculous in a world where from the very first day the student is split in two: the inner, natural part, fenced off by an invisible mesh, a secret refuge in which to come to terms with one's passions; the other part, that of appearances, the outward image. Two forces in everlasting conflict, whose cruel, protracted war has no predictable outcome.

Seminarians moving on either side, nearby and in the distance, were enjoying their two hours of recreation time under the surveillance of *maestrillos* with whistles around their necks. Arturo, back at the wall, searched the length of the road on the off-chance that the impossible might happen. As he stood waiting, his wandering thoughts flowed back to the day he said good-bye to his home town on the morning he left for the Seminary: *You'll find perfection there with God by your side and you will now be devoting yourself to Him forever, my son... Yes, mother...* and my eyes went chasing after my friends on their way to the river... *Be a good boy, study hard and, with the help of the Virgin, you will want for nothing...* The boys were carrying fishing poles and lines and must be in the park by now... Laly and her girlfriends will be going to the waterfall later on... *Come, have a bite to eat, Father Santiago said he would stop by for us at twelve o'clock...* I gave my slingshot to Leonel but I told him he had to lend it back to me to use when I am home on vacation. For sure, he'll be bringing back *rolones* today, he's such a good shot, he's the one who taught me. He also showed me how to tarzan on the vines at El Salto. He'll be coming back along the road showing off his strings of *ciguas* and *rolitas*, there's lots of them near the river bank now... *Think of me always while you are at the Seminary and I will pray to the*

Virgin every day to help you... Yes, mother, and will it be all right if I take my comics along? What did Father Santiago tell you?... That they'll let you know what you should read when you get there. Leave them here, I'll take care of them for you... Good Father Santiago arrived at twelve on the dot and right after him all the ladies of the choir besides Doña Casilda, Doña Josefa, and others who were always petting me like I was their own grandson, and... *How clearly the lad says the rosary! And...Come on, Arturito, give us a sermon, you're so clever at everything!* And they'd die laughing their little old-lady laughs, always dressed in the same mourning dresses, always smelling of the vestry. Though I was the one they were saying good-bye to, this wasn't a thirteen-year-old boy they were seeing off, but a grownup priest. And while Father Santiago was giving me little pats on the shoulder with his soft hand that smelled of sacramental wine, the women were acclaiming the town's first priest, their very own first priest, and... *What a lucky woman you are, comadre!...* and my mother, bursting with pride, a great big smile on her face.

Arturo was sixteen in March. In celebration, his mother sent him cinnamon candies made with her own hands, together with a tender little note. His sister wrote to him also but, unlike their mother, told of worldly things: that she had a boyfriend, an outsider, whose surname Cronos-vino (winetime), as he himself said, was meant to suggest pagan gods in orgy. A ruddy-faced young man, he came galloping in one day on a spirited mule, determined to carry off the prettiest girl in town. Also, as she confessed in the letter, it was impossible to resist a man who was able to stand off the rest of her numerous suitors with no more then a few words. Those others, armed with shotguns, surrounded him one day in the town square fully intending to blow him off the face of the earth. They had joined forces in a disorderly gang and appeared before the mayor, brandishing their weapons, to demand that, once and for all, he issue a

23

decree forbidding entry into town of such intruders who come to steal their girls from them with sorcerer's spells. Cronosvino, flaming with rage, stood up on the back of his mule and let loose a tirade that stopped them in their tracks: "Assholes, if you had any brains and the balls to go with them, you'd take those shotguns of yours and blast open the doors behind which they lock away the girls of this town!"

Arturo was so intrigued by his sister's story that he scarcely paid attention to the news he really wanted to hear: "With vacation time getting so close, Laly is out of her mind waiting to see you!" There was also a letter from his friends containing an account of their latest adventures, as well as the lyrics of Lucho Gatica's newest hit, the bolero *Amémonos* (Let's Love One Another) which they had copied out for him on a sheet of paper.

Arturo, concealing his eagerness, would be waiting for his package every Monday during the nearly three years he spent at the Seminary. He picked it up each week at one o'clock, hid in his dormitory, and keeping a weather eye open with bated breath, he ferreted out the letters that came hidden in a trousers pocket or buried deep inside starched shirts. He uncovered them with a roguish sense of wrongdoing, savoring the wickedness, for it was the only way of evading the Prefect's censorship. This inquisitor opened the mail from the post office and, as though this were a perfectly acceptable procedure, passed the letters on in that form after he had read them. All outgoing mail, as well, had to be turned over to him unsealed.

Arturo tore up his letters and threw the scraps down the toilet but held on to Lucho's song until he had a chance to memorize it. He had hidden the paper inside a corner of his mattress but, unfortunately, Father Sáez discovered it a few days later during one of his regular inspections. The Prefect went immediately to Arturo's classroom, summoned him with a crook of the finger, and marched him to his office. Waving the paper in the boy's face, Father Sáez said, "You're a good poet, Gonzalo, romantic and mellifluous" and with a mordant, sarcastic tone he began to read, *"Amémonos, mi bien, en este mundo/donde lágrimas tantas se derraman/las que vierten quizás los que se aman/tienen un no sé que de bendición."* (Let's love one another, my dearest/in this world where so many tears are shed/perhaps those spilled by lovers/ have, somehow, a touch of blessedness.) And giving the screws another turn, he leveled a question at him: "Is it conceivable that a full-fledged seminarian, a student like you with a true vocation for the priesthood, could find inspiration in this sort of thing?"

"I didn't write it, father. It's a song." A shadow was beginning to darken his upper lip and his voice of incipient manhood was hoarse. "I brought it with me from my vacation and put it aside without any improper thought. I never looked at it again. I forgot about it, father, I swear."

"You may go now, but see to it that no such thing ever happens again. If it does, you will pack up your things and leave at once." The poem was converted into a little paper ball in the prefect's bony hand, and he did not take his eyes off Arturo until he had thrown it into the wastebasket. "One thing more. Go straight to your Spiritual Father, have a talk with him, and confess."

"Yes, Father."

The Spiritual Father had already been informed. He was a short, thickset man with sensual lips, a toad's huge bulging eyes, and not a hair on his head. He was the scourge of the student body, a kind of mill wheel between whose stones seminarians were ground up to be molded into tamed, timorous creatures.

Arturo left the Prefect in the certainty that this was not one of his lucky days. He was no more than a minute away from the Spiritual Father's combination quarters and office, but he walked down the hall slowly, making time. He had no need to look back to know that the pistol in Father Sáez's eyes would be leveled at him all the way. He had to recover from the shock and get his thoughts in order but, being unsuccessful in either case, he barged into a toilet. Every second of delay, however, made it worse for him. He was headed straight into the hangman's hands, and the thought chilled his blood.

There had been a drastic deterioration in Arturo's relations with his Spiritual Father. He had received a very stern warning from him in the month of February when he confessed to having masturbated for the second time. "If it happens again I am ordering you to report to the Prefect before you come here and tell him that the priesthood is no vocation for you." Arturo promised him it would never happen again, that it had been a terrible weakness of the moment, and that he was praying very hard not to give in to temptation. The boy was sure the matter would not go beyond the confessional but, subsequently, he sensed that he was under even closer surveillance by *maestrillo* Ordóñez—who made the rounds of the dormitories at night—and Father Sáez.

Peering down the hall as he knocked on the door of the Spiritual Father's quarters, he could see the frail figure of the Prefect at the door of his office, still watching him. Arturo felt himself cornered.

In February, before going to the Spiritual Father to confess his second masturbation, he had spent long hours in deepest despair. The incident had occurred at night, and not being in a state of grace, he would be unable to receive communion the next morning. All seminarians were required to attend chapel and participate in the daily mass. As they filed in, they took their places according to height from the first row of pews to the last. They proceeded to the altar in the same order to receive communion and those who were unworthy had to remain in their seats. This made it awkward for the others to pass, and the "sinners" had to stand up in place pressing back against their seats to make room, the rest glancing sidelong at them as they squeezed by. Then, they remained isolated in the emptiness until the others finished communion and returned to their places. Meanwhile, the Spiritual Father traveled up and down the aisle with his short little steps, taking note of the most insignificant details. Arturo, alone in the anguishing solitude of the chapel, the world swirling round and round him, was distraught that day, wishing the earth would swallow him up. He realized that he had no alternative. He would have to go before his confessor at once so that he could take communion but, dreading the encounter, he remained another time without receiving the sacrament. This was too much for him! When the religious rite was over that second day, Arturo, an automaton, headed for the confessional. He promised everything just to escape the unbearable humiliation of isolation at mass and, even though the priest proved to be exceedingly harsh and menacing, he left feeling that an intolerable burden had been lifted from his shoulders.

Those were his distressing thoughts as he raised his knuckles to knock at the spiritual father's door. He was confident that the priest would not link up the matter of the song with that of the masturbations or give it much importance but, knowing him as he did, anything could be expected, including being expelled then and there. However, one thing was certain: to find him in a generous mood would be out of the question. What could be expected of a man who had never been seen to smile, the skin on that rotund face of his taut to the bursting point, a man who never failed to reprimand? Arturo hesitated when he saw the door swing open but finally entered. He was surprised not to find the Father behind the door nor seated as usual at his little desk.

No one seemed to be anywhere around. There was nothing but silence in that room, no sound, no movement... nothing! An eternity a few seconds long passed, and just as he had made up his mind to slip out of that stressful atmosphere of suspense into which he regretted having entered uninvited and in which he had begun to feel the first chill of terror, he noticed the crucifix on a nail in the wall in front of him begin to writhe convulsively. The youth received such a shock that he became paralyzed with fear. He wanted to run away, but as in a nightmare, he couldn't move. Then, at the same moment, there appeared in a corner of the room, apparently materializing out of thin air, a round mass of flesh with what seemed to be two huge eye sockets from which there spewed and retracted a stream of something like blazing embers aimed right at him, trying to set him on fire. Regaining control of his senses after a moment, he tore open the door, and still stunned by the vision, he bolted out only to come face to face with Father Sáez who seemed to fill the entire hallway. "Oh, Father!" he shrieked. The priest seized him by the shoulders with both hands, cutting off escape, swiveled him around to face the open door, and thrust him headlong back into the room.

The apparition was no longer there, the crucifix was bloodstained but motionless, and now all he could see was the Spiritual Father seated at his desk, in apparent calm, immersed in a thick book with black covers. Arturo dared make no reference to what he had experienced but did stare in fascination at the smooth skull before him; he could not help noting that it bore a vague resemblance to the specter that had frightened him out of his wits a moment before.

"I'll leave Gonzalo in your hands, Father," the Prefect said, "he would like to have a word with you." As usual, the confessor proved ruthless, but Arturo only repeated in a trembling voice what he had said to the Prefect. Although the priest browbeat him unmercifully, he made no charges and did not send him to see the Rector. The boy concluded from this that he had escaped expulsion, at least for the time being.

At midnight on the second Sunday of January, 1950, Santiago Alfonso de la Caridad Bell changed into a man saddened for the rest of his life. He had heard a knocking on the door and thought it was friends on a spree, still abroad celebrating the cock's victory. He groped for his matches and lit the lamp. The voice that called to him was familiar but its tone gave him an uneasy feeling. He leaped out of bed in a sweat and flung open the door without any precaution. He was given the news that fifteen minutes before his son Cástulo had been picked up by an army patrol, that is to say, under the worst possible conditions.

All efforts to find out where he had been taken were in vain. Months went by, and only one vague rumor turned up that grew more and more nebulous as time went by: that there might have been a political motive behind his arrest and disappearance. Antonio's grandfather, however, felt it in his bones that some other element was involved that he could not fathom.

"That morning dawned so clear, the sun was so mild, and such a sweet breeze was blowing that it made a man wish he was a poet. The cocks were impatient, waiting for me to let them out into the warm sun. What a celebration they made when I turned them loose! I live only to remember that day, Antonio. I can't tell you how often I've wished I had the magical power to wipe away all the time that came after and go back to that glorious morning. Your dad was with me a little later, and I brewed him his coffee. He never got out of the habit of stopping by for his first cup of the morning, always very early, at first cockcrow. He continued it even for the years after he married, even after my dear one was

29

gone and I was left alone in this big place with plenty of room for all of us, but where he never wanted to come with his family to live. That was his way and I respected it. Always very independent, Cástulo was. He couldn't have been more than your age, maybe nine years old, when he got me to build him a little house in the back patio, a hideaway under the rose bushes where he'd go in the afternoons to do his homework."

"You're old enough now for me to tell you about it, Antonio. I know you've asked me to in your way a number of times, and I would never give you more than vague answers. That was so as not to contradict your mother. She says you and your sister Aurimaría are too little to understand certain things. She's mistaken, though. Poor Alfonsina! Cástulo's disappearance made her so fearful that all she does is try to keep trouble away from you. She doesn't want you to grow up knowing the truth or to find it out in such a way that could make you bitter and vengeful. But I think differently. I know you'll understand perfectly well and that whatever you decide to do when you're grown up will be your affair to deal with as you see best. I'm convinced that children understand from the time they're born; they have their own way of knowing. I don't think that in order for children to understand they have to be spoken to in the language of their age. I used to talk to Juanito, my favorite cock. I know he understood me, and he was only an animal.

"At the time of Cástulo's calamity, cockfighting was one of the main pleasures of my life. It was a fever my son caught from me. I recall that he owned a *pinto* at the time, a little speckled bird that was a marvel, and on that Sunday we took him to the cockpit to match him up. Juanito was born out of a crossing with that beautiful *pinto*. There was an individual at the cockpit that day, Cocolo Cantera, a loud-mouthed braggart and mean bully, whose nickname was The

Snake. He was parading a 'cinnamon' with good strong spurs, holding it up in his two hands challenging all comers, but getting no takers. Actually, just to bring that brute down a peg, I picked up Cástulo's *pinto* and said to the loudmouth, 'I have this bird here that'll take you on. How about it?' The Snake just laughed and a good number of the others joined in. Then the man answered me in a sneering tone, 'And like how much were you figuring to drop on that chicken of yours, Don Santiago?' It was Cástulo who answered, 'There's two hundred pesos on him and that's because I don't have anymore.' It was a sizable amount. Cástulo's friends there and I raised the ante to three hundred and fifty. So's not to string the story out too long, I'll just tell you that the *pinto* tore The Snake's 'cinnamon' to pieces. It brought the house down. What a surprise that was! We left happy and Cocolo Cantera must have crawled home with his tail between his legs. But, that was the beginning of the end for my son. I realized that a year later.

"I've already told you the story many times about the fight between my cock Juanito and Cocolo Cantera's and what brought on the challenge. It happened exactly a year after Cástulo disappeared. I told you that the day of the calamity dawned as sweet as a blessing, but by nightfall the sky began to close in and it got so dark you couldn't make out a sign of light up there anywhere. The downpour came at ten o'clock, more or less. I was already lying in bed, the way you see me now, smoking a cigarette, listening to the first raindrops pattering on the galvanized roof and going over in my mind all the things that happened that day. I was in a cheerful mood, calm, the music from the good clean rain on the metal making me feel even more contented. A while later, I put out my cigarette and settled in for the night. I slept maybe an hour, something like that...and then I suddenly woke up...not feeling anything out of the ordinary at the time, not having any premonitions. Outside the rain was coming down even heavier. I was smoking another cigarette and thinking. And then, I remember as clear as if it was today that my thoughts turned to my dear departed, your grandmother, and it seemed to me as though she was right here with me, chinning like we always did before we went to sleep. It might sound like a coincidence, but who knows? The fact of the matter is that she was here with me when that knocking came. To me the strange part is that my departed hadn't given me some sign, or maybe she did and I couldn't understand. It never crossed my mind that anything was wrong, I simply thought it was Cástulo's friends celebrating with their winnings from the cockfight. I should have realized, though, that in such weather nobody would be out in the street just for the fun of it. Then, when I recognized my *compadre* Ramón's voice, it dawned on me, or I had a suspicion, that they weren't coming around for any ordinary reason. My *compadre* was a man who retired early and wouldn't be at my door at that hour looking to have a chat. I thought: Something's up, dammit! But not for a minute, not even remotely, could I have imagined that it might have to do with my boy's calamity. But that's what it was. My *compadre*'s son had waked him to give him the news that Cástulo had been picked up, and he came to let me know. What happened from that moment on is a nightmare that has never ended.

"Such is life, my boy. It's when you least expect it that something awful will happen to you. Well, I'll continue the story tomorrow. And, another thing, don't let your mother know about what I've been telling you. If she finds out, she won't let you sleep at my house any more."

"No, grandpa, I won't tell mom anything, I promise you. Good night, grandpa."

"Good night, my son."

On Sunday, January 14, 1951, a year after the night Cástulo disappeared, grandfather was up early to give the cock his last minute attentions. He didn't know why but he had a feeling that something special was brewing that day. The fight had been set up with The Snake, Cocolo Cantera's famous "Killer Feet" since the week before. The town's top experts were against it being held for the reason that one of the two finest and fiercest fighting cocks in the history of the region would be lost. But what started out as innocent cracks on Santiago Bell's part ended up provoking a challenge there was no walking away from once they reached Cocolo Cantera's drunken ears on the other side of town. Santiago had said in front of several persons in his yard, as he stroked his *pinto's* feathers, "No cock alive can beat my Juanito," and added that, in comparison, "Pig's Feet" would be a more appropriate name for Cocolo Cantera's "Killer Feet," plus a few other joking remarks. Actually, his words didn't really amount to more than kidding, a way to praise his own cock. The fact was, however, that in less than half an hour, The Snake had gotten wind of what Santiago said, as well as things he didn't say. Cocolo Cantera's reasoning power didn't go much beyond that of his cock's. To make things worse, he was roaring drunk at the time he was told. Besides, there was an old grudge against the Bell family over a woman. It went back to when a cousin of Santiago Bell's threw Cocolo out of a dance by the scruff of his neck in the days before he enlisted in the army. The violent nature of that former Nigua Prison guard had heated up to fever pitch and he stormed over to the other side of town to demand satisfaction from Santiago, using his foulest prison-guard language. Before a dozen onlookers, he yelled that either they shoot it out or have it out the following Sunday in a cockfight for a stake of no less than 500 pesos in gold. Without taking his eyes off him, Santiago Bell answered coolly: "I can't accept your challenge to a duel, Señor Cocolo

33

Cantera, because in the first place I don't use guns and, second, because a duel calls for two gentlemen. Furthermore, I consider that we're too old to be brawling. I went off the rum a long time ago so that the hot blood shouldn't rush to my head when I'm faced with ignorance or lies. But, by all means, my *pinto* is available, so have your cock ready and we'll meet on Sunday."

Everything was set for the fight to take place at five o'clock. People had come from the farthest points of the county, as well as from other cities reached by news of the match between the two famous cocks. The arena was jammed to capacity with onlookers perched in the most unlikely places. The yard outside was also packed to bursting, even as far as the gates, and draining like an abscess into the neighboring streets where bets on that Sunday's contest were being laid and expert opinion argued. It was the same as on the night before and every day of the week on the park benches, in the whores' bars, and everywhere else.

The shout that went up exactly at the appointed hour could be heard at the four corners of town. Santiago Bell, held the *pinto* in his hands, waiting to toss him into the pit. He had prepared him with all the skill of a great master of the art and something besides: the unending devotion that's needed to train a child destined for a spiritual mission. He had worked on it since long before Cocolo Cantera's challenge and foresaw a momentous encounter. The past two months had been spent in daily training sessions to strengthen the cock's leg muscles, wings, and beak. He was fed a special diet and every aspect of his physical condition, including the sheen of his feathers and his reflexes were carefully checked. But there was more to it than that. He treated him with love, instructed him with words, kissed his comb as one would the cheek of a child, and had gone as far as to give him a person's name—Juanito.

Santiago preceded the tossing of the cock into the ring with a sacramental ritual: He rubbed his beak, legs, and spurs, lifted his wings, and blew gently on his trembling muscles; next, both remained looking into each other's eyes; and, finally, he stroked Juanito's body gently from his head to the end of his tail. Then, as he was sending him into battle, Santiago said to him, "Dammit, Juanito, lose if you want to." And with a grand gesture, turned his back on him as if to say that he had done his job and the rest was now up to him.

True to his name, "Killer Feet" brought his most powerful weapon into play at once. He used his armored spurs without leverage, hanging in the air, rapidly repeating the thrust: two, three, four, without touching the ground. He had put away twenty-five local and national-class rivals in a matter of seconds with that technique. But, the *pinto* dodged this first broadside, falling back and leaving his opponent to slash with his spurs at empty space and landing in the sand on his tail. "Killer Feet" attacked again and Juanito again evaded. Without himself launching a single kick, Juanito spent the first minutes of the contest studying his opponent's fighting style, deciding how to proceed. This was a departure from the customary behavior and it confused the spectators. But the *pinto* had adopted a strategy that not only brought the public to a pitch of frenzy (Niño Juan de Dios was later to admit that he swallowed a lighted cigar butt without even realizing it) but left them convinced that he was possessed by the spirit of a man who was really doing the fighting that afternoon.

In fact, when Juanito decided that it was time for him to fight, he maneuvered with the judgment and guile of a rational being. He pressed up against the wall, and when "Killer Feet" unleashed his barrage of kicks, vacated the spot as fast as lightning, moving to a point right behind him, and the moment "Killer Feet" turned around, seized that disordered mass of legs and feathers with his beak, pinning it to the wall in a masterful stroke. At the same time, he plunged in his armored spurs repeatedly with astonishing swiftness, not giving his enemy a second to breathe, and neutralizing his leg action. Juanito's beak was his most formidable weapon and having once gotten a grip with it, it was very difficult for an enemy to shake him loose without losing a great deal of blood in the process. "Killer Feet" was badly wounded by the *pinto's* first charge, but he was a courageous fighter and, weakened though he was and with skin dragging on the ground, he kept charging at the *pinto* with unabated fierceness. Juanito not only left him no opening but began to circle around him in what appeared to be an attitude of mockery, doing nothing but looking at "Killer Feet" sideways who, although weak and bleeding, still showed reserves of kicking power. The *pinto* repeated his tactic of hugging the wall in preparation for resuming his previous attack and "Killer Feet" flew at him along the ground in a dying thrust, shrieking like a karate fighter. It was no more than a final act of confused desperation which Juanito easily sidestepped to pin him against the wall again, seizing him with his beak, which seemed more like a fish hook jammed into his crop, and proceeding to methodically dig in his spurs all over the enemy's body. "Killer Feet" had already been dead for some time without anybody realizing it. Although apparently still standing, he was actually being held up by the *pinto's* strong beak from which the pit judge had to disengage him by cutting away the skin with a butcher knife.

It was at this point that something so mysterious and unclear took place that even now, years later, the testimony of witnesses cannot be explained except in terms of speculation and fantasy. The actual, tangible circumstances were as follows. At the end of the fight, Juanito remained standing soaked with "Killer Feet's" blood, and it was the consensus of those present that the *pinto*, quivering as he walked around the dead cock, gave vent to a hollow, guttural cry that seemed to come from another world. His eyes were two fiery points scanning, radar-like, the space around him. As soon as Cocolo Cantera jumped into the ring to recover the remains of his cock, a force of nature took over the pit and nobody could prevent the *pinto* from hurling himself upon The Snake like a creature possessed to destroy him before the astounded eyes of the paralyzed onlookers. Those who were in the front rows relate that the spur blades lengthened to the size of daggers which the *pinto* stabbed with bewildering rapidity into Cocolo's heart, then into his eyes and all over his face leaving it a bloody mask and the man stone dead in the middle of the cockpit.

"Grandpa...grandpa..." whispered Antonio, wide-awake, eyes bright, disturbing thoughts fluttering through his little head, banishing sleep.

"Yes, Antonio, what is it?" said his grandfather, still half-asleep.

"What did they arrest my daddy for? What did he do?"

The grandfather sat up, struck a match, lit his cigarette and then the lamp with it, got out of bed, and opened the window. Huge stars were out and they seemed close enough to touch. He calculated that it was after midnight.

"Everybody assures me he hadn't done anything. He had his political ideas, his disagreements, but he never advertised them. I was the only one he opened up to. We came home together from the cockpit, the two of us, put the cock in his coop, and went to the kitchen to fix a bite of supper. We sat around until about eight o'clock when he got up to leave, and I went out as far as the street with him. "We're in for some rain," I commented. Both of us looked up at the sky. "You're right, it's going to rain," he said, "surprising, when it's been such a beautiful day all along." I should have walked him home but didn't. I don't know what stopped me. As a rule, I would stay around at your house until ten or so but that day I didn't go, maybe on account of the shower that was on the way...I don't know. The fact is I didn't go. I'm sure that if I had, Cástulo wouldn't have gone out on the town. In any case, it's strange that he did because we had to be at the shop bright and early the next morning to finish up four doors for Monday. It was a firm promise, and he never stayed out late when there was work waiting the next day. Seems like he was real eager to get together with his friends to hash over the cock's victory and celebrate. People talked of nothing else that Sunday, it had the town on its ear.

"According to what I was told, Cástulo stopped in at a bar where he sat down at a table with friends and stayed on with them, all enjoying themselves. It was later on, much later, that a patrol walked in. There were three police with rifles and two men in plain clothes with pistols under their shirts whom nobody had ever seen around here before. They went straight to Cástulo and took him away in the same car they arrived in. That's all anybody could tell me.

"He was never seen again...not ever again. My only son, my hope, the apple of my eye, the light of my life. Sometimes, I blame myself for not getting him out of this swamp in time, but I wanted him by me always. I taught him his trade and he became a first-rate carpenter, but it really wasn't his calling. The same thing had happened with me. I followed in my father's footsteps because nothing better was open. But as time passed, I got to love the smell of wood. Cástulo never really adjusted, his eyes were on the city and he had a bent for reading. I'd leave books on the table, and he'd pick them up and study them because that's what he wanted to do. And so he got to be more and more dissatisfied and convinced that his future and his family's was on the other side of these mountains. He kept saying that time seemed as though paralyzed here, that the people were breathing the same polluted air all the time, and that our society is stagnant, a society that measures a man's worth by how much land he owns or the guts he has to stand up and kill or be killed. Cástulo kept dreaming of colleges and getting to know the world he had learned about from books. They were fantasies, yet I do believe he had the talent to make them come true. But every man has a destiny and your father's was to die an early, senseless death that was the outcome of an evil brute's grudge and the barbarity of this shit-hole of a country."

Arturo Gonzalo's great distress as he left the chapel after mass was somewhat eased by the day's busy schedule but night brought it back with redoubled intensity. He had committed the sin of the flesh again the day before but now no longer had the strength to go to the Spiritual Father and confess. He had not received communion that morning and was well aware that this relapse could mean immediate expulsion and that confessing to another masturbation would entail exactly the same punishment. Furthermore, how long could he go on taking the malicious smirks of his companions as they made their way to the altar, hands clasped like archangels, while he, kneeling on the prie-dieu, leaned back to let them push by him, hanging his head, feeling as though an eagle were gnawing at his entrails? No question but that his fellow students were mentally stripping him naked, morbidly visualizing him, member in hand, manipulating it, quivering with excitement at the illusion. What else could possibly drive a seminarian to pass up the chance to receive the Sacred Body of Jesus through the Sacrament of the Eucharist? What other kind of sin could he commit in a world made up of nothing but studies, rituals, surveillance, and long nights of sleep. On rare occasions when some other seminarian missed communion, he would have the same thought and be asking himself the same questions. And yet, this was mere conjecture because not even once in his three years at the Seminary had he had an opportunity to dispel his doubts by talking to a fellow student. Confidences never went that far. It was forbidden terrain. The darkness of the dormitory aggravated his problem. Morning was imminent and he would have to face reality without seeing a solution to the dilemma. But, he was certain of one thing now: Under no circumstances would he put in an appearance before the Spiritual Father. The most sensible thing was to go to the Prefect's office or preferably the Rector's and say to him: "Father, I wasn't meant for this calling and so I'm going back home, today." That's what the Spiritual Father had ordered him to do if he masturbated again. The Rector wouldn't try to hold him back. On the contrary, he would say to him, "Pack your bag and get out of here...by way of the Upper Seminary while classes are in session, so that nobody will see you." He would go as far as La Fama Hotel by bus and at two o'clock in the afternoon take a taxi to his town. And when he got there what could he tell his mother, and what was he going to say to Father Santiago and Doña Casilda and Doña Josefa, and Señorita Cristina, and the others when they saw him appear at this time of the school year and began to bombard him with questions? They threw me out for being a masturbator. Good little Arturo, their dear little priest they were so proud of, in contrast to so many of today's youth running amok nowadays, expelled like that from the Seminary. For what? For being a masturbator! Good God in heaven! The world must be coming to an end! No... preferable to say that I... Yes, I'll tell them that I...

But, Arturo Gonzalo never had to tell them anything. Actually, he didn't have the courage to return to his home town under such a cloud. He couldn't bear to think of the look of anguish on Father Santiago's face, who had believed in him and given him such guidance. It terrified him to imagine his poor mother's grief and shame. Her lifelong dreams all centered in him and confided to him on the day he left for the Seminary! *"Son, my only desire is that you become a priest; the day I stand at your side after you hold your first mass in our town I will be the happiest woman on earth. Then, my son, I can die in peace, for there's nothing more I will want from life."*

No, no way could he go back to his town. And no way, either, for him to go in repentance to the Spiritual Father and say to him, "Father, with deep pain in my heart, I want to confess that I masturbated again," and to have him turn red in the face and say to him "Get out of my room at once and tell the Rector that you are leaving the Seminary immediately!" To make promises and beg for absolution would be useless and serve only to humiliate him more, and leave him wallowing in his tears. No! No! What, then...?

When the *maestrillo* rang the bell in the hall at 5 a.m., Arturo, in his sleep, thought he was hearing the trumpets of the Last Judgment. He had spent a sleepless night interrupted by occasional spells of scary dreams and had barely begun to get some rest when the shrill alarm drove him leaping out of bed as though he were on a spring. However, he had made much progress during his anxious hours of wakefulness. He had hit upon a clear plan of action he was sure was the best and only feasible one.

Mulling over what steps to take in the skirmish that faced him, he remained seated on the bed collecting his thoughts. Finally, his spirit buoyed by his new found determination, he jumped to his feet and set out for the washroom with the solemnity of a gambler hiding a card up his sleeve, determined to win.

He had a feeling that everything around him was different. The light beginning to flood the world was of a brighter hue and seemed a life-giving emanation that did not reach the rest of his companions hurrying to or from their ablutions, toothbrush and soap dish in hand, towel around the neck. Looking at them, they seemed to him children penned together in a corral, automatons, their wills controlled by brains trained to manipulate.

As he went through his daily routine, each aspect of it became an extension of his increasingly supercharged thoughts. He brushed his teeth vigorously, intense inner forces, not anger, being the motor of his exaggerated actions. In the toilet, he moved his bowels with fury: "Shit, that's what those priests are, shit!" Consciously or unconsciously, he was resorting to the time-honored device of self-justification. Little wonder, for what he intended to do in just a short time called for strong convictions and considerable courage. He was about to set off a soul-searing blast within himself intended to expunge from his being a moral principle by which he had lived since childhood. This would be a move to break free, to make up for three years of anguished inner struggle and, at the same time, spare him the disgrace of expulsion. He sought to extricate reason from the talons of doubt and fears that clamored for a terrible revenge to be exacted by blind, instantaneously effective forces. But there was nothing to hold him back anymore.

Secure in the course he had chosen, he set up a barrier around himself and lined it with slabs of steel. Emerging from the dormitory in his best cassock, he passed *maestrillo* Ordóñez who was checking on the seminarians being dismissed from the North Pavilion and greeted him with uncommon warmth. Before getting in line to enter the chapel, he went to the Spiritual Father's room, where he had evidently being expected, and said to him. "Father, I want to confess, or rather, to have a talk with you since I don't believe that what happened to me calls for confession." The Spiritual Father kept his head tilted downward at exactly the same angle he had been holding it, not disturbing a single crease of his habit for as long as he remained seated behind his desk, until finally he rose and looked up and down at the source of that self-possessed voice, his huge round eyes bulging from their sockets like fists. But no reply seemed to be forthcoming. In view of the priest's silence, Arturo met the confessor's inquisitorial gaze squarely and continued his statement along these lines: "Father, once again the night before last, I was tormented by temptation of the flesh. For a moment, I felt myself weakening but managed to resist the devil's first onslaught and to drive him off with a long and resolute prayer. But, that was not enough for me. I had to convince myself that I wouldn't fall an easy victim again to that terrible temptation so I spent most of my time in meditation and prayer from that moment until now when I've come to tell you that for the first time in my life I feel myself a free man, without doubt in my spirit, without fear, and with such strength that I consider myself capable of overcoming the greatest obstacles that I may come up against. What I wanted to tell you, Father, is this, that I feel myself free of sin and with a conscience clearer than that of a newly baptized child."

The Spiritual Father remained standing, hearing him out. Incredulous as he was astonished, he proceeded to search Arturo's eyes for the truth. Lending himself to the scrutiny, the boy widened them, with perhaps excessive candor. Yet, in their depths the priest recognized Arturo's honesty. His statement held no contradictions. Its logic, his serenity, and the details all dovetailed except for something elusive, hidden beyond tangible reality. Lost in the abyss of Arturo's composure, the priest sought it, probing desperately, sounding the unfathomable depths of the soul in vain. Finally, he had no choice but to accept Arturo's declaration.

"My congratulations, Gonzalo," he said, at last, "you are very courageous. Be at ease, now, and go to hear mass.

Should any doubts trouble you, feel free to consult me."

"Thank you, Father," he replied.

During mass, when it was Arturo's turn to receive communion, he did so with utter conviction and not the slightest remorse. He returned to his seat revitalized and with a sense of power that possession of an extraordinary secret imparts. As he knelt, he could not resist looking towards the aisle where he met the skewering gaze of the Spiritual Father who had been observing him closely. Arturo held his head between his two hands and recalled the episode of horror in the confessor's office. He figured, as he had many times before, that it couldn't have been anything but a ghoulish trick on the priest's part. In retaliation, as he turned his eyes toward the aisle again, he thought, "You didn't get away with your magic tricks this time, did you? Hah! Not this time!"

How had Arturo arrived at the determination to lie or doubletalk the spiritual father and then receive communion while bearing the sin beyond redemption of masturbation?

For months he had been devoting much thought to himself and his behavior. He had brought himself under self-analysis but never so deeply as on that night of torture just before his confession. Was the uncontrollable desire to masturbate that would overwhelm him almost without his realizing it—as though the urge were lurking in some corner of his body, suddenly demanding release, bursting outward—a dangerous symptom of sexual aberration? Was he abnormal? He looked back over his life as far as memory would permit and found nothing of concern. He recalled his first erotic experience with the same naturalness as the time he climbed through a barbed-wire fence to fill his pockets with pomegranates and gooseberries in a field guarded by vicious bulls. It had been an enjoyable and healthy adventure like the one of stealing mangos—using a pole fitted with a blade and a tin pitcher—from a tree in a walled yard that belonged to a lady who was so stingy with her fruit that she would send her servants up the tree to pick them before dark while she watched them from below. Such escapades formed part of the daily routine, like eating, going to school, fishing in the river, and hunting on the mountain with slingshots. And all of them were group activities, including masturbation, in many cases, shared without reticence or shame, which became anecdotes to be told around park benches, in the shallows at the river's edge, and bragged about by boys beginning to be men.

If he was abnormal, then all his friends in town were a bunch of degenerates from birth, starting with Leonel, whom he remembered years back puffing out his little chest in the schoolyard, and saying, "Hey!...this morning I did it to myself and listen...some gooey stuff came out...and it stretched like about so far..." And he made horizontal movements with his index fingers, pressing them together and separating them, to demonstrate the extension and strength of the substance which he heard named for the first time as "the come." That afternoon he tried to emulate Leonel, who was two years older, but nothing came out, it just swelled up and got red as a tomato. But he liked the way it felt.

Weren't those urges stirred up by human nature in dreams when not satisfied via normal channels? But there was a difference. Dream fantasies are not sinful because they take place beyond the control of the will. Therefore, if they occur by involuntary command, as in the case of heartbeats, doesn't that mean that they are an inseparable part of the spiritual fabric?

Arturo Gonzalo whiled away the interminable hours of his sleepless nights mulling over such rationales. And, though he foundered in a muddy lagoon of confusion at times, he managed in the end to summon the strength to swim his way to the surface as if between the strands of a web.

His thoughts took many different twists and turns through the hiding places of his mind and in each he came upon real flesh and blood enemies waiting to crush him pitilessly. Those were the men of the Seminary, specific, tangible figures to whom no appeal was possible. They had their daggers out for him, ready to plunge into his breast, and he must lose no time in getting the best of them.

"If I don't go to mass and receive communion today, they'll expel me. If I confess so I can receive communion, they'll expel me, too. But throwing me out of the Seminary is one thing I can't let them do. Oh, my God...! The Lord's wrath and the eternal flames! Fire? Hell? The Infinite and the horror of torture by fire for all eternity are concepts beyond my grasp. But one thing I do understand is man's punishment: It's for now and there's no escaping it. God's punishment comes later. But, what is my sin, anyway? And supposing I'm not really in a state of sin? Of course, I'm not. What in my life is there for me to repent? And even if I did have something to repent... which, as a matter of fact, I do...? And besides, since that's the case, what stands against me in God's eyes? Nothing whatsoever...And if there's nothing... Aha! Then I'll fake a confession! Because, the hundred-percent sure thing is that I must go and see the Spiritual Father... I must... Otherwise, how can I justify not having received communion yesterday? If I didn't, it was because I was not in a state of grace. That's it...! I'll go, and confess, telling a lie...then, I'll receive communion and, after that..."

From that day on, Arturo Gonzalo felt liberated, able to study and to dream. He had neutralized the threat of man. He possessed himself of Laly Pradera and the neighbor of wingéd footsteps whom he kept seeing from the shadows of the pine trees at four o'clock, and made them his with not a twinge of conscience, contemplating from his window other heavenly bodies that dwelt among smiles out there in the world's immensity.

Weeks went by and he was scarcely aware of God's displeasure, yet His presence and the probably implacable condemnation of His wrath weighed on his mind as the one still unresolved woe. It was the only thorn that pricked somewhere in his spirit from time to time and kept annoying him like little festering sores impeding enjoyment of his new state and which—there was no telling—could unexpectedly worsen.

Early in June, shortly before vacations, with the dream of Laly Pradera's kisses a reality soon within reach, with the recurrent mental images of his home town and its surrounding lushness, the streams clearer and softer flowing, the mountains greener and more idyllic, and the great laurel tree in the square like a monument in a garden of love, he resolved to set himself free at a single stroke from his one source of anxiety. Accordingly, he asked himself: "And what if, after all, there were no God? Then, all at once, as though he had come upon the philosopher's stone, he suddenly considered it confirmed: "There is no God."

"This is the time of year when the whole town seems a garden giving birth to flowers and rainbows, the earth drenched with good rain, the yards in the early morning covered with tiny worm houses, and the girls singing their innocence at church and school, and sighing with love. In Maytime, the town's essence, heavy with fragrance, seeps sweetly into the very marrow of one's bones. May, here in the Seminary, brings me emanations of the world, those from close by that reach me through my ears, as well as distant ones in my memory. This year I had the good fortune to be assigned to a dormitory on the third floor in the north wing. It is cooler and from there I can see the buildings of La Feria and, a little beyond, the whitecaps of the Caribbean, and hear them crash against the cliffs. It's Saturday night and Ramón Gallardo's merengues carry clearly all the way from the *Típico Quisqueyano*. The boys raved to me about his music during summer vacation. Bunches of them would barge in at my house and try out the latest steps, dancing with one another. They'd come in the afternoons, drink fresh coffee, smoke a cigarette, passing it around till there was practically nothing left of the butt. Then, they'd take off to make the rounds. I usually stayed home because I couldn't keep up with the supercharged activities of those guys. They always went around in a group, with pockets empty, but happy as larks. Sometimes, they'd club together with the "old guys" to make up a kitty for a bottle of rum. The first slug would bring out the lyrical vein and they'd lose no time breaking out the guitars and singing; later they'd gather under the girls' windows and serenade them in the moonlight. Those serenades sounded beautiful in my town at night, and I had to hold myself down to keep from jumping out of my bed. There were times when Laly's image would be with me gnawing away at my mind until the first wisps of the morning light.

"It must be ten-thirty or eleven. The *maestrillo* put the lights out a long time ago. Ramón Gallardo's merengues float up to me along with a smell of fried fish. I can hear *maestrillo* Ordóñez's footsteps. They are unmistakable, he walks like a cat. *Maestrillo* Garmídez's are heavy, these are not. They are like a mist filtering even into the seminarian's sleep. I turn over in bed and make believe I'm asleep. I picture him cautiously parting the curtains that serve as the dormitory doorway to feel out students' faces with his flashlight beam. He's been checking on me lately but can never catch me. Less than a month ago he caught my neighbor, Jacinto Coronado, doing it to himself. I'm sure that's what must have happened. *Maestrillo* Ordóñez fell on him that night like a shadow. I put my ear to the partition and although I didn't hear anything at first, I knew something was going on next door. I could make out low voices but not what was being said, and then there were receding footsteps and faint sobs as though smothered under a pillow. I looked for Jacinto in line next morning but he wasn't there, nor was he in the washroom. After that, I didn't see him anywhere, not in the chapel, at breakfast, or in class. In the afternoon, I heard somebody say that Coronado had left. Hardly a whisper. That's the system. When the authorities decide to expel a student, they do it in the strictest silence, without anybody knowing what's happening, and then they turn his name and his memory into dust. He is never mentioned again. I stayed in bed, hesitating, annoyed at the rounds of that phantom. My ears have become so sensitive that I am now able to recognize footsteps that are leaving for good. I have the urge to do it to myself but don't dare to even though I've figured out a system to keep from getting caught, but I'm afraid that little guy can smell it. It wouldn't surprise me if the Jesuits had trained that bloodhound to sniff out the stuff. Besides, his presence breaks my concentration. I like to take myself on long, relaxed trips. It's a strange thing, but no matter how hard I try, I can't switch phantom lovers and make it work. I take different tacks, but it's Laly Pradera, like a mythological goddess, who's always there crossing my path with her spiky little nipples and luscious, bouncy rump. I guess the reason it happens that way is because that's my experience, the only reality I know."

"Who was it, grandpa? Who was to blame?"

"Now, don't be getting yourself worked up, Antonio, you'll get to know the whole story soon enough. I'll let you in on things when necessary and trust you to tuck them away in a corner of your mind. It'll be just between the two of us, our secret until you're older and then you'll know yourself what to do about it. By then, I'll be dead and you'll be Cástulo reborn and roaming the world in search of a better life. I swear to you, son, the only reason I didn't put myself into bed to die of rage, of indignation, of powerlessness was because you existed, because I had to wait for you to grow up a bit so's I could turn over to you all of what I'm carrying around inside me, that's not mine anymore but yours and that I couldn't leave for somebody else to give you...

"Now, who's to blame? I've had my suspicions since the first moment, more of a hunch, let's say, but where was I going to find justice?"

"That same night, the night of the calamity, I took off a second after my *compadre* gave me the bad news, running in the rain like a lunatic all the way to the army guardhouse. There I found only a couple of soldiers who grunted at me like pigs. 'Wait for the Captain or the Lieutenant,' was all they'd say. When I got to see the Captain and asked after Cástulo Bell, he answered, 'Cástulo who? Ah, they transferred him to the city. Business for the tops. I don't know anything about it.' 'What do you mean, you don't know anything about it? What do you mean you goddammit to hell don't know!' Luckily, my *compadre* Ramón had came along with me. Otherwise, they would have killed me on the spot. I went so crazy he had to grab me around the waist and drag me out with all his strength to get me back home. 'And don't go nosing around or the same'll happen to you,' the Captain yelled at me. I could hear him as my *compadre* was pulling me out to the street."

"Who do you think it was, grandpa? Who do you suspect?"

"Listen carefully, Antonio. Listen closely to what I'm about to tell you and then wipe it from your mind until such time as you have need to remember: the vile human being behind your father's calamity was Cocolo Cantera.

Much as I suspected, I didn't get to be really sure until Juanito killed him in the cockpit. Now, I want you to hear this other thing: It was Cástulo who killed Cocolo. After finishing off Killer Feet, Juanito spoke and I was the only one who realized that it was Cástulo talking. I was already aware of what he wanted. You know what happened after that. In the midst of all the tumult and confusion Juanito flew straight to where I was, I grabbed him out of the air, and handed him over to my *compadre* Ramón, standing next to me, to put him back into the same sack we brought him to the cockpit in. I told my *compadre* to take him away and hide him. Of course, nobody was accused of The Snake's death. The talk that went around made it all the more mysterious. As time went by, things quieted down and pretty soon I brought Juanito back home. You got to know him real well, playing with him as much as you did, and you remember when he died and that funeral we gave him."

A young man from Cuba entered the Seminary at the same time that Antonio Bell was beginning his first year there. He was a *maestrillo*, as that teaching level is known in the Jesuit educational system. Fabricio Paula y Céspedes, 23 years old, was from Havana, and unable to come to terms with the discrepancy between the perfection of the celestial kingdom and the abominations of the world in which we live. His departure from Cuba was headlong. He had to be whisked out of the country before Baptista could change his mind about yielding to pressure and granting an exit permit to an individual suspected of being one of the sinister brains behind terrorism in Havana. His family's social position and wealth had weighed heavily in convincing the Dictator and in reaching an agreement with the Jesuits without prejudicing their relations with him. Fabricio had always been a bit of a headache to the Company of Jesus and its authorities were rather at a loss in coping with his rebellious spirit. Twelve years had gone by smoothly since he had entered the Seminary. Fair-skinned, the unmistakable stamp of Miraflores aristocracy in his bearing and the light of intelligence in his eyes, he possessed all the essential attributes for development into a Jesuit stalwart. Such paragons, however, were not always sufficiently malleable and Fabricio was certainly made of more refractory materials. This was not viewed with any great concern at the outset; in time they would press him into the desired mold. The important thing was talent, a natural quality that is not inoculable. Sanctimonious hypocrites lacking that gift were a waste of time. The same held true for the effeminate. It took a seasoned eye to identify them before they crossed the threshold and the astute Jesuits rarely erred. What they required was the genuine article, the diamond in the rough to be put through their laboratories for polishing into a rare gem. The dull-witted or unmanly were not admitted into the exclusive club of the sons of Saint Ignatius nor were the unrefined, blacks or mulattos. Those could join the brotherhoods of other orders and even become secular priests should their intelligence be sufficient to see them through twelve years in a seminary. There was room for everybody but each in his proper place and Fabricio Paula y Céspedes was well endowed to be a privileged member of the General's service. However, after twelve years, with eight still remaining for ordination, the young man had not fully conformed to the accepted model. He held independent opinions, mainly in the social area, and he clung to them stubbornly. With four centuries of experience behind it, the Company was secure in the belief that it could bring out the luster of this gemstone and that there was ample time to do so.

Fabricio Paula y Céspedes was able to spot undercover policemen at a glance, a capacity developed in Havana. It was purely a matter of instinct. He noted that the ones in the Santo Domingo airport might as well be wearing a sign around their neck. On entering he would search one out and eye him challengingly, contemptuously discharging the full load of rancor he bore inside. He went through the red tape of immigration and customs with this provocative mien as though he were invulnerable or indifferent to danger. He was met by two priests who drove him to the Seminary. As they rode, Fabricio intuited the new dangers that awaited him in this new country, this Caribbean trap.

Upon completion of his seclusion in the Manresa spiritual house, he was assigned to teach world history in the Lower Seminary, launching a new phase of his life.

Open, communicative, earthy in speech, he quickly established rapport with his students, particularly because he had no compunctions about telling racy stories. A favorite subject was an uncle of his. A world traveler, he would suddenly appear in Havana like a comet and disappear again for five years at a time without a sign. As Fabricio described him, he was a charming, roguish man and a confirmed bachelor. Tall and slender, with elegant manners, he had an endless fund of incredible tales. One day he returned from his wanderings to announce his intention of never going off again. He was nearly fifty years old by then. They said that he had come back insane and at the insistence of his brother-in-law was committed to a mental institution. He had no objection to this and accepted the family's decision as if he were being sent to a hotel at Varadero Beach. Within a week he was a kind of monarch at the institution. He became an adviser to the psychiatrists, lover of several nurses, spiritual guide of the nuns, and performer of magical tricks for the inmates. Fabricio related that when he was nine years old, he tried to convince his mother that his Uncle José was the least crazy man in the world. He had reached that conclusion one Sunday when he went with one of his cousins to visit him and found that he had exchanged the white linen suit he had brought him as a present the week before with one of the cooks for a couple of ordinary spoons. Fabricio's mother did not accept his reasoning, and when she went to visit him the following Sunday with her husband and other family members, all were prepared to reproach him, but were taken aback when Uncle José related anecdotes of personal experiences in the Arabian desert which demonstrated the relativity of values. He presented irrefutable arguments to support his point and, in conclusion, with the lucidity of a mind at its soundest, said to them: "What the hell am I going to do with a fine linen suit here in this slaughterhouse for the insane? These ordinary spoons are of much more use to me." His sister who heard the first sensible pronouncement ever to have come from him, spoken with the seriousness of a bishop, removed him from the place that very afternoon, against her husband's advice, without benefit of an exit pass and, eager to right an unhappy injustice, installed him in princely accommodations on an upper floor of the family home.

It was at this time that Uncle José got into the habit of rising at cockcrow to go down into the kitchen, and after stirring up the maids by smacking them on the behind to make them run off squealing, he would install himself at the dining room table. Seated there with a huge white napkin embroidered with the family coat of arms spread across his chest, he would be served a hearty breakfast during which he missed no opportunity to slip a hand into whatever forbidden area of female anatomy came within reach. While the other family members were still asleep, Uncle José, equipped for a foray into the countryside, would leave the house not to be seen again until late afternoon. He would return with a British-detective aura about him, slip through the patio to avoid indiscreet questions, and disappear on the upper floor until, having washed off the mud in a rose-scented bath, he went down directly to the dining room, whistling a Lecuona tune, his expression guileless as a babe's. Since his absences were entirely in character and no worrisome changes in his customary volubility were discernible, the family continued to treat him as the same Uncle José of his globe-trotting days.

Time passed in this way until one Tuesday in June when in the middle of supper a hollow, ghostly sound of a bass voice threw the diners into a panic. Fabricio related that his parents, at either end of the ancestral mahogany table, who, having finished their meal, had at that moment risen halfway from their seats, remained frozen in that position, while he and his two little brothers, no less terrified, jumped up in their chairs. This happened just as Uncle José, drawing up his quixotesque figure to its full height, had launched into a weird and cryptic tale that was a melange of three ancient dead Spaniards, a moonlit night, a rumbling river, a mysterious ceiba tree upon a hillock in a little field, and the voices of those dead men who, coated with a white substance like lime, approached the ceiba in slow motion as he, José, stood at the foot of the tree petrified with fright, where they named him custodian of a vast fortune. That is to say, José was charged with digging up a treasure that had lain for some two hundred years no more than inches from his feet. It wouldn't have taken much more for the brother-in-law himself, growling in Basque-Spanish, to have dragged José off to the asylum in a strait jacket. This, not so much for the wild story of the buried treasure as for the shock to his nerves when he rose from the table to hear José delivering unexpected words of introduction..."Ladies and gentlemen... Ladies and gentlemen..." in a voice like thunder but which at the same time seemed to be coming from far away, the voice of a midnight spirit that boomed suddenly from his throat and was further dramatized by a movement of his bony right arm, which swept up slowly from his waist as though unsheathing a sword from his belt and brandishing it aloft.

Calm and good humor were restored the next day as he continued his story. It was heard first by the immediate household, then by family members, including nieces, nephews, and cousins, and little by little, friends who tiptoed in to listen to Uncle José's spoof about a buried fortune. These were all people who considered Uncle José a harmless lunatic, a story teller of great imagination. At the same time, however, he kept alight a tiny flame of greed hidden deep in their souls since such a story carefully examined, with the hallucinatory overlay removed, might possibly have some truth to it this time. Why not? This time, it could well be part of often-rumored treasures of gold hidden in olden days that turn out to be real. Each one said to himself inside, deep inside: "What's to lose in having a look?" even as they proclaimed their disbelief with raucous laughter at the comedy.

Meanwhile, Uncle José started coming down to the kitchen again before the sun awoke and, scarcely relaxing his ramrod posture, continued to grab at the female servants' bottoms with ever improving aim. They were a black girl and two mulattas from Oriente, young and toothsome, who began to get fun themselves out of the sly rump hunter's game and when they heard him coming would pretend to be busy while, at the same time, tilting up their outboards for him to grope more accurately. The rest was routine: breakfast, departure from the house, return at dusk. He always entered through the patio gate, his boots covered with mud, his gait no longer a stiff, tense march but rather a relaxed amble. As time went by, Uncle José's behavior also changed. He talked sparingly but sensibly and instead of slipping away after supper to the solitude of his room he sought that of the city's streets; no one in the house knew where he went and he offered no explanation. This lone, wandering wolf was up to something!

Those sorties—as was later learned—were for the purpose of holding secret rendezvous—in a park, a church alley, a dimly lit bar...with each of six people, separately, who had made the most disparaging comments about his tale of apparitions and his sojourn in a mental institution. A seventh person—his brother-in-law—was approached at home. Uncle José was suggesting to each the possibility— merely the *possibility*—that an incalculable fortune in a two-hundred-year sleep might be buried on the property he owned along the Rincón. Each, of course, was unaware that Uncle José had contacted the others. Uncle José advised every one that he alone was in on the secret. In this way, each was quite proud to accept the reasons for having been selected that the owner of the treasure put forward.

His powers of persuasion were apparently irresistible. They stemmed from a small manual published in Mexico on how to search for buried treasure. It bore allusive figures in gold leaf on the cover and was illustrated with drawings that appeared to have been made centuries ago. Particularly worthy of note, as the sites became known, was their remarkable correspondence with the indications in the book, that is, the similarity between the sites described as potentially explorable and the spots where the dead Spaniards had indicated a fabulous treasure chest was buried. The manual specified that the sites chosen for hiding bullion or other golden valuables followed basic rules that made it possible for the treasure to resist the ravages of time and the elements. Thus, appropriate locations were considered to be, for example, at the foot of a long-lived tree or on the peak of a promontory, which would be always accessible and protected against soil erosion by rain and wind; and the orientation in a straight line from a bend in a river since its course never changes. These were some of the basic indications. Another highly recommended procedure was to conduct anthropological and historical research on the area to find out who its inhabitants had been, the financial standing of the property owners and their economic activities, and the presence of ruins in the surrounding terrain. In short, all the guidelines for identifying a likely site were set forth.

After Uncle José had brought the victims there, one by one, ignoring disguises (wide-brimmed hats pulled down over the eyes, false mustaches, dark glasses...) so that they could see for themselves that the place certainly seemed to have been created precisely for the purpose of burying treasure. They then dipped lavishly into their pockets to hasten the digging, it being fully understood, of course, that the appropriate security measures for this type of operation were being taken and that absolute secrecy had to be observed, a point specially stressed. Uncle José would allow himself to be buttonholed while the investor-in-turn would say, "Not a word to a soul! Understand? To nobody!" These were, of course, not brusque admonitions but rather orders delivered in the form of pleas. Uncle José assented docilely, with a sob of gratitude when one of them, under sacred oath, promised him a life of unending delights, a world at his feet. The amounts invested varied according to the vigor with which faith had blown upon the embers of their ambition.

The brother-in-law, on his part, was apparently interested but kept stalling on his participation. One day he got Uncle José into his van at dawn and drove him to the Rincón property. He had heard about this field (the only one inherited by Uncle José that he had not combed) and wanted to have a look at it and perhaps consider the possibility of building a summer retreat there if he could negotiate a good deal with Uncle José. He brought all this up along the way but the only reply he could elicit was silence. Even though the brother-in-law was a stranger in town and despite having arrived before the sun was up, he took the unnecessary precaution of avoiding the main streets by skirting the cemetery and driving along a dusty road that brought them in a matter of five minutes to the wire fence that enclosed the land. It was a well-tended property (Uncle José had devoted the last few months to making it presentable) partly level then rising like a dromedary hump to slope down on the other side to the river bank. The brother-in-law would not allow himself to be directed and what he did not negotiate on foot he scanned with his bird-of-prey eyes. He took note of the many fruit trees and made a mental estimate of the acreage. Then, shadowed constantly by Uncle José, he approached a recently built hut disinterestedly, regarding it closely without asking questions. He then climbed to the top of the hillock and exhausted by the effort leaned against a tree which was so old it seemed that it must have been born at the same time as the very soil from which it had sprung. It was the ceiba already well known to him from Uncle José's stories. His glance followed the river which widened as it flowed past the plain, observing that were it not for the bend, if the flow had continued in a straight line the waters would have poured over the hill, their center passing right over the middle of the fantastic ceiba. He took in all this with no change of expression. Uncle José, on his part, did nothing but keep his eyes on his brother-in-law, observing his slightest reaction, sizing him up. When they came down to flat ground, retracing their steps, Uncle José contrived to edge the man (now more manageable though manifesting the same indifference) towards a nearby woods to show him the remnants of some thick stone walls covered with moss and vines. These walls that had withstood the pressure of centuries bore evidence to the fact that people of substance had lived there.

"This property fulfills all the conditions set out in the manual," said Uncle José. And, as though talking to himself, added in a loud voice, "Down below are the ruins of the sugar mill and these appear to be those of the residence of the owners, who obviously must have been people of considerable fortune."

"Yes, seems like the soil is good and virgin, besides," the brother-in-law replied, veering away from the other's comment. Uncle José had only to raise his arm to pick a mango off a neighboring tree.

"Here, brother-in-law," he said, "they grow close to the ground, the kind you don't even have to reach for."

On the way back to the city, the brother-in-law suddenly asked Uncle José, "How much are you asking for that land?"

Meanwhile, Uncle José who was enjoying the view through the window of the van, answered offhandedly, "After I've dug up the treasure, I'll make you a present of it."

That is exactly what he had told the other "partners." When they got home, the brother-in-law invited him into his office where he handed him a sheaf of bills without counting them, as he said, "Here's an advance. When do we start digging?"

"Soon. Work starts this week."

Uncle José was going to be away in the city for a few days. To arouse no suspicions he notified the "partners." It was a Monday and he expected to be back by Wednesday. He went to the Morón area where he hoped to find a Haitian who would have the necessary attributes for the job he needed done. It was harvest time and there were many Haitians in the sugarcane zones but those he interviewed were in such deplorable physical condition that he had to reject them one after another until all were eliminated. The army corporal who had acted as his guide more than earned the hundred pesos he received when he appeared at his little hotel early Wednesday evening with a herculean black man whom he had tracked down on the coffee plantations. Early on Thursday morning, Uncle José and the giant Negro set off for Havana on a bus whose top was covered with bleating sheep and cackling hens. That same day, he continued on with him to Rincón and, at five in the afternoon, installed his man in the hut he'd had built shortly before. He told him, "You are going to live here as lord and master of this property and you will lack for nothing, because you will be my other self." As they strolled around the fields, he chatted with the black man, making him feel secure and at ease. Before dark he went to a crossroads where he waited for a car and late that night was back in Havana.

The new occupant of the treasure fields had not yet recovered from his initial bewilderment when Uncle José appeared the following morning at the wheel of a rattletrap jeep piled high with staples and supplies necessary to sustain life in a rural area. Bending way down to get through the door to greet his boss, the black flashed him a gleaming smile, obviously pleased with his new situation. Uncle José spent the entire day with his man, giving him instructions, breaking him in. New trees were to be planted and existing ones pruned and tended, he would have to prepare seedlings for an orange grove, cultivate a vegetable garden, clear the grounds of brush and weeds, and mend fences.

The man was an ebony colossus, slow but precise in his movements, and tireless. A machete hooked at his waist, he went about his tasks doggedly, carrying out orders so effectively that by the fourth day not only had he cleared the land from one end to the other and installed new fence posts, but had the seedbeds ready for the orange trees.

This was really not his true mission, at least for the moment. He was there for another purpose which became evident on a Friday. Uncle José had prepared his man, telling him that certain individuals wanted to get their hands on the property and that it would be necessary to throw a scare into them. He explained all this, not in so many words nor all in one day, but in various forms. He wanted the black man to have his heart in the task, to feel that he was defending his own property, which in a way did belong to him. Uncle José's method, overabundance—of food and, promptly on Fridays, rum—was effective.

A new member joined the cast that day, a former mental patient by the name of Venancio Alofuente with whom Uncle José had dealings before and after being discharged. Venancio was a stringy, melancholy figure, the color of a wax candle, and so cut out for his part in this enterprise— because of his histrionic talents—that Uncle José had no hesitation in enlisting his services to play the role of a hanged man. Furthermore, since he looked for all the world like a Spaniard fallen on evil days, he could not have been more aptly cast.

The first act of the play began to unfold at eight o'clock in the morning of the appointed day. At that time, Uncle José was welcoming the first of his "partners" at the entrance to the property. The man arrived in work clothes and, as usual when he visited that place, wearing a wide hat and dark glasses. Appointments had been made with the other five, separately, to come at intervals of an hour and a half, so that, as Uncle José calculated, the curtain would be ringing down by five o'clock.

A woodpecker was patiently at work hammering out a hollow in a tree. It was the only sound to be heard in the woods except for the echo of the rat-a-tat above the other trees. The light filtering through the foliage transformed the dew into myriad tiny rainbows. Two men went into the hut and soon came out with picks and shovels, ropes, a lantern, and a pail. Their task was to finish, unseen by anyone, the little that remained to be excavated from the hole Uncle José had ordered to be made, instructing the men to stop digging when they had reached a depth of half a meter above the treasure, taking into account the approximate height of its dead owners. The "partners" had advanced enough money for that much, that is, for starting the hole, for building the shed, and for purchasing a vehicle. Shouldering their tools, the men walked among the trees on the flat land getting wet from the droplets that fell when they brushed against the leaves. As they approached the hillock and were about to climb the slope, Uncle José suddenly dropped to his knees and looked up in ecstasy towards the ceiba whose top was barely visible. He shut his eyes and strange words that sounded like a prayer issued from his mouth. The "partner" asked him what had happened and Uncle José replied that as he was climbing he felt the dead graze by him and that was why he prayed, to pacify them. The terrified man looked all around him and remained rooted to the spot, unable to continue, but Uncle José pushed him ahead, urging him on. They continued upward and almost at the top of the rise, a shriek like that of a wounded animal broke the silence. A scene of horror from another world greeted their eyes, once more paralyzing the "partner" with terror. There, alongside the ceiba a few yards away, was a circular pit and above it, hanging like a snake from a branch, was a taut rope with a hangman's noose around the neck of a white man. His tongue sticking out and his eyes bulging out of their sockets, his body was suspended up to the shoulders in the hole. At the other end of the rope was the hangman, a gigantic black figure, naked to the waist, head shaven. The body belonged to a human being while the head was that of an ape. This outlandish creature roared like an enraged beast as it went about its grisly task. The "partner" watched Uncle José standing beside him begging for mercy in a shrill, bloodcurdling tone as he pointed at the hanged man with a trembling finger and repeated over and over again, "It's the Spaniard...! It's one of them...! It's a dead man...! Ay, God in heaven...! Yes, it's one of them...! Ay, Ay, Ay...! Suddenly, the "partner" came to life, dropped to the ground, propelled himself backwards on the seat of his trousers, then, getting back on his feet and staggering like a drunkard, flung himself down the hill as though the devil were chasing him. After a few moments, Uncle José could make out the sound of a motor and then a cloud of dust rising from the road below. The black man removed his ape mask, the hanged man slipped his head out of the noose and was helped off the platform he had been standing on in the hole. Uncle José joined them, all bursting into laughter. They celebrated their success with a round of rum and looked forward to the next performance of their magic act to be repeated every hour and a half until five o'clock. The platform was to be set up again for the last show at daybreak the following day with the brother-in-law as actor-spectator.

Early the following Monday, Uncle José said good-bye to his sister and nephews in their respective rooms and went down to conclude his farewells to his "girlfriends" on whom he lavished money, kisses, and bear hugs that had them flailing their heels in the air. He was unable to take leave of his brother-in-law who had kept himself locked in his bedroom since Saturday morning. His wife said that he had returned in a vile temper from she had no idea where, his face out of joint. Uncle José was to set out that same sunny morning, destination unknown, carrying a small fortune in his billfold, having left a similar amount in a bank minus three thousand pesos he paid the Haitian to cover his needs and for working the land until he returned. His traveling companion was Venancio Alofuente whom he had promised one day in the mental institution to show the wonders of the world. All that money was the balance of what he had received from the "partners" who seemed to have disappeared since Friday. The brother-in-law ended up more convinced than anyone of the existence of the fabulous treasure but Rincón left for Havana on Saturday, preferring to die rather than return to that place.

Such were the stories Fabricio told his students with great gusto and a racy Cuban sense of humor. He had reams more that he had written for his own amusement when there was nobody to listen to them. He was very popular among the students and this talent that distinguished him from the other *maestrillos* automatically exempted him from the hateful task of disciplinarian, which called for a much less sensitive temperament. No whistle was ever draped around his neck. He devoted himself to teaching his world-history classes and a good part of his free time to maintenance of the athletic fields with pick, shovel, tamper, and wheelbarrow for carting sand and gravel. The students were inspired by his example, and he was able to recruit work brigades that labored happily under the hot sun. When the field was leveled and tamped down and goal posts repaired, he organized football, basketball, and volleyball teams which served to instill a healthy spirit of comradeship and competition.

The Rector, Prefect, and Spiritual Father did not fully approve of this outburst of youthful vitality but it was in line with the dictum of *mens sana in corpore sano*. Though they considered that it might tend to foment an unseemly cult of physical development and concomitant arrogance, they did not interfere with his activities. However, what they could not tolerate was his boldness in having gathered together priests, *maestrillos*, brothers, and seminarians at a bonfire of an evening and singing, the Chilean song "*Yo vendo uno ojos negros* (I have a pair of dark eyes to sell)" with guitar accompaniment. They warned him: "You cannot make yourself into a magnet of licentiousness." They bore down on him unmercifully. He was interrogated as to whether he thought that, in addition to constituting a living example of its preaching, the Christian vocation of priest-hood could also include encouragement of the carnal transmission of worldly passions. They pressed him to be on guard against the temptations of the flesh and to tread cautiously in the sphere of modern technology which, in its indifference to the intimate sensitivities of men, women, and the innocent, thrusts upon the atmosphere their provocative messages of brash sensuality by means of the radio and the infestation of jukeboxes. They concluded by reminding him that a Jesuit's every action must be governed by the Christ-like motto of *Ad majorem Dei gloriam*. He was packed off to a two-week spiritual retreat at Manresa for rehabilitation.

By the time the retreat was over, Fabricio Paula y Céspedes was even more deeply convinced that the way this world operated was decidedly wrong. Upon his return to the Seminary, his mind seethed with ideas of social re-demption to even a greater degree than in the fervent years of political agitation in Havana. The passion that had been temporarily quiescent flamed anew and the idealism that boiled up in his guts again like a volcano impelled him to put the conspiratorial abstractions into action that had occupied his mind much of the time in the solitude of his stay at Manresa.

On the 17th of April, it could not possibly have crossed Antonio Bell's mind that he would be spending his fourteenth birthday under the lash of tyranny. On the morning of that spring day following Fabricio Paula's history class on the exploits of Hannibal, every aspect of which he had purposefully stressed and magnified, Antonio's name was called out as the students were filing out of the room. It was the teacher asking him to come to his desk. Addressing him in a conspiratorial tone, he said, "Bell, I'd like to explain chess strategy to you. I'll look for you in the chess room at four-thirty, if you can make it."

The chess room was on the first floor close to the southern wing. It had been a storage place for discarded furniture which Fabricio had been given permission to clean out and set up as a small center under his responsibility where he could teach seminarians to play chess. The authorities viewed it as a worthwhile project for fostering the development of logical thinking. Fabricio's intentions, however, went beyond that. It was to be a place where two or more persons might hold discussions for hours if necessary without interference and without arousing suspicion. An ideal spot for conspiring! What other pretext could serve him better to talk at length during the recreation period with boys who were under constant surveillance? To meet in his room was very risky. To begin with it was forbidden and, furthermore, if such a meeting were to become known, what was to prevent malicious tongues from wagging? And so, having succeeded in setting up the chess club, Fabricio went over the qualities of the students he had dealt with so far, estimating their aptitudes and possibilities as prospective proselytes. A film of the most likely candidates was rerun over and over again before his mind's eye as he feverishly sought to detect even the slightest clues of rebelliousness in any of them. It was played out again in his dreams with new characters as well appearing in distorted form: the Rector with a vulture's crest; Tirano, in gold lace, kneeling erect on a prie-dieu as he heard a Te Deum in the Cathedral; the Archbishop Metropolitan using the affectionate diminutive of Tirano's first name in the course of a sermon, referring to him as "Rafaelito"; a potbellied Seminary cook throwing swill to the pigs. In short, a jumble that was of no help to him in reaching a conclusion until, at last, one name that had been in the forefront of his thinking since the beginning, stood out as definitive—Antonio Bell. He was his best student and helper in the reclamation of the athletic fields. Furthermore, although there had been no more then incipient brushes of conversation between them, Fabricio felt that Antonio held him in highest esteem. It showed in his silence, in his seeking guidance whenever in doubt about complex historical concepts, more as a pretext to talk to him than because he was unfamiliar with the material. What impressed him most about the boy, however, was the scarcely veiled fire that flared up in his eyes during an athletic game at a moment of rough or unsportsmanlike behavior. The same was true in class in his boundless, almost neurotically passionate interest in the great rebels of history. The day's lecture provoked that kind of reaction in Antonio. A transformation took place that disassociated him from the present and took him back through time and space to play an active role in wars waged close to the dawn of history. Fabricio caught this metamorphosis in the embers that glowed in the boy's eyes, and it ignited in the teacher the impulse to bring a different aspect of his profession into play.

"Antonio, would you be willing to take part in actions to overthrow Tirano?"

"Just tell me what I must do, Father. I believe I have been waiting for a long time to hear just that."

Such was the teacher's question and the boy's answer on the second day after the inauguration of the chess club.

Antonio Bell was so eager to get to the chess lesson that he tried to mentally force the hands of his watch ahead to 4:30. The month before, while lost in a moment of anguished daydreaming, he had wished that Fabricio were not a priest but his real father, a son of his grandfather, the replacement for his dead father. He saw himself as a child running about on the grassy plains of his home town, playing with his reincarnated father at being a little boy, indulged with tales and fantasies. His grandpa's hearty laughter was a constant accompaniment, and he was awash in the tenderness of a dry-eyed young mother whose tears, so often shed, had left her barren of joy, her skin aging and her disposition turning glum. Untroubled by twinges of conscience, he imagined himself going off with Fabricio Paula, father and son fleeing the Seminary, to re-encounter things lost, to recapture delights that had been snatched from him. So dreamed Antonio Bell at his desk in the classroom; at chapel, on his knees before the bleeding Christ; in the solitary grotto of Our Lady of Mt. Carmel; dreaming himself back like an inverted river flowing to its source, like a light consuming itself in its own fire.

At four-thirty, he sat down at the table opposite the teacher to receive his first lesson in chess: the pawn, which moves forward and captures diagonally; the knight in L-shaped flight; the bishop, with a long, diagonal trajectory; ponderous rook, devastating queen, and the king, ranks protecting him in his elephantine movements. The next day, as Antonio was setting up the pieces on the board, Fabricio asked him to describe to him how he had spent his childhood. The king sprang from Antonio's hand and rolled on the floor. Fabricio retrieved it and placed it on its black square. Without answering, Antonio moved PK4, his head bowed over the board. In silence Fabricio countered PK4, waiting for Antonio to answer his question. KnB3, attacking the white squares. Fabricio defended with PQ3. Antonio continued the attack with BKn5. Fabricio Paula was amazed at the speed with which Antonio had grasped the game. Actually, he was no novice but had kept his mouth shut about it. His grandfather, an advanced player, had given him his first lessons when he was eight years old and not long after that they were playing even. In addition, he had devoured his grandfather's chess books. He had said nothing of this the previous day when he sat down to be shown the abc's by his teacher. The game ended in a draw but the amazed teacher surmised that it had been a condescension on his opponent's part. It was at the end, after he repeated his question, that Fabricio learned the background of

Antonio's knowledge of chess as well as other things. He started his life story from its least tragic aspects but inevitably it entered thorny pathways and soon his eyes reddened and his face began to twitch. Antonio confessed that since he was a small boy he had mourned the death of his father—of whom he had only a hazy memory—and suffered his mother's grief, and the gradual deterioration of his grandfather. He related the story of his father's death in detail as his grandfather had told it to him. Fabricio listened to that voice laden with unceasing pain, saw the boy's effort to hold back brimming tears, and understood that no prayers or pious counseling would heal his wounds. Those tears would have to be drained off through other channels that could provide him a purpose in life. The memory of the boy's loss would have to be converted into an inspiration, into something that would be helpful to him as a step towards achievement on a higher plane, that would fulfill his need for assurance that his father's death had not been in vain. He was encouraged. And when he had finished, Fabricio stood up and embraced him with all the warmth that parent and child feel when they embrace, and Antonio was strengthened.

Fabricio Paula waited two days before initiating a conversation of a political nature. He spoke to him of what had taken place in Cuba where the youth had risen up in the countryside and the cities to overthrow a blood-soaked butcher with an insatiable lust for money. He theorized on the subject of the fundamental rights of man; on liberty and the pursuit of happiness; discoursed on the concept of equality that shook France in the eighteenth century; pointed up the need to eliminate the shame of material and spiritual poverty in which our peoples have been stagnating for centuries, evils battled against by Cuba since the revolution. He touched on those subjects in measured tones, cramming them into Antonio's brain word for word, as though he were driving iron bars in with a sledge hammer. Then, with great tact, he went on to lay out the differences and similarities between Tirano and the dictator of his own country. Having done this, he fell silent for a few seconds in expectation of Antonio's reaction, which was: "Tirano is a criminal, Father, and no less evil the power-hungry and pharisees who support him."

Several weeks had passed since he organized the chess club and although he had managed to attract some two dozen seminarians interested in the game, he was greatly disappointed to find that the students he had contacted, the best of the crop in his estimation, showed very little interest in politics and, what was worse, lived in ignorance, indifferent to what was happening beyond the walls of the Seminary, as if they were two unrelated worlds. At best they were snails—Fabricio calculated—curled up in their shells, afraid to poke their heads out into the light or else, out of habit, their minds had lost the faculty of open exchange with their fellows, distrustful of any unfamiliar ideas, shy of the threat of a disconcerting thought. To be sure, he handled the matter with extreme caution, making the most uncompromising probings, being careful not to share confidences with weak spirits who might judge a thought to be sinful and feel impelled to run to the Spiritual Father to confess, for instance, that under Father Paula's urging they had found themselves tempted to take part in one thing or another. But all was not lost, Antonio Bell alone was worth the rest of them put together. On various occasions Fabricio had managed to elude surveillance to instruct him in what he called "modern methods of white terrorism." This involved setting fire to public buildings, government vehicles, and businesses connected with Tirano, followed up by telephone calls claiming the acts to have been committed in the name of a powerful organization of thousands of brains working to take power. With a watch-maker's meticulousness he had taught him the use of phosphorus, the candle, and the formula for delayed-action, spontaneously-igniting devices. He had schooled him in the art of disguise: how to look ten years older, to dress like a woman, a beggar, an upper-class youth. When he was through, he contemplated his handiwork like the Lord of Creation, and found it perfect. Yet, at the same time, something strange occurred, a sudden reaction that shook him to the depths of his being. The perfectly coordinated weapon of war fashioned by those skilled hands of a craftsman of redemption aroused an overwhelming sentiment of love in him that he realized was incompatible with the nature of the intended action. The father surrogate Antonio had sought in Fabricio, a yearning that had blossomed with association, was a sentiment that took possession of Fabricio Paula as a paternal love that caused him to see in Antonio the son denied him by his religious celibacy. But now, with the conclusion of his task, repentance suddenly set in.

Sensing the solitary nature of his mission, Antonio tried to convince Fabricio to talk to Arturo Gonzalo; assuring him that his friend would not refuse to go in with them. He had talked to him about it earlier, but Fabricio would not take him on because he had decided not to involve any but first- or fourth-year students with whom he had closer contact and could influence more readily. Arturo Gonzalo was a third-year student whom he knew only by sight. Besides, the school year was ending and with vacation soon to begin, it was better to cancel or postpone plans. That was Fabricio's frame of mind and although he had said nothing to Antonio, he actually did not have the stomach to mark the boy for such a risky future. Sentimental weakness is the worst possible companion of revolutionary action, and Fabricio Paula was now suffering from that failing. When he tried very subtly to convince Antonio that it would be convenient to put off summer action for a more appropriate time, it was too late. He realized as much in the determination of the boy's glance, in that special blaze in his eyes so familiar to Fabricio. He could see that it would be impossible to dissuade him and ended by authorizing him to proceed as scheduled. The volcano's mouth had caught fire, and there was no stopping its eruption.

Bearing suitcases and bundles, excited students rushed back and forth, faces radiant, saying good-bye to one another like good friends, like brothers—as they had never treated each other during the school year, acting like people from the same neighborhood who, although they never speak at home, throw their arms around one another if they meet in another part of the world. The last hours of the school year had come and the month of June was opening for them like a glowing fan, like a tempting assignation for which they were headed, fearfully, as to a pleasure in which desires, lubricious emotions, swirl, but while receiving parting counsel from the Spiritual Father and the Prefect, the boys were the personification of virtue.

Antonio and Fabricio had been looking for one another and met in the corridor where they gripped each other's hand tightly in a farewell that was chary of words but charged with emotion.

"Don't fail to call me as soon as you get back to the capital. When do you think you might be coming?" Fabricio asked.

"In July, Father. In July," he said, compressing his lips and looking into his eyes. "I'll call you when I get there, Father."

Fabricio watched him climb the stairs, following him with his eyes until he was gone, remaining there until he was quite sure not even his footsteps were to be heard. He tried to resist an onrush of emotion but couldn't escape it. He thought of the boy whom he had turned into an adult for good, prematurely, perhaps. He decided to return to his room but stopped on the way, hesitated, and turned toward the pine grove of the yard. The noise of the cars driving in and out, of the voices that would soon be echoes in the dining hall, the chapel, the classrooms, and in all corners of the immense cement cross, reached him there.

Antonio Bell was at the entrance with his suitcase, saying and receiving good-byes, staring vaguely, restlessly looking at the wall clock that crowns the image of the Virgin of Altagracia. All at once, anxiety switched over to pleasure when he saw Arturo approaching along the corridor. He ran to meet him, restraining the desire to embrace him but pronouncing the word "friend" joyfully as he said, "What took you so long in coming down, friend? I was waiting for you. Couldn't leave without saying good-bye." They chatted as they returned to the vestibule. Arturo put down his suitcase and, violating an unwritten law, hugged Antonio. That was a key moment in which the two boys sealed a friendship that could not be outwardly manifested for nine months but which had been communicated in the secret language of the heart. Yet, at this ultimate moment, Antonio had to curb his tongue to comply with Fabricio Paula's order not to tell Gonzalo what he intended to do during vacation, not to invite him to participate. Finally, he got into the car that was already there waiting for him, and was still waving good-bye when he caught sight of Fabricio's figure on the roof, his right arm raised limply, as the solitary car moved up Cordell Hull Avenue going northward... northward... Viewed from the roof, it became no more than a tiny black dot disappearing...

II

...The pussycat's coat was so wonderfully glossy and alluring, as she lay nestled in the warmth of his arms, that he kept smoothing his hand over the fur as though it were a woman's hair. Under the hypnotic drowsiness induced by the man's light fingers the pampered little creature lowered her eyelids slowly till they closed over her huge green eyes while the lids of his own meek eyes drooped shut in tandem, and he fell sound asleep upright in his desk chair, dreaming of the precipices and splendors of nearby mountain peaks. His secretary noted that the pained grimace was gone from the man's lips which now seemed to her to be smiling from off in another world.

Dr. Ramos was aware that the "granite will" had begun to crack, the "iron grip" to slacken, and that the infallible "political wizard" had made his first blunder that day. The time for replacing him had come. At last! "I shall carry his glowing ashes on my shoulder to sprinkle them like volcanic dust upon the air so that his deadly presence will forever be breathed. My Epoch (a dream patiently nursed since I was born!) is at the threshold but, oh Caesar!, my *coup de grace* will be invisible, and like devout Aeneas I shall enter Dido's city wreathed in a mantle of mist. Then will I erect for my kingdom wonderful monuments of stone and cement and all other materials that perpetuate themselves in the memory of man."

And the secretary continued to marvel at that happy, distant face with the unwavering smile that was positively not of this world.

"What a strange fellow," Tirano kept thinking as he sat in his generalissimo's armchair pondering the possible consequences of the war against the church he had now launched and in which Antonio Bell was really no more than a convenient pretext.

Dr. Mario Ramos was constantly ridiculed. His people, those fated to launch him on his rise to power, were on the boorish side and unable to accept his affectations without a snicker. In greeting, he extended his hands like consecration wafers, with little energy or enthusiasm, the long fingers drooping listlessly. His gait was rhythmless, ungainly, as though he were walking in outsize shoes. His eyes were mute, the pupils unchanging, with perhaps sudden forbidding flashes that momentarily accentuated the triangular eyelids. From the time he was a young man he had made it a point to hide his tired puppet body under a stifling costume of jacket and necktie. Those of his own generation derided such garb but older people, unprejudiced by suspicion, grew to respect him as a matchless model of wisdom and responsibility. His voice in conversation no more than a trickle of water from a calm stream scarcely emerging between motionless lips was in oratory a roar. He had cultivated the art of public speaking ever since ambition first stirred within him, practicing from perches high on the chalky promontories around his native town from where he addressed nothingness to an intangible audience in an indeterminate location. When his fame as a silver-tongued orator had grown to national proportions, people never ceased to wonder how a leonine roar of that volume could possibly issue from the throat of such a fledgling.

As a teenager, while his schoolmates were reciting "The rose fell into the water, its petals, though, did not fall," and such anthological favorites at their gatherings, he declaimed poems of his own creation which always ended with a kind of premonitory peroration: "There lies Glory!" Having pronounced those words with his forefinger raised to point at something beyond reach in the far distance, his figure took on the semblance of a Jupiter, Lord of Thunder. Transfixed by the upthrust arm capped by a fist with a protruding biblical finger, listeners looked up to follow its indication and came to rest upon a large, speckled spider, hypnotized, suspended from the highest ceiling beam. That mysterious refrain with which he ended his poems was inspired—as attested to in his oral biographies—by an encounter with a beautiful young woman; attracted by the force of his inspiration, she rose from the bench where she was sitting with her boyfriend, approached him as he strolled down the street, alone as usual, to bestow upon the boy the caress of an older sister. One of the young men present called out to the boyfriend, "Watch out, man, or they'll be stealing her from you." Blowing out a lungful of heavy cigarette smoke, he replied, "No problem, man, faggots don't make it to Glory." A serene, scathing glance from the insulted victim cut through the gust of guffaws as he continued on his sphinx-like way, impassive and enigmatic.

Apparently, nothing could ruffle his composure, but he did assiduously collect those gibes like cords to be braided into a lash.

Despite his aura of wisdom, he was underestimated during a considerable portion of his life by both the military and political cliques who looked upon him as no obstacle to the furtherance of their own ambitions. Furthermore, when it came to women he never aroused jealousy; he was able to conduct his liaisons without attracting the slightest attention from other men, remaining thereby aloof from the beehives of passion.

As a young man, he prowled the edges of his native barrio with extreme caution, entrapping solitary little alley cats, regardless of color or condition, and rendering them helpless with the venom of his forked tongue. As the years went by, he developed into a consummate practitioner of the surreptitious conquest. Finally, a personage of prestige with impeccable social credentials in the capital, he took to hovering about public squares of nocturnal wanderers and, as if in another world, reciting litanies from a heavenly limbo, he was able to arrange the most outlandish encounters with randy servant girls. A bystander might have thought that this solitary man walking slowly and apparently deep in thought was probably enjoying a stroll before turning in when all of a sudden he would veer off into the cemetery on Independence Avenue. However, he was not just after a fast bang; those encounters were deeply, passionately relished on a bed of wild lilies prepared for the purpose under a coverlet of pansies.

Eventually, when he could no longer go about alone because of his high position, he wielded so much power that Estanislao Elermoso, then the sole purveyor to his libidinal needs, would slip the ladies—more carefully selected and ever younger—into the royal bedchamber in the middle of the night.

When Arturo González returned from summer vacation and entered through the vestibule, his little leather valise on his shoulder, he did not experience the same thrill of expectation as in his first year, nor the excitement of seeing in others what he himself had felt in his second year nor, in his third. It was a feeling of nostalgia for lost innocence and of pity for the freshmen, but now his sensation was rather one of being drained, of total apathy. He was a remote being, indifferent, making his way through the sacristy hubbub of entering students and their cohorts of weepy mothers.

The taxi that brought him had been late in leaving town and, according to the driver, was making the trip only because he had promised to, since this was no day to be out on the highway. His mother, on saying good-bye to him felt a stab of anguish just as she did every year, but this time it was not accompanied by the usual resignation to the pain of her son's absence counterbalanced by the consolation of his missionary destiny. She realized this time that the lad was getting into the car against his will with a look in his eyes of mute supplication, seeking comprehension. Yet, she made no move to detain him, hoping and having faith that when he was back at the Seminary a miracle would take place there. On this trip, however, a mother's infallible instinct told her that Arturo was without doubt a different person. She was haunted for many days by the fear that her son would have his way, that he would refuse to return because now that she saw him developing into a man, his character taking on a form of its own and new muscles bulging out of his skin like an awakening of serpents, she knew she didn't have the strength to impose her will on him. Life was sabotaging her chance to make her dream of a life of purity for her son after all her suffering, all the tears shed over her husband's drunken bouts, his desertion; he had abandoned her entirely to her own devices, a woman condemned to pedaling and pedaling away at the machine where she was losing her eyesight in the mazes of embroidery, trapped in a remote corner, piling up accounts of secret hatreds for those who considered her an interloper, even though her son was their own flesh and blood, notwithstanding the marks branded into her arms by the kitchen griddles, the coal-heated clothes irons, the harsh laundry soap...

She wanted a son untainted by any vice, who was a priest, at the opposite pole of her drunken, brawling husband; it was as though in some dark, unconscious way she wished to create a weapon of vengeance against the indignities of that man, of all men. That was the reason she felt so sad as she took leave of her son with a hug and a kiss, understanding that it was only out of love for her that he was returning to the Seminary so as not to slay her dreams, her yearnings. Actually, it was merely postponing the agony, because the Arturo who was saying "Good-bye, *mamá*," as he buried his head in her breast, pressing her tightly to him, "I'm going, *mamá*," as though prompting her to say, "No, son, don't go, stay here with me," was a soul torn by the tears of the one who was torturing his heart. His was a spirit that had been butchered, a heart that was spilling blood, the hot blood of a macho who had now tasted his first bite of a woman's lips... *"I love you in the light of the round moon that etched out the peaks of our town, Laly Pradera; I saw you through the gates walking in the garden of your big house, I, shielded by the solitude of the street...Laly Pradera...I escaped the vigilance of the bricks, was made invisible to your eyes, and in the fragrance of the jasmine, the bronze notes of the church bells calling to rosary were the texture of your skin, the sweetness of your trembling lips... Laly Pradera... Not the smoke of the incense burner, nor the dark transparency of your mantilla, could hide the glow of your face when for the first time I held the tray of the Eucharist close to your velvety neck and saw your enchanted little pink goddess's tongue appear, as though yearning for me, stretch out to receive the host from the priest's fingers... Laly Pradera... When you were just blooming into a woman and we were offering our eyes in innocent love glances like daily bread fed by time till the garden gave me your kisses... Laly Pradera...Laly Pradera."* And the echo of the voice of Arturo's thoughts carried from the seat in which he sat huddled all the way along the highway to the town. *"I love you skating in your little striped skirt, the boys' choir singing: Clock, stop telling time, for I'm going to lose my miiiind. I'll be waiting for you in the park after the sung mass. The girls in Parque España are so looovely, and you were walking with your eyes lost in my eyes, smiling angel smiles... Laly Pradera..."*

Arturo never noticed the storm brewing as they drove at a snail's pace through the foothills of the mountain range and when the trees began to show signs of growing restlessness his thoughts were far away. His traveling companions thought he was asleep even when the wolf whistle of the wind began to be heard, and continued to think so when they stopped and got out along the coast to watch the threatening waves show their claws. Worse still, he remained lost in thought, deep in his memories, when they reached the Seminary. He had not yet fully returned to this world at the moment the *maestrillo* handed him his room number which was no motive for celebration since it was in the same dormitory in the north sector as the year before. He had been glad about it at that time because it was on the third floor, and with the windows thrown open to the night he could feel the vibrations of that bit of the world stretching out before his eyes. After receiving his bell code—two shorts and a long—he went to his room in silence, greeting fellow students on the way with no more than a nod or a flick of his hand. He threw his suitcase on the bare bed and it was not until he tried to push open the window and was struck full in the face by a blast of rain-laden wind that he returned to his senses. The courtyard was under a head-on attack from the hurricane that came roaring in through the pine grove.

A little later, he set out to find Antonio. He had had no word from him since his last letter received early in July, although he had written him twice in August. He was anxious to find somebody to whom he could speak freely and unburden himself of so much that was weighing upon him. He could have used the inside stairway, passed through the dining hall and from there into the main corridor, but he preferred to go to the roof, open to the rain. He had mentioned Laly in his August letters, in a casual way, and perhaps that was why Antonio had not replied, perhaps it was terrain his friend preferred to avoid. Yes, that must be the reason Antonio hadn't written and might not want to listen to him now. He went to the room in which *maestrillo* Ordoñez was greeting students, waited around for a time, and when Antonio didn't appear, stepped into the recreation room where he found only a few seminarians at the window watching the trees in the yard sway in the storm. On his way back, he looked into the chapel without entering. There seemed to be some traffic in the vestibule but the corridors were as dark and deserted as the uninviting outdoors. It was still early and Arturo dreaded looking forward to the afternoon that would stretch into a long evening with nothing to do unless he met Antonio. He didn't want to ask anybody about him lest they might suspect his purpose. He wandered back and forth, upstairs and down, revisited the same places he had already been before he at last made up his mind to go to his room. The supper bell finally drove him out. He didn't see Antonio in the dining hall, nor at the ceremony that followed to officially inaugurate the new term.

It was as though he were entering a new world. He had been saying good-bye to Laly on a park bench only the night before, after the rosary, gaily, their hands brushing innocently, fleetingly, with no opportunity for even the fleetingest of kisses. Accompanying Laly, in addition to her younger sister, was a neighbor her own age, a city girl with a skittish imagination, who was vacationing in town, on whom the boys had pinned the nickname "The Watch Tower" because she would hiss "Watch out, watch out!" when she spied Laly's parents approaching. That had been the previous night in the town square where the people walked round and round in a great circle, winking or flashing little smiles at one another as they listened to Lucho Gatica singing his syrupy boleros on the nearby jukebox, melodies that blended uncomfortably with the classical pieces played by the municipal musicians for the traditional Sunday evening promenade. But this was something that had happened to Arturo at some distant time, in a remote and fantastic world, like a dream, that had nothing to do with the formal, austere, blindingly lit hall filled with dark cassocks that he now had to deal with.

The welcoming address was delivered by a bishop who was officiating for the first time at a ceremony of this nature. He was flanked on the right by the Rector and on the left by the Disciplinarian Prefect and the Spiritual Father. At the doors and in the aisle stood three *maestrillos* who could have passed for policemen, whistles around their necks, notebooks poised. The event, although the same as usual in its general thrust—stress on spiritual fortitude, discipline, rejection of worldly vanity, detachment from family ties, stalwart resistance of fleshly temptation—bore a direct and graphic threat and that was precisely why such a high dignitary was there. He had not been invited for the purpose of repeating things the Spiritual Father could have told them more dramatically and with greater effect. His role was to address the audience, backed by the full weight of his ecclesiastical investiture, for the purpose of urging, ex-horting, obligating them, as the integral sector of the Church that they were, to subscribe to each and every one of its tenets, including that of absolute, unconditional loyalty to Tirano's regime, which had bestowed so many favors upon the church and to which it owed the construction and support of the Seminary. There was a burst of applause and huzzahs, and at the end, a long lineup for the humble kissing of the Right Reverend ring.

All these things happening around Arturo Gonzalo were re-echoing in his distraught mind in a frighteningly distorted form, like in a nightmare. His eyes continued the fruitless search for Antonio during the ceremony, but it became less and less important, finally turning into something vague and meaningless.

On that first night at the Seminary, he slept uninterruptedly with the placidity of a tired animal lost in limbo, but he awoke spontaneously towards morning before the bell sounded and went to the window to look at the ravages of the storm. The yard was a swamp, the trees in their usual place, the sky gray, the sun unable to filter through the heavy clouds. As he peered through the hazy pane, he tried to piece together the images of his dreams during the night, but they were disjointed and he was unable to fix on them. Instead he began to daydream: Laly Pradera was at his side, her brow and enormous eyes illuminating the world. He called up his mother in his mind but devotedly dismissed her because she made him feel sad. All very well for afflictions to spring from reality, out of life's events, but they shouldn't be dragged in as thoughts. And so, he preferred to keep his mind on Laly and hold her there until he was obliged to return to Antonio; Laly would reappear and then his mother, but his friend came to occupy the forefront of his mind. He was there at five o'clock in the morning, the world shaking with terror: *maestrillo* Ordoñez had made his devastating presence known. Retreat was soon to begin.

When he finally spotted Antonio, a black dot in the long rosary of seminarians, they were already on the way to the chapel, committed to silence. Days were to go by before the students were permitted to speak again.

It was the first Sunday in October. The afternoon sun shone with all the intensity of a summer day, the air was crisp and clear and the wind howled in the pines. The almond trees, in a long line that followed the right angle of the building, were shedding their large, heart-shaped leaves already forming a carpet. Arturo had been feigning diarrhea for which he was given pills but he tossed them down the toilet.

His malingering won him an excuse for the time being from the evening walk which followed an established route along the oceanside to the Feria and finally El Embajador Hotel's polo field. At other times, it went directly to Manresa. This was the customary Sunday stroll for the groups of silent boys, wearing blinders, who set out through the streets closely shepherded by *maestrillos*. Arturo watched them go down Cordell Hull Avenue and when he saw them continue downhill without turning right, he realized that they were not headed for the polo match. "Then I'm not missing anything," he said to himself, "this is the third outing of the year and they still haven't been to watch the polo." It was refreshing to be there. Surveillance was somewhat relaxed, and one could let one's thoughts roam in and out of the bright colors as the horses raced around. On their return, the seminarians went about in a near daze. Tirano, a polo fanatic, almost always attended and was there to watch his son play. Porfirio Rubirosa was also a member of a team and the girls there, besides looking beautiful, were deliciously perfumed. The group was swallowed up at the bottom of the slope and all he could see from his dormitory window was a bit of the city he was familiar with down to the minutest detail stretching all the way to the sparkling blue sea.

Arturo left the dormitory section and on his way down the main stairway felt a subtle stirring of happiness that prompted him to sing out loud and leap at each landing. Suddenly he stopped and cocked his ears; he could hear nothing but the echo of the silence. He continued on his way without a sound, slowly, alert, somewhat ashamed at his momentary excitement. "That was much too risky!" he scolded himself. On reaching the door to the yard at the north end of the Seminary, he went through nervously and made his way to a rock under some trees where he sat uneasily for a time. The view from that point took in the full expanse of the Lower Seminary, as well as the various entrance doors of the area, to which his eyes returned from time to time as he listened to the familiar, distant, seductive drone of the city without letting his eyes and attention stray from his objective.

Waiting made Arturo impatient. He had stood up from the rock and sat down on it again several times and though he had intended to walk to the other end of the Seminary where he thought Antonio might be, he decided against it. Actually, he was afraid to cross the open field. Besides, that wasn't what had been agreed on. He had said he would wait for him under the almond trees in the north sector while the seminarians were on their outing and that was it. Yet time was passing without a sign of Antonio. And more serious than that, there wasn't a single cassock anywhere in sight, and he was beginning to feel the pressure of the solitude. Behind him lay a broad wooded area with blue mountain peaks looming in the misty distance as though suspended from the sky; in front of him, the Seminary which despite its reality seemed to transform itself into an abandoned edifice looming up from past centuries, and Arturo began to feel a sensation of loathing.

A month had now gone by without Arturo having been able to talk to Antonio and share the events of the summer with him. Antonio's contact with the other students was restricted. He did attend classes or stand in line with them at the dining hall but was strictly forbidden to talk to others, except for whatever brief exchange about a common activity might be necessary. A contagious pariah, he had to remain apart from the group during recreation, isolated in his dormitory, the chapel, or on the grounds. Sunday was the most bearable time. He was permitted a visit from his mother in the morning, but the cauldrons of hell were fired up for him again in the afternoon. The students took off on their outing, leaving the Seminary an empty unbearable maze of sepulchral echoes.

The two boys had agreed to meet that Sunday between two-thirty and three. They had been able to talk the previous Thursday on the way out of the dining hall. His friend's voice sounded as though he had something the matter with his throat.

When his retreat ended in mid-September, Arturo sensed an atmosphere of extreme tension in the Seminary, with constant whispering and redoubled surveillance everywhere. It had never been easy to learn the truth about anything there, but now it was impossible to hide the fact that Antonio Bell was the center of attention. There were rumors that he had been arrested in July for political reasons; that he had been caught planting bombs in public buildings; that it wasn't bombs, but that he had tried to set all the buildings of the Feria on fire with gasoline; that he had been tortured in Tirano's prisons, at Victoria, Cuarenta, the National Palace itself; that he might be insane. The Seminary was a beehive buzzing with speculation.

Communication between students was hampered not only by the constant proximity of a *maestrillo,* but also a strict order prohibited discussion of politics. Everyone was living in fear.

The situation was even worse on the Sunday Arturo decided to feign illness and remain on the grounds. When he had talked to Antonio the Thursday before, they had both decided that it would be best for them to meet in the adjoining wooded area. It was a hasty decision reached in the few headlong seconds available to them.

Antonio was not there when Arturo arrived at the appointed place at two-thirty. The were no sounds to distract his uneasy thoughts but those of Sunday revelry wafted from the Malecón and the Feria. Lying on the ground, angry and frustrated, his head pillowed on a fallen tree trunk, his eyes lost among the clouds, by four o'clock he had given up expecting his friend.

On Tuesday, they were able to communicate briefly again under the same pressure. The opportunity came after supper as it had the week before. Distracted as he frequently was by trifles, in the manner of small boys, *maestrillo* Garmídez started comparing his old-fashioned pocket watch with a wrist watch belonging to a fifth-year student. He was defending the virtues of his ancient relic with such passion that a ring of boys formed to listen silently to his expostulation which he clinched with a comment that caused the owner of the wrist watch to turn pale. He said, "An article of that kind is nothing but an instrument of vanity." It was a gold wrist watch with a very flashy gilt band, a present from an uncle in New York. The student had brought it with him on his return from vacation and prompted by the relative freedom enjoyed by fifth-year seminarians was evidently unable to resist the temptation of showing it off. After this fit of pique on the part of *maestrillo* Garmídez, he had to put it away, not so much because it was forbidden, but because he was more concerned about his companions' ill will than he was about the *maestrillo*.

Taking advantage of the barrier that had formed around the watchdog, Antonio whispered, "I couldn't get out, they took me to the office. Doctor Mario Ramos had been there."

"Who?" Antonio asked in surprise.

"Doctor Mario Ramos. You must have heard of him?"

"Sure, but..."

"I'll explain later," Antonio interrupted, moving away. Arturo took a step forward as if to follow him but swiveled around immediately at the sight of *maestrillo* Ordónez entering the area.

Dr. Mario Ramos was a man for whom every moment of his life represented a unique and irreplaceable value, all of which were carefully counted like newly minted coins, greedily as a miser, rigorously as an ascetic, each particle, each link nurtured as though it had a life of its own. He did not share even the most fleeting instant of intimacy with anyone. And so the obscure seeds were sown of an arcane life that knew neither embarrassments or exaltations, like an overblown vegetable turned to stone. His activities, the purpose of which only he knew, were carried out with mechanical rigidity according to a strict schedule.

The chauffeur opened the door of the car at two o'clock in the afternoon. Dr. Mario Ramos thanked him politely, stepped slowly out of the vehicle with the calm of a Buddhist monk in nirvana, and stretched out his right hand to the waiting Rector, his left gripping a black felt hat. The effusiveness with which the priest took the Doctor's hand between his froze upon contact with those exhausted fingers that seemed barely sustained aloft: a dead, glutinous hand.

"Good afternoon, father." The piteous voice of an expiring ventriloquist.

The priest's answering words stumbled out, lame and disconnected. Afterwards, having recovered from the initial disagreeable impression, he repeated them in a firmer tone inside the Seminary as the two of them climbed the broad marble staircase.

"Good afternoon, Doctor Ramos. Welcome to the Santo Tomás Seminary."

The priest heard a faint sound that appeared to have issued from alongside him and, bringing his deductive powers to bear, inferred that his companion had said, "Thank you." Actually, the plaintive moan emitted by Dr. Ramos resembled no intelligible sound and though the Rector quickly twisted his head in the hope of deciphering a syllable or two by lip reading he saw that those lips were tightly sealed.

The bishop and Papal Nuncio were waiting for him in the Rector's office. The tenseness of the preambles was somewhat alleviated by a statement from Dr. Ramos that was audible this time.

"Right Reverends, in your cordial company and in this holy place I feel spiritually at ease as on few other occasions."

The observant Rector wasted no time watching those stiff lips with a one-millimeter crack between them through which the visitor's guttural articulations issued as though having originated at that very point. He had previously observed his handshake with some curiosity and now noted with satisfaction the same drooping and flaccid hand he had seen when he entered. "It's a mannerism of his," he concluded. He immediately stepped over to direct him to one of the armchairs by the desk. Before sitting down, however, Dr. Ramos took a few steps along a diagonal to the bookshelves where, assuming a beatific stance, he let his eyes glide over the titles. The office into which he had been introduced was formally elegant: a small circular rug on the floor, serving as base for a low, solid table that stood on six sturdy lion's paws; at one side, a lustrous mahogany desk; covering the broad windows that faced the front garden, a great curtain in a single sheet of a shimmering ivory-white fabric. The furnishings consisted of four armchairs with tall backs and padded seats, a few side chairs around the little table and bookcases against one wall. On the opposite wall there hung a medium-size crucifix flanked by images of Saint Thomas Aquinas and Saint Ignatius Loyola. A colonial porcelain amphora stood in one corner. It was in this setting that the first of a series of meetings took place between Dr. Mario Ramos and high dignitaries of the Roman Catholic Church of Santo Domingo at two o'clock on the first Sunday of October.

No sooner had they taken seats than the Rector asked leave to open the windows and the curtain. A soothing breeze entered the room. The Rector approached the distinguished guest and offered to take his hat but the Doctor gestured his refusal by grasping it more firmly as one would a talisman of some sort, saying, "Thank you, Father, don't bother," and resting it on his knees, kept continually rubbing it on both sides of the crown with his two hands.

"Doctor Ramos," said the Rector on returning to his seat, "I welcome you in the name of Holy Mother Church and of the institution of priestly education that you honor with your presence."

"Thank you very much, Father," he whispered, bowing his head slightly.

The priests were assuming that Dr. Ramos would initiate the conversation, but he did not so much as look at them. His head then turned toward the bookshelves and with his eyes on the books once more as he revolved the hat in his hands, he scarcely took notice of his hosts. To break the silence, the Rector blew his nose loudly into a handkerchief, as thoughts unbecoming to his calling crossed his mind: *"This bastard is either a horse's ass or making himself out to be one."* At a moment when Dr. Ramos appeared to be glancing toward him, the Rector made a gesture with his hand inviting him to speak, but Dr. Ramos seemed not to notice, prompting the Rector to think again, *"What the bastard is doing is playing dumb."* The Doctor then turned his attention to the Nuncio, whose diplomatic stare appeared to engage him, and bobbing his head gave to understand that he was correctly interpreting his expression, but even then he kept his eyes on the ceiling for quite some time. Finally, separating his legs, his chin thrust forward, a detached expression on his face, he said to the group, "I have come to hear you out, Right Reverends. Against my will I must carry out the thankless duty of mediating in such an unhappy dispute. Speak out, Fathers, I am all ears."

It was the Nuncio, an almost excessively handsome and elegant young man, probably not even thirty years old, who, addressed Dr. Ramos in a heavy Italian accent.

"Doctor Ramos, the Holy Father is concerned about the possibility that an isolated factor...an act of madness on the part of a simple seminarian"—the Nuncio made a move of disparagement—"might result in deterioration of the traditionally good relations between the government and the Church." And stressing his words to make the message sharp and clear, he went on, "It is a concern that His Holiness conveyed personally to me and which I, throwing myself upon the mercy of your good offices, Doctor Ramos, would like to be brought to the attention of His Excellency, the Generalissimo."

"The task that has fallen to my lot, besides being thankless, is a difficult one. I don't know, to be sure, with what success, but it will give me great pleasure to be the bearer to the Generalissimo of His Holiness's well-justified concern." His words were delivered in the faint, expiring voice Dr. Ramos adopted for dialogue. "And what shall I say to the Generalissimo regarding the status of the seminarian Bell?" he added, as though letting fall a droplet of poison.

It was the Rector, now, who reacted. "I will send for him immediately, Dr. Ramos, if you consider it appropriate to talk to him...to question him in any way." And he went to his desk where he pressed a bell, giving the signal agreed upon with the Prefect to bring in Bell, who had already been sitting in his office for some time.

"Not necessary, Father, not necessary. What you all have to tell me will be enough," Dr. Ramos hastened to answer. However, the rector did not cancel the order to bring in the seminarian.

As for the Bishop, he remained silent, nodding his round skull, in turn, as each man spoke. A flabby, potbellied sexagenarian, his acquiescent nature had made it possible for him keep afloat and rise in the priesthood over the years, his placidity never varying. Now, however, he found himself embroiled all at once in this annoying controversy. He was accustomed to steering his portly, cask-like figure through the salons of high society as well as at occasions of major public rites of the Church resplendent with uniforms, the aroma of incense blending with Parisian fragrances, but he no longer commanded his earlier pastoral instincts and the necessary capacity to cope with conflictive situations.

The atmosphere in the room turned tense undoubtedly because of the suddenness of Dr. Ramos's question, unexpected, at least in that form and right before more tranquil discussion of weightier matters. The Doctor's question revealed to them how seriously the Bell affair was being taken at the top. It was as if this thorn in the Church's side had become the center of everything in a very suspicious effort to activate and spread the venom produced by the discord. A knock at the door broke the ensuing silence. Seminarian Bell entered, followed by the Prefect, a pompous little man, languid in appearance but with a purposeful mien and a steely glint in his eye. Actually, there had been no point in bringing the seminarian to this meeting inasmuch as the very sight of him caused a rash to break out among the priests and besides it was not in Dr. Ramos's interest, who was annoyed to find, on turning his head, that he was confronting a kind of prisoner. Was he being taken for a prosecutor, he, a dignitary on his way to the top being placed in the crude and odious role of policeman? By no means did he wish to project such an image but rather one of an arbiter in a situation involving unavoidable circumstances of some importance. But he, Dr. Mario Ramos, an interrogator of boys, never! How little these priests knew him. He was, however, satisfied with their initial reaction to his question. That was his primary objective: to have them keep in mind that the sword of the devil was poised upon their necks. The next thing would be to dispense with the unexpected presence of the seminarian and to pursue his strategy at this meeting which he knew would occupy a good part of the afternoon.

"As far as I'm concerned you may take him away," Dr. Ramos said. "I don't think his presence makes any positive contribution to furthering our discussion. I would greatly appreciate it if..." He moved his head sideways and swung his hat to the right.

Dr. Ramos took longer in indirectly manifesting his wish to have the seminarian Bell removed than the Rector did in giving the Prefect the sign to get him out of the office. It was then that the Ambassador of the Vatican and the bishop, as if to clear the air, asked for orange juice. From the pitcher beside his desk the Rector served them both and Dr. Ramos, as well, who had not indicated that he wanted any. Following the Nuncio's example, the Rector sipped his juice in quick, measured doses while Dr. Ramos barely tasted his. The thirsty bishop, however, clutching an enormous white handkerchief that he kept rolled up in a pocket of his cassock for mopping brow, neck, and cheeks, absorbed glassful upon glassful as avidly as parched earth. His movements were out of character with his usual serenity, a fact that did not escape Dr. Ramos's notice. The atmosphere cleared little by little and faces reflected a return to relative normalcy, but no one ventured to reopen the dialogue, frozen since Antonio Bell's exit. It began to seem as though the group would remain indefinitely mute, each loping the track of his own thoughts, when Doctor Ramos, sitting in a peculiar half-arc position, hat squeezed between his hands, an expression on his face that moved to compassion, addressed the others, but not actually them alone, his voice pitched to other audiences, other timeless echoes.

"I, too, feel with deep regret the pain that has lodged in your hearts. Perhaps the sacrifice upon Golgotha was, among other things, the infinite wheel, the unending immolation of the Just, at whose forge even the right hand of the Lord will be raised up, amends having been made for the errors and wrongs that have been visited upon us human beings by circumstances of ill omen. We must keep in mind the transitoriness, the short-lived flight of shadows, and evoke the Eternal and, in so doing, combine our present and our future to attain thereby the wisdom of that fusion. He who addresses you has remained in the darkness like an idol of death, like a Jonah many times over, who has dwelt in the belly of the whale for eleven hundred days and eleven hundred nights, his spirit shackled to a monstrous enigma, without the right to the merest beam of light in this tropical maze. But he has walked over the mire and emerged unstained, over the upright lances without being wounded. And, oh Lord, prudent and magnanimous, cause the redeeming shoots of bliss to rise out of the foulness of the swamps! I have no fear and, fear not yourselves, whose sacred mission projects the faith and reason of salvation, princes of the true Church, the eternal constellation of institutionally established love. The harpies will fly over your heads like a fiery flock but, by the divine hand, a breeze of hurricane force will come to sweep their foul wings and drive them into an imminent hell. Let us have no fear, now that the fates are smiling upon us, and I will be always at your side, forged into a spiritual link, foreseeing hatred's end."

Having so spoken, Dr. Ramos curled up into a ball in his seat as though to hide within his own body, anticipating with some misgivings the reaction to this fuzzy erudition that had kept the Nuncio's eyes alight, the Jesuit's skeptical, and the bishop's face flushed.

The Rector was about to say something but before it could come out it turned into a cough and then a sneeze that he trapped in a napkin with a prestidigitator's skill. He excused himself and moved to the window to watch flocks of pigeons flying over the treetops along the avenue. Black and white, the birds came and went. He said to himself: "Behold the birds of the sky... Your Heavenly Father nurtures them." And then: "...I will be like the prudent man who built his house upon rock." He was immersed in these musings when he heard the Nuncio's voice.

"Whose is this image and inscription? Render unto Caesar that which is Caesar's and unto God that which is God's." And taking into his two hands the crucifix that hung upon his chest, added, "Presuming upon your proverbial benevolence, I would like to beg you once more, Dr. Ramos, to convey our respects to the Generalissimo and our assurances that the temples of the Church will never become a center of conspiracy, but a fountainhead of peace, enlightenment, and harmony for our people."

With a somewhat delayed reaction, Dr. Mario Ramos assented to the Nuncio's words. The essential ground had been basically covered, but it took another half hour for the departure to be consummated.

It was four o'clock when the Rector accompanied Dr. Ramos to the Seminary entrance. The soft, lifeless hand held out to him again did not surprise him, but he was taken aback at the sight of a cat in the back seat of the car from where Dr. Ramos picked it up tenderly and cradled it in his lap. Equally unexpected was seeing him get out of the car slowly and painstakingly after having settled back, to say to him in a secretive whisper, "Father, I neglected to tell you that the Generalissimo will ask me concerning the seminarian's mental condition. What shall I tell him?"

"That he's crazy. Tell him that he's simply crazy, Doctor."

"Yes, Father."

The priest, curious about the cat, looked through the car window and saw that the animal lay in the Doctor's lap again, hypnotized by the man's fingers making furrows through the little animal's black fur. "I wonder if he's a witch doctor?" he said to himself as the car bounced away over the speed bumps.

Seen from the study hall windows, the trees in the garden were still, the leaves glinting in the bright sunlight of the early afternoon. The haunting cry of the *botellero*, the bottle peddler, "*Llero... Llero...telleeerrrooo*, penetrated the room, clearly amplified by the hermetic silence, the hawker probably climbing the hill from the Feria, the barrio of Matahambre, from where he would go on buying bottles, sacks over his shoulder, his melodious call cutting across the city, till he was far, far away... Many of the students had to hide their heads behind their books, biting their lips to keep from laughing at the unbearably funny effect of this outlandish voice suddenly shattering the solemn silence of established order. The *maestrillo*, pretending to be reading, sat behind a desk on a low platform facing the students, got to his feet and stretching out his bird-of-prey neck, poised himself to pounce at the faintest sound, the slightest movement. The hawker's cry was fading but still audible far away like a moan from another world. Having spied something, the *maestrillo* stepped down from the platform, claws unsheathed, and slinking to the rear of the room where a student's head nodded over his desk, thrust his club under the boy's chin and lifted him in the air. This action was followed with a notation in his class book after which he returned to his place with the same catlike tread. A pale, bewildered-looking boy who occupied the seat directly in front of the proctor's desk was now the object of his special attention. The man's stare flamed. An expert in the power of concentration, he held his eyes on him for minutes at a time without blinking, without dissimulation. The victim of this methodical frontal assault was the seminarian who had been in prison the previous summer charged with an attack against state security. Now, with malicious intent, Tirano had turned him over to the priests who were tossing him in their hands as though he were a hot coal they were desperately looking to drop into a tank of water.

Antonio Bell, unkempt, head down, left hand over his eyebrows like the peak of a cap, right hand clutching a pencil, was noting down in a copybook bits of the thoughts that were churning in his imagination and which he sought to cover up as best he could. However, the eyes across from him seemed to have the power of drilling through matter and appeared in the book that lay on the student desk jumbled together with the words on the page...

"Lose if you want... My grandfather. Who's going to make his coffin? He must have made it himself and put it somewhere, waiting to die... My grandfather. Who killed my dad, grandpa? 'Cocolo Cantera denounced him.' Denounced? Arturo will come back to stay... Maybe this Sunday... We'll hide in the brush... Maybe he knows where Father Paula is. Arturo, where's Father Paula? *Mamá*, please bring grandpa to me. Please, *mamá*. If I were invisible and could fly, I'd go right now through the sky and find out where Father Paula is... Grandpa must be in the patio. *Mamá* told me he was laid up. 'He's in bed. Antonio, and doesn't get up.' When she comes this Sunday, I'll tell her, '*Mamá*, beg grandpa not to die...' He buried Juanito at the back of the patio in a little box he made specially for him as if he were a child... My grandfather. I wonder if Doctor Ramos knows who killed my dad. Who murdered my dad, Doctor Ramos? Was it the one who denounced him? The one who put the knife or the bullet into him? The one who ordered him to be killed? The ones who know about all the murders and sleep side by side with the murderers? Doctor Mario Ramos. They say he isn't a bad person... He wrote a book of poems when he was thirteen years old.. I'm going on fifteen and never wrote a poem... Father Paula wrote stories. I liked to hear him tell us the story about the treasure, the things about his uncle. I would like to meet Father Paula's uncle. I'm sure Uncle Papo doesn't want to have anything to do with me. *Mamá* didn't tell me so, but that's how it must be. When she comes to the city, he doesn't want me to visit her. He must be very scared. I have to go to the city for a few days, Mamá. "Go to Papo's house," she told me, "you'll be more comfortable there than with Floripe." And that's how it was. Uncle Papo liked me very much and was very happy to see me when I came in July. How was it possible that they caught me? Father Paula told me that day in the morning, "Antonio, go back to your town, I'm having trouble at the Seminary. Go right now, today." But I stayed that night and the next in the city and then didn't have time to go back to the town. Uncle Papo must be scared...and angry. I wonder what Uncle Papo must think. What did he think the night I didn't show up."

Arturo Gonzalo, kept watching the *maestrillo* from the middle of the room. He caught the glare in his eyes, the fiendish will to destroy Antonio Bell. It worried him to see the way the hollow in the nape of his friend's neck kept deepening. If he had had to give an account of the destruction that he saw taking place in the boy, the first image to come to mind would not be the emaciated face or the prominent bones of his arms but the nape of his neck. It was the image that became most dominant, that appeared before his eyes for hours each day in the study hall. It was painful to recall him on the basketball court months ago: fast, almost vicious in his aggressive style of play. He seemed to grow when Father Paula was there. He was inspired by his presence. He found it hard to imagine him involved in underground activities, in the nightly acts of terrorist arson of which he was accused. He marveled at how difficult it was to really know a person. He pictured him at four-o'clock recreation, an innocent-looking, timid figure. It was only in the course of the game that a certain quality of heroic violence came through. The drama was hidden, lodged deep inside like a silent ulcer. He was always neat, his shoes shined. *"Sometimes he lent me the shoeshine liquid and paste, and he would give me part of whatever his mother brought him. He was the only one with whom I shared my things, too. He must really have balls. I'm dying to know all about what happened."* He was thinking of him as though the Antonio sitting a few yards away was different than the Antonio of the term before, as though this one were a figure out of another time. *"He looks sick, poor fellow, as though his hopelessness was eating him up."* No doubt about it, they were two different beings. The priests had set about driving him out of his mind and were well along in the process, as if reconfirming their words to Tirano: "He's out of his mind... Crazy... A lunatic!" *"Poor Antonio, they're giving him the business and the worst of it is that I don't see how he can escape it."* As soon as the bell rang to end the period, Arturo Gonzalo hurried ahead to wait at the door to talk to Antonio but was unable to do more than greet him timidly before the *maestrillo* broke in and ordered him away. He went off through the crowd in the hall, not reviewing in his mind the theorem for his geometry class, but pondering the vacant look in his friend's eyes.

"My Uncle Julio tells me there's no loneliness like the loneliness of New York, but I don't understand him. He says it in a sad kind of way, his face very pink like when he comes back from vacation every year. 'You stay in your apartment for months while it's cold or snowing outside. Your neighbors are like ghosts, always in a hurry, who don't even say hello to you. You ride in the subway, going and coming, and you have a crowd of people for company who are either hostile, alienated, or asleep. And where are they going? Into the void!' My uncle talks so nice, like he's reciting, and I love that theatrical quality of his when he says, 'And where are they going? Into the void.' But I go on not so convinced of that New York loneliness he claims, when I compare it to mine. Not this city's but my own. New York must be under that star over there and with snow piled up in the streets now, early in December. My town is over here where pretty soon in the cool evenings the boys will begin tuning up their guitars as they get inspired by dreams of sunrises and flaming sunsets: Blanco Castillo, Rafael, Timo, "Jusepelloro" (the name Papito took on now), Claudio Ortiz. Blanco will get drunk as he keeps searching the face of the moon that outlines the curves of the mountains and polishes the river to a shine:

> *For loving so much, my heart one day*
> *could love no more;*
> *So heavy it was with love*
> *that its vessels to the brim were filled,*
> *and with no more honey in its combs*
> *the contents then were spilled.*
>
> *And filled to the top now*
> *with bitterness,*
> *of the juice from its fount of bile*
> *if sated with the taste of gall, I say*
> *its coffers with honeycombs*
> *will refill one day.*

"Claudio will recite his poem 'Juan and Amalia,' so sad, so tragic!

> *In a soiled and dog-eared book*
> *Tossed away in a corner*
> *I thumbed the crumbling pages*
> *that broke my poor heart.*

101

"And so, I will go on to the end singing of the ill-fated love of a young couple, and bring tears to your eyes. Those young people were so gay and smiling, there was such sadness in their poetry as though they inhabited two worlds at the same time. Well...here I am, too, waging my war of two worlds. There, New York will be pulsing beneath that star, and on this side, the streets of my town will be asleep under this other star... Laly Pradera. I love Laly as a reality, and I love the girl in the neighboring house, too, who passes by in the afternoons like an illusion. I love them both. Yesterday, we looked into each other's eyes, yesterday for the first time, and a beam of light entered my heart; today you hid them. At what time will you be going by in the mornings? If you want me, I'll come down at night, crawl through the bushes and steal in close to your house to kiss you, take you by the waist and draw you close in my arms... I'll leave a dummy in my bed and fool the *maestrillo* when he checks... That's it! Antonio could do the same, prepare a dummy, put it under the covers, and sneak out... Of course, it would be harder for him, he's far gone... In any case, I'll play sick this Sunday...cramps or whatever...The thing is it can't be later than this Sunday. It's urgent...I have to get to talk to Antonio."

By early December, Arturo was convinced of the need to deal immediately with the situation that was clearly ravaging Antonio. He was thinking that his physical deterioration, which had advanced with obvious rapidity in the month of November, might not only be due to intense emotional suffering but to some sickness, as well.

November was a disastrous month for Antonio Bell. He had spent most of the time writing letters to his grandfather which he would roll up and hide in the cavity in a leg of his iron bed. On Sundays, when his mother visited he would spread them out on her lap and repeat, "*Mamá*, tell grandpa to write me." She would steel herself and tell him that soon they would all be together and that was why he had to eat and get strong.

"Are you taking your tonic?"

"Yes, *mamá*."

"Come on, son, eat these biscuits I brought you...look...with some of this cheese on them...and then drink this juice. You are very thin. You'll die if you don't eat."

"Later, *mamá*, I promise."

"But eat something now...come, my boy, eat while we talk." Antonio nibbled at the biscuits and drank the juice, finding it difficult to swallow. His mother saw the menacing lines of death in his wan, emaciated face as Antonio struggled to down the juice.

"But what's the matter, Antonio? What's happening to you?" And she shook him gently, holding back the tears as she rocked him by the shoulders.

The tears flowed on the way out, but she put on a brave front at his side: "Are you going to let yourself be beaten down, dammit?" And she looked around as though to make sure she was not being overheard. Actually, nobody entered that prisoner's room to which she was led by the Prefect every Sunday for as long as the visit lasted. They remained together there until noon. During those two hours, the vestibule had filled up with relatives who used the time to chat with sons, brothers, nephews, to give gifts of a razor for one beginning to show a downy upper lip, of perfumed soaps, deodorants, or sweets for the younger ones, and to offer hope and encouragement for those who showed signs of faltering for reasons they couldn't say, which were interpreted by the visitors in every other way except that the flesh was weak.

Antonio was relaxed as long as his mother was at the Seminary, apparently sedated by the caresses of that loving hand. It was a kind of hypnotic regression that led him through passageways of fleeting enchantment only to return him with the abruptness of an avalanche to the foreshadowing of an imminent nightmare. His mother contemplated him as her fingers flitted over his damp forehead and hair. She saw how restless he was, that there was no serenity of spirit there, that these moments were nothing but a brief truce. As the hour of separation neared, the wrenching nightmare gripped Antonio ever more tightly, and at the noontime good-byes, the curtain began to rise again on the ineffable drama of his anguish. She would return to the town heartbroken, more convinced each day that her son was on the verge of madness, but thanking the Lord that he was, at least, alive, protected by the fathers of the Seminary and out of Tirano's clutches.

The Prefect lurked at his office window each Sunday waiting for her to arrive. The moment he saw the sad, black-clad figure step from the taxi, he would rush to greet her deferentially, help her with Antonio's package, and escort her to his desk where he would tell her about her son and how concerned they were about helping him recover from the traumas of imprisonment and torture; about how they intended to call upon professional help, if necessary, to ease him through the crisis; and for her not to worry, that the worst was over, and that even if Antonio were to express aversion for them, the priests of the Seminary, and behave in a manner evidently detrimental to the institution and its good order, they would never forsake him. The mother's eyes filled with tears of gratitude as she brought her damp lips to the priest's hands and begged him on her knees, for the love of God, to do everything in their power to see to it that her son, whom she had torn from her side and delivered him, her mother's heart bleeding, into the service of Our Lord, would never be sent back to Tirano's dungeons. Afterwards, Doña Alfonsina joined her son, not in the common visitors' hall but in another place they were allowed to go to, a small, solitary room, behind a closed door where they would be alone and spared the ogling of the curious. Antonio would try to explain to her, often incoherently, about the iniquities to which the priests were subjecting him. She never paid due attention because of her concern that what her son was trying to tell her was no more than a sign of a gradually deteriorating mind. Hadn't she known over the years the dear little fathers of her parish who would take the last bite of food from their mouth to feed a hungry person? How could a priest possibly tell lies or harm an innocent being? When she asked herself those questions, the sparks of doubt that arose within her seemed to have been struck by the devil, and she rejected them automatically. To dwell on them for even an instant would place her in jeopardy of sinning. Antonio asked after his grandfather, and she would lie, telling him that he was not well, ailing, and that was why he hadn't been to visit him. And she also lied to her father-in-law, telling him that Antonio was fine, that thanks to the priests, his life had been spared, and that he sent regards and asked his blessing.

At the end of November, it seemed as though even the shadows were conspiring against Antonio. He lived on the ragged edge, trembling, withdrawn, terrified at every corner, at turns in the staircase where he thought he was seeing the Prefect, the Spiritual Father, or one of the *maestrillos* appear like figures in a horror story. He would imagine that they were tying him up, hanging him, putting him in a straitjacket, and sending him to Tirano's dungeons; that they were burning him as a heretic in a roaring bonfire, cutting him up like a side of beef, boiling him, feeding him to the dogs. It was then, when he was going through spasms of terror, that he attempted suicide, or thought he had killed himself or was being murdered, or when he felt that his life was about to be ended by a confused combination of murder and suicide.

It happened on a Sunday afternoon. The seminarians did not go on their outing that day because a baseball game between Santo Tomás and La Salle was scheduled. What could have impelled Antonio Bell to go upstairs to the first floor, then to the second, and finally, in a burst of impulsiveness to climb the steep overhanging spiral stairway to the roof? He had never gone there before or had any desire to be there, but an irresistible force drove him to see the game that day from the top of the building. He distracted himself by watching the planes as they came in and took off at General Andrews Airport, concentrating with special interest on the windows of the outgoing aircraft. As though possessed, he watched the tiny human heads, each in its particular universe, eyes fixing on something or other, a hand moving, thoughts or imaginations turning on matters in which he, Antonio Bell, meant nothing. That is, he didn't exist, as if he had never been born. At one point, he began to stare at the palms of his hands trying magically to decipher his uncertain future, then, turning them over to observe the knuckles, the joints and then the nails, which seemed to him rather pale. He felt that he must be very thin and touched his face to again discover what the image in the mirror had told him so many times before. He found himself up against the low guard rail which didn't quite reach his knees. Seen from the playing field he stood out against the gleaming white sunlight in a long, narrow silhouette suspended in the air like a figure in levitation. From that height, Antonio was able to see the general movement of the players without sharpness of detail as blurry images moving about in a dizzying scene, their voices reaching him as faint overlapping echoes. In a fleeting instant of concentration, like an animal hypnotized by a bright color, the boy fixed his eyes on the player up at the plate, when in an ecstatic upsurge, he felt that the hands swinging the bat were his hands, that he was in the other boy's place, his misery transmuted into happiness. Under those circumstances he was enveloped in a joyous aura except that, as in the case of the sensations of peace imparted during his mother's visits, consciousness with menacing fangs crouched too near. These were cases of lethal happiness in which, given the impossibility of disconnection, every atom of pleasure bore the macabre seal of impending death. Despite everything, he managed to reason, looking at his hands again, blurred in the mist of his pupils, that within one, two, ten years, or at some point in the future, he would inevitably be something different, miserable to some degree, but not this unfortunate wretch now seized with a desire to throw himself from that height and to fall to his death in a matter of seconds in plain sight of everyone, rescuing himself thereby from his cursed misfortune. It was then that he looked down and saw himself stretched out on the dark green grass, smashed. Suddenly, instinctively, he turned his head and was confronted almost head-on by the eyes of the Prefect. His flesh crawled at the sudden contact with those lizard eyes emanating from which he felt a force that pushed him toward the edge. As though awakening with a shock from a horrible nightmare, he leaped away and fled, stumbling, from the priest. Then, utterly terrified, he ran into the building, down the staircase, and out into the yard. Gonzalo, who had been shocked to see him on the roof, saw him again at a distance under the almond trees, but then he was gone.

The whores, drunken and coarse, dancing *habaneras*, stark naked, breasts swaying to the accompaniment of their own hoarse, raucous voices in chorus in a wild, lewd carousal in a moonlit yard, disappeared when the Seminary windows became crowded with incredulous onlookers. They reappeared three days later accompanied by men, obscenely uproarious, took possession of the saints' grottos where, howling like cats in heat, they fornicated. The last thing they did before the orgy ended was to paint beards on Our Lady of Mount Carmel and Our Lady of Sorrows, and to dress up the Holy Child of Atocha as a Mexican movie bandit with mustaches, a big sombrero, and a couple of toy revolvers. The next morning, the priests inspected the vandalism and, in addition to empty rum bottles, found hair-raising messages in the form of dead dogs and cats hanging from the trees. Outraged, they protested this sacrilege to Dr. Ramos, who answered with a phrase that in time became part of the Dominican anthology of political folklore: "They are uncontrollable wild animals, but beyond my reach." He repeated as he got to his feet, "They are beyond my reach," and with a dramatic pause, slammed his fist down on the Rector's desk making the objects on it dance. Then he added, "I don't know whether it will do any good to take up your complaint with the Generalissimo but I will try." Poor Dr. Ramos, like Sisyphus condemned to move wild beasts like the rocks around him for the rest of his life! In any case, the women did not reappear in November, but the black Volkswagens of the Secret Service came. When the whispering breeze in the pine grove deepened the silence of dawn, the lugubrious rumbling of the prowl cars could be heard along the avenues of the yard, making rounds, lying in ambush behind trees, menacing.

Arturo Gonzalo kept his fingers crossed on the Friday he appeared at the Prefect's office to request a Sunday pass for the city. With luck, individual passes could be obtained only two or three times a year. They were generally given for a family visit to see an uncle or aunt, or to spend an afternoon with a mother who had come to town. The last was Arturo's pretext and since it was his first application of the year, the pass was readily forthcoming. The excuse was false and so was the destination. He had other plans for that Sunday, the sixth of December. On Saturday night, however, when he saw the sky covered with dark clouds, he was afraid that a bad storm was brewing. That morning he had been able to slip Antonio a note indicating that it was urgent that they meet in the usual place. Antonio confirmed with a nod in the afternoon in the dining hall. But the threatening sky worried him. He hoped for rain during the night to be followed by a bright, sunny morning. Impossible otherwise. It would mean another delay. Rain on Sunday signified a sea of red mud and cancellation of the Seminary outing which would make it impossible to meet in the scrub. Now that he had specific plans it was important to let Antonio know. At his usual spot by the window of his room, his bleak mood was not receptive to Ramón Gallardo's heady music, to thoughts of Laly Pradera, to anything but those dark clouds that kept shutting out the sky. Disheartened, he lay down and tried to sleep, to seek oblivion as he waited for what the morning would bring. It rained in the night and although the early morning sky was gray it cleared up and further showers seemed unlikely. Slowly, the sun began coming out. At ten o'clock recess there was no doubt that a fine day was in store. As the vestibule filled with visitors, Antonio went to the yard. The ground was soft and spongy, but the sun was heating up nicely. During lunch, Arturo had no idea what might be the cause of the expression of virtual happiness on Antonio's face. Possibly his mother had brought him good news, thought Arturo. "Remember," he told him on the way out of the dining hall, "two-thirty."

"It's been thousands of years since the sea was here, but it left its traces." Arturo tried to calculate the distance but didn't know if it was now two, three, or four miles away from the place where he lay in the scrub scanning the horizon and reflecting. "How much of this part of the island was once under water?" The cliffs were tall and stretched out for a long distance and the rocks looked like sharp teeth. He had heard it said that there was a an enormous cave further up as big as El Embajador hotel and that it was inhabited by huge snakes. The only snakes he was familiar with were small, green, and harmless, but people say that the other kinds eat chickens and eggs and are dangerous. "But there are no chickens here," he reasoned, "yet they could slither as far as the Seminary looking for food." The ground is clay and the flora a mixture of low and reedy plants. There is no explanation as to where the seeds came from for those great trees, mangos, mammies, and tamarinds that are sparsely scattered around the countryside. He had ventured quite far into the woods and got scared when he realized it. He had no watch and tried to guess the time from the position of the sun which, however, didn't tell him much, except that it had passed the meridian. He figured that an hour had gone by since he had left his building, which would make it about twelve-thirty. At worst, then, there was still ample time for him to be where he was supposed to meet Antonio. He hurried back, whistling, as though to ward off evil spirits that emanate from excessive silence. When he had arrived at a point where he was able to see the Seminary yard and the almond trees where Antonio would be, he sat down and waited. Before long, he saw a figure come out of the north section. He wasn't sure but thought he recognized one of the cooks who usually went about unkempt, un-shaven, and in dirty clothes but who now looked clean and neatly dressed in shirt and trousers. He had seen him a number of times carrying large cans of slops on his shoulder for pigs he was raising somewhere in the brush. He watched him walk through the yard to the avenue. He looked so spruced up that he thought enviously that he must have a girlfriend in the city.

The day had turned out to be beautiful with a warm sun and a cool, pleasant breeze. As he waited, he reflected on the qualities of nature and how it was impossible to explain why each day of the week should have distinctive features. He thought, "It must be that the human mind creates the differences, but it's a fact that a Sunday is unlike any other day. I will invent the colors of abundance with my mind, the colors of happiness...I will invent love." Furthermore, he knew that beggars often came into the Seminary through the main entrance and gathered in the yard, as pesky as flies, men and women, young and old, naked youngsters and infants. The kitchen nuns herded them together on Mondays and Thursdays under the oak trees on a rise at the Upper Seminary and fed them there, but only on those days. It seemed strange to him, therefore, that on a Sunday a very old man should be picking his way painfully through the yard toward the almond trees in the north sector. He wore a battered hat, his bent body advancing with the help of some sort of a cane, and he carried a bundle in his other hand. Arturo watched as he reached the edge of the brush where he saw him hide behind a tree and look back and then off to both sides as though he were expecting something or somebody. It wasn't until he took off his hat and straightened up that Arturo suspected that the old man could very well be Antonio. Nevertheless, he didn't move from where he was until there was no doubt about it. Then, he hissed and made signs at him until Antonio took notice and came running.

"Holy Jesus!" said Arturo admiringly. "Your own mother wouldn't recognize you."

"A remembrance from Father Paula," Antonio replied, smiling wanly.

The two made their way through the thicket, Arturo going ahead to push the branches aside till they came to a familiar little clearing. So far away from the world and so close. The faintest whiff of the city, the slightest murmur of the traffic reached them remotely, very remotely. They sprawled out on the ground, puffing a bit, the silence so intense that their very breathing seemed a disturbance.

"What a great day it turned out to be! I was afraid it was going to rain," Arturo said, looking up at the sky. "If I only had a slingshot I'd pop that *cigua*," he lamented, pointing to the little bird that was pecking at a custard apple on a nearby branch. "Beautiful afternoon, isn't it?"

"Yes," he answered clutching at his waistline with both hands, "I ache all over, it's so long since I've had any exercise."

"Don't worry, you'll make up for it." Another *cigua* joined the first in dismembering the fruit. "I could get them both with one shot," he thought. Then, at last, he went on to say, a note of alarm in his voice, "You look like you're dying, brother. Once and for all, tell me what's happening to you, Antonio."

Antonio pressed his lips together, bowed his head, bobbing it up and down for a few moments in tiny movements of assent.

"I'm going crazy, Gonzalo. I don't know what to do anymore."

"Forget that! You're not crazy and you're not going to be! But tell me...from the beginning. How much truth is there in all this?"

"Before anything else," Antonio asked anxiously, "tell me what became of Father Paula?"

"He's out of the country. They say he went to Puerto Rico. Well...at least, that's the talk at the Seminary, but a little while ago I learned that they got Paula out of the country before you could bat an eye. He was the one who trained you, right?"

"Who got him out? The priests? When?" Agitated, Antonio got to his feet.

"Yes...the priests. When we came back he wasn't there any longer. It must have happened during vacation."

"How did you find out?" Antonio, relieved, seemed to take on new life. At moments his eyes flashed the way they used to.

"That's what I wanted to talk to you about. Don't be alarmed but you're going to have to escape from the Seminary. It's dangerous for you to remain here. Now, don't get alarmed. If the priests don't succeed in driving you crazy, they'll kill you some other way, maybe even by witchcraft. Don't look at me like that. You don't believe me. You think I'm exaggerating, don't you? Well, listen to what I'm going to tell you. The priests are deeper into witchcraft that anyone could imagine."

"I do believe you. What comes as a surprise is my having to run away from the Seminary. Do you realize what that means? But you haven't told me yet how you found out about Father Paula."

"Frank told me, Frank Bolaño. But that's not so important. The main thing is you. If you don't get away, they'll give you the business. I have it practically all set up." There were flashes in the atmosphere, in the trees, on the ground.

"Who's Frank Bolaño?"

"A kind of off-beat guy but I've gotten to trust him. A first-year student. Maybe you've noticed him, a tall fellow with a round face and sort of hefty. He's the one with whom I'm planning your escape."

"Come on, Gonzalo, you must be kidding? Planning my escape with a first-year student! What's this all about? I don't get it. And how come he was the one who told you about Father Paula?"

"I'm not kidding, Antonio. It's on the level. I know this is all going to sound weird to you, like it did to me when I first got to know him a couple of months ago. I was at four o'clock recess, over by the pine trees...you know...early in

October. Frank was there, too, a well-built guy in expensive clothes. He approached me. To begin with, it struck me as very odd that anybody his age would be entering the Seminary. I have to tell you he's seventeen. What kind of age is that to be entering the Seminary? He told me he was from here. "Ah, a blue-blood from the capital," I said to myself, "conceited and stuck-up, like the rest of them." At first, I thought he was a drag, but after a while, no. He came back the following day and again the next and we talked for a while each time. I warned him that it wasn't advisable for us to be seen together every day and in the same place, that the priests didn't approve of that. So we agreed to meet every two or three days and that's what we did. We discovered we had a lot in common and lots to talk about. He fired questions like a machine gun but when it came to answering, he was more deliberate. I gave him my ideas, like I did with you, and he appreciated it but I had a feeling he was treating me like a kid. At least, that was how it seemed to me. We talked a bit about our own lives and then I spoke about you, about our friendship, and what you went through and the things that were happening to you, now. At one point I told him that I thought that if you didn't escape from the Seminary you were going to die. It was like serving up a meal to a starving person. No sooner did he hear the story than he was already beginning to figure out how to save you, an automatic reaction. He took your case on himself. The guy is a genius, lots of imagination and, at the same time, methodical and organized. He's been to the city three times. I don't know how he does it, but the priests don't interfere much with him. One of the seminarians from here told me that he comes from a wealthy family in the city. This week Frank let me know that he had it all arranged with an aunt of his to hide you. That there was no problem. She is absolutely trustworthy and loves him very much, he said. She's a woman who is up on what's going on in this country. She even knew that a seminarian had been arrested for political reasons. Your case, of course. And Father Paula's, too. She's taken you on...for Frank. It seems she got information through priest friends. Frank tells me that his aunt pays the tuition for several Seminary students whom she doesn't even know. Imagine! And she does the same kind of thing in other Catholic schools. That's a great lady! So, what do you think?" There were four or five *ciguas* now hopping around together on the branch after polishing off a custard apple.

"I appreciate this, Gonzalo, but I really don't know what's best for me anymore, whether to die, to stay, or to go. Frankly, I feel a terrible emptiness, unable to decide anything. Like I'd lost my will power. It's hard to believe. Even the beatings in prison didn't break me. They didn't get a word out of me. And, now..."

"Yes...and now you're willing to let yourself be the fall guy for these priests, right? You're going to let those priests give you a screwing, right? Don't be naive, Antonio..." Arturo threw his hands up.

"It's not that..."

"Yes, it's just that." Arturo's tone hardened. "Make up your mind. Either you let yourself be killed here without firing a shot or you go down fighting like a good soldier."

He went on more gently, "Okay, that's just a manner of speaking. But what I want to get through to you is that you have to take the plunge, have faith, don't die before you have to. I'm going to repeat to you what you once told me your grandfather said: 'Antonio, life always begins today. Tomorrow will be its today and you can live those different todays of tomorrow in the present-past which is a way of making you forget the troubles of the past-present.' Remember? You used to tell me those things, and you spoke so eloquently as you remembered your grandfather's philosophy. Wow, what a problem that was for me in the beginning!"

"Okay, Gonzalo, you're right. When do I have to be ready?"

"I'll let you know, brother. I had to get your consent first." A stone in his hand, Gonzalo stood watching the *ciguas* but ended by throwing it against the rocks. "All right, let's be getting back. I'll see you later. But, tell me, how did you manage to put that disguise together?"

"Easy, nothing to it. I'll show you one of these days. Now, before going into the yard, I have to change to ordinary clothes." And he proceeded to remove his clean clothing. As he dressed, Arturo could see the welts that crisscrossed his back, tracing out a map of pain on that body, the bones still not yet fully developed. Arturo's face became a mask of pity, then of horror and rage. "I'll talk to you about that stuff, later." Antonio, uneasy, hurried as he pulled on trousers and shirt, combed his hair, and scrubbed the old-age lines from his face with a handkerchief and water from a small jar. In a few moments he was another person, said good-bye, and took off. Arturo watched him disappear into the brush, then looked around till he spotted a proper stone, picked it up and flung it with fury at the *ciguas* which scattered in fright. "Shit! Missed!" he grumbled.

Frank Bolaño had entered the Seminary at a glacial point in the cold war between Tirano and the Church. He was admitted through the good offices of the bishop out of regard for the Bolaño's family tree of sturdy trunk, noble roots, and splendid ramifications, particularly in the case of Frank's aunt, Doña Amelia Bolaño, a young widow with honey-colored eyes and a heart of gold. She was a friend of the bishop's who was so fond of her that any request issuing from those incomparable lips was immediately and generously granted by His Reverence with almost playful pleasure, a flickering little smile, and a tone of voice soft and sweet as a rainfall of sighs. And so, through Doña Amelia's intercession, young Frank Bolaño Caprino bounded straight from worldly turmoil into the priests' cloistering hands. Whether as a disciplinary measure, a precaution in an ever more threatening environment, or perhaps for fear that the lad would continue indulging his mania for tapping telephones, a dangerous hobby that had signified more than one headache for the family, his parents decided to clap him inside the walls of a boarding school. His mother envisioned a uniform, his father preferred a cassock.

We'll lose him if he continues the way he's going," Doña Kiki Caprino said to her husband. "I didn't want to say anything to you, but he spends his nights with the whores on Eighth Street. I'll talk to General Cortalejos about getting him into the Military Academy."

"Nothing of the sort!" Don Fortunato cut her off. "Do you want to see him end up an enemy of his own parents? I want no policemen in the family. Damned if I wouldn't rather see him a priest!"

Doña Kiki lost no time in picking up the ball. "Fine, let him be whatever, so long as he gets on with it. If that's what you want, the best thing to do is to talk to Amelia. We've got to get her busy on it. We'll go see her tonight."

Amelia, married at eighteen and a widow now at twenty-two, her body in fullest splendor, was lithe as a schoolgirl in her bearing. Though the youngest of five children she was the hub of the family. When she was out of sorts, depressed, bored with the world or at odds with it, all hurried to her side to dispel the dark clouds, going to any lengths to find diversions for her, even during the dog days. Amelia imparted a sense of freedom, opened windows for them on a social world other than the accustomed one of a sanctimoniousness fit to kill. Her husband had died of an aneurysm at the age of 36 perhaps from over-enjoying a wife whose power of attraction was magical. It was said that he departed this world, clutching Amelia's hands, hating with every fiber the thought of being in any other world. Her youthful, festive mien remained unaltered either by marriage or the depression that followed her husband's death. "Poor little thing," her father used to say when he was alive, "she hates unhappiness." After her husband's death, a family council tried to convince her to move in with her mother who lived alone and was beginning to get lost in the ten rooms of her sunny old mansion, but she fought for her independence, facing them off with a fierceness that made them think she might be going through a change of character. However, it was only a passing phase. She remained in her colonial house on the banks of the Ozama River and it was there that her brother Don Fortunato and sister-in-law Doña Kiki came to beg her to talk to the bishop about getting Frank into the Seminary.

"Frank, a priest. Ha, ha, ha! You're kidding, of course," said Amelia. "Make a priest out of Frank? But Fortunato....but Kiki...whatever put such a fantastic notion into your heads?"

She was his favorite relative. They had played together their entire childhood at all sorts of games and engaged in mischief of every kind in Amelia's parents' spacious house. Frank's big frame made him look older than she with her slim, adolescent's body and spirit. Their closeness never lessened even after her marriage, Amelia would often leave her husband at home to go off with her nephew to a matinee or an afternoon get-together with former schoolmates who continued to treat her as though she were a single girl.

"But, Amelia, you don't know the half of it. Have you any idea what your favorite nephew is up to? He taps telephones and spends more time at a fancy Madame's place than at home. Can you imagine such a thing, Amelia?" said Doña Kiki pressing both hands to her head.

"I questioned one of his sidekicks, a fellow who goes by the name of Renacer," chimed in Don Fortunato with a grimace of disgust, "and he told me how they climb up telephone poles with those irons repairmen put on their legs, and hook on to the lines with one of those apparatuses for taping conversations. He also said that they have a connection with a girl who works at the phone company and helps them out with the recordings. God knows what kind of a woman would be capable of such a thing! And that's not all. Don Teodoro Barbosa came to the house three days ago to complain that Frank was tapping his family's conversations. Imagine that, a person as decent and respectable as he is! I didn't know what to say, I was so embarrassed."

"Wow, Frank must have heard some fascinating conversation," Amelia chortled.

"You treat everything as a joke, Amelia," complained her sister-in-law. "This can lead to trouble and steps must be taken." And in a barely audible whisper, she added, "The next thing you know, he'll be tapping Tirano's telephone. Imagine what could happen then, God forbid!"

"And what does Frank have to say to all this?" Amelia wanted to know.

"That they are lies spread by Don Teodoro's daughter. That one, the youngest, seems to have Frank loping after her with his tongue hanging out. They tell me the poor fellow is climbing the walls." Bringing her right hand down to her crotch, Doña Kiki added, "You know how those things are."

"That young rascal is going to get a fever, and I've told him so," said Amelia as she served the coffee and cookies. "I'll talk to the bishop. School starts pretty soon, around the middle of September, I think."

For the last several months Frank had been suffering one of those serious amorous obsessions that play havoc with a man. It all began one night during an evening social at the San Antonio church in Gazcue. The drama group was presenting a play, *Los Inocentes* by Father Gutiérrez Santovenia in the parish house with a cast of all neophyte actors. A showing of the movie, *On the Waterfront* with Marlon Brando, was to follow. Frank preferred going to the Malecón but let himself be inveigled by a group from the Colonial Zone to take a ride with them to Gazcue and take advantage of a free party. They wanted to see the film but had no interest in the first part of the program. They arrived late, the room was full, and each had to grope around in the darkness to find a seat for himself. The projector made a noise like a locomotive, the subtitles were barely legible, and clothing clung damply to the body. It was such an uncomfortable situation that Frank decided to take off and tried to locate any acquaintance through the fog of the projector who might accompany him. It was then that he began to feel a spider of subtle fingers climbing over his leg. He had been there a while without taking notice of the girl beside him, whom he now recognized out of the corner of his eye, keeping very still, fearful of making a movement that might scare off that hand that was resting on his leg. His member began to bulge and the hand advanced to cover it. Daintily, the fingers unfastened his fly to open the way to delight, remaining inside to perform a deft, caressing action over the tight skin, over the erect head. Then, collecting the secretion that oozed from its mouth, she smoothed it onto the palm of her hand and brought it over the shaft of the organ now close to the bursting point. Frank tried desperately to hold himself back, shutting his eyes as every muscle in his body went tense in an effort not to explode in a paroxysm of pleasure. But the girl applied cunning devices of dilatation that held it back at the beginning and then sped up the climax of spasms that emptied him in a volcanic eruption. Frothing, the member drooped, relapsing exhausted into lethargy. Frank did not wait for the showing to end. Soaking with perspiration and sticky as he was, he wandered through the streets to his house, the image of Carmen Isabel Barbosa, scarcely fifteen years old, throbbing in his brain, penetrating him in every breath he took, feeling her in his every action, first with delight, then with the vengeful anguish of the disappointed male. It was his first youthful experience but, from that very moment, he became a creature thirsting for sex, of the kind she could provide him, because he could think of none other. The following night, certain of success, he set out to find her. He strolled by her house directly behind the Olympia Theater, where she lived with her parents and a spinster sister. Carmen Isabel was the unanticipated fruit of a late rush of fertility. She had grown up spoiled, her headstrong nature battening upon the debility of others. Frank walked to the corner, stood there for a while, then retraced his steps without having seen her. It was not yet seven o'clock. Disappointed, he tramped through the Colonial Zone and when he was about to go into his Aunt Amelia's house, he stopped at the stairs and returned to the sidewalk, thinking. He wandered the neighborhood, but it was too early to find friends out on a street corner anywhere. He returned automatically to Carmen Isabel's street and this time did see her behind the trees in the garden, sitting on the balcony beside her sister. He was sure his presence had not gone unnoticed by her and began to kill time chatting with an ice-cream vendor down the block until he saw a pair of girls enter Carmen Isabel's house and come out almost immediately together with her. He followed at a distance, watching them cross Independence Park and continue on towards the Malecón. He quickened his pace until he overtook the group. They knew each other. Any of the girls would have welcomed the possibility of a romance with a young man of Frank's position. He treated them to ice cream on the Malecón, and they all strolled to the boulevard and sat on a wall. She invited no intimacy, however, treating him as though no such thing as carnal contact had ever taken place between them. Rather, her attitude was impudent, indifferent, mocking. Confused, Frank tried to get some sort of explanation from her but she stopped him with a good-bye kiss on the cheek, saying, "*Ciao*, darling, see you tomorrow."

He watched her, dainty and coquettish, as she disappeared in the maze of vehicles that crawled along the avenue. A horn blowing close by made her turn her head. A hand waved at her from the car, signaling to her, and she raised hers in answer but kept walking, continuing to wave her hand as she drew away. Then, she was swallowed up in the shadows of Ranfis Park.

A hoarse roar came from the horizon, a huge ship was approaching the port, a great black cloud behind it as far as the eye could see.

Frank remained floating in a limbo of uncertainty for several days. He had no idea what sort of role he was playing in the vague maze of a drama in which the secret portals of pleasure were opened one day and magically slammed shut the next. Dusk of every afternoon found him standing somewhere on El Conde Street, the customary gangway to hopeful fulfillment, watching with his friends as the interminable parade of upper-class girls went by. He was hoping to catch a glimpse of Carmen Isabel in the last light of the setting sun, in the midst of the multitude that jammed the sidewalks in slow, aimless progress to nowhere until dispersed by oncoming darkness. After eight o'clock, the two-miles-an-hour caravan of automobiles appeared, loaded to capacity with young men anxious to make their presence felt, to display a symbol of power that would be a talisman for attracting the girls who vied for the glances, smiles, and poetic gallantries so lavishly strewn along the route by those tropical Casanovas. Following this, came bedtime for him, a swollen night of torture because today, yesterday, and the day before, he had been told that Carmen Isabel went to the 7:45 p.m. movie at the Olympia Theater in the company of a fellow from Ciudad Nueva, that she had also been seen around the Pony Club in the car of a certain Paquito... He would go to bed squirming with his Aunt Amelia's warning in mind, "You can't trust her, that little cookie is hornier than a bitch in heat." But he was not for listening to advice since she had kissed him torridly just the Sunday before in a cave at the zoo. Moreover, although it was quite true that no matter how hard he pressed her, he could get no serious intimation of love from her, it was no less true that those hungry-wolf bites she gave him or the way she allowed him to bite her back, breasts, belly, and the curves of her silken thighs, and the ferocity with which she committed all her acts, must mean that there was something in her heart throbbing for him. She had to be having some feeling for him, dammit! But his illusions were promptly dispelled. He could find neither hide nor hair of her the following Sunday and then at night he learned that somebody had taken her swimming in the warm waters of Boca Chica. And so he was provoked to such a pitch of exasperation and jealousy that he hired an apprentice detective for a few pesos. This was a certain Tony Tomasa, aka "The Private Eyelash," who owned a raucous motorcycle which he maneuvered in and out of certain streets dogging Carmen Isabel's footsteps, revving up the motor to the maximum when he saw her getting into somebody's car. But the results obtained in that manner did little to clear things up for him. It was at this time that he met a telecommunications engineer who taught him the skills of telephone tapping, a hobby which with every increasing technical sophistication was to serve him in many facets of his life. With the assistance of a beefy young electrician, who worked as helper for a pole climber, he went into a new field of information gathering. It was so effective that within three days he was able to find out on his own things that he actually knew but, in his senseless attempt to becloud the harsh light of the sun, could never resign himself to believe.

While her house slept, Carmen Isabel engaged in feverish masturbatory telephone conversations using the most sagaciously unbridled language imaginable with boys whose names were all familiar to Frank. New appointments would be made and previous ones recalled with erotic excitement whipped up to a frenzy. Each partner tried to outdo Carmen Isabel in lewdness but her vocabulary of licentious profanity was so rich and imaginative that she bested them all by far in her infernal capacity to provoke the most violent orgiastic effects. On listening to the tape, even Frank was shocked out of his rage at the morbidness of it. Overwhelmed by this unbearable reality, he lost his appetite, scarcely ate at all, became morose and swamped in an inferiority complex. No matter which way he turned the problem around in his mind, he was unable to pinpoint the flaw for which he was being rejected: his masculinity was unassailable, though no fashion plate, his appearance was, at the least, acceptable, his social position enviable, and his breath fresh. Overwhelmed by his inability to have her to himself (there was no question about his having had her, though shared on a broad front), he believed that his stock would go up with her if he acquired a sports car. Finally, he approached his father on the matter who said no just by looking at him. Irrationally, he began plotting revenge of the most sinister type, but the heat of his ire remained at the same pitch of intensity as his desire to possess her and this, in a way, minimized the possibility of a confrontation with her. He was afraid to lose her and for many days preferred silence to creating a situation that could alienate her. He was able to have her from time to time but, then, for some reason, she began to avoid him and he, as a consequence, to seek her out more persistently. And the more ardently he pursued her, the more he made a fool of himself, so much so that he became the laughing stock of the Conde and Malecón cliques, until one night he gave full vent to his bitterness by running off tapes that he had recorded of her midnight conversations for a group of friends out in the open on the avenue. It was a bombshell. When Carmen Isabel's parents found out, they wanted to pillory the boy there on the lawn of the house.

Frank, on his part, abandoned his usual haunts in favor of Herminia's whorehouse, located on the city's heights, where he nursed his disillusionment. It was an exclusive establishment of fresh, refined young women who danced *guarachas* by Daniel Santos and Toña la Negra's *Salomé* with harem-style undulations. They took their upper-crust category very seriously and the lowly were excluded. "High-class and high-style" was Herminia's motto and her instructions to her stable. "It's orchids we're selling here, dammit, not cabbages!" Meekly, they took their guidance from this short and dumpy drill-sergeant, her flesh now in its irremediable fifties, her face thickly powdered, a false Marilyn Monroe birthmark on her cheek, both forearms dripping bracelets.

Early one evening, Herminia saw the faces of a pair of young men peering in at the portal of the establishment. Judging from the angles of the stance, bodies half-hidden around the corner of the door jamb, and the beadiness of the eyes, she took them for a couple of nosy locals and went on placidly filing her nails, seated in the shadow on a bar stool. She was all by herself for, at that hour, not even the regulars had yet appeared. The girls were bathing, freshening up, having supper in their rooms in the rear patio, getting ready for the heavy-traffic hours. She looked towards the portal again and her attention was caught by one of the faces which together with the rest of him was now almost entirely visible against the light at the threshold. She was now able to deduce from his appearance that he was nobody from the area but a rich boy from some distance away. When she saw him take two steps in, shadowed by the other boy trying to hide behind him, she called out, "Come on in, boys, nothing to worry about. We don't eat children here. That is, not raw. We have them for dinner, but fricasseed." This was accompanied by a feline gesture with red talons extended, sausage fingers wiggling, and a great big mouth opened to roar like a lioness.

Since they remained where they were, talking in a whisper and not daring to come forward, the madame slid off the bar stool and approached them with a come-to-mama gait, took each by the hand, and steering them toward the swimming pool, as she hummed a honeyed wolf-to-Red-Riding-Hood tra-la-la, deposited them there before a platoon of the gayest, friskiest of whores who were splashing water on one another and laughing.

"How many pesos do you have," Herminia asked the prospective customers who, groping in their pockets, quickly said, "Seven."

"Enough for a fast piece each. Which ones do you like?" she asked in a peremptory tone.

Timid and taken by surprise they didn't know what to answer and Herminia ended by choosing for them. She then went off to the bar where she waited for them. When they returned she invited them to her table and ordered drinks.

"On the house," she told them. "Come back whenever you want. Junior hours are until eight o'clock." And looking at the one whose clothes smelled of money, she said, "You, big boy, what's your name?"

"Frank Bolaño."

"With a name like that you should make general." Turning to his companion, whose darker skin, jeans and neat white shirt spelled lower class to her tart's sharp eye, she asked, "And yours?"

"Renacer, ma'am. Renacer Mateo. I'm a cousin of Joseito's. Pleased to meet you."

"You look like a nice guy. Come along with him whenever you like."

Drawing Frank towards her she planted a motherly kiss on his cheek and when they had finished their drinks showed them to the door where she sweetly bade them good-night. After taking a quick look up and down the street, she returned to the bar, saying to herself, "That young turkey's going to end up bringing in the family jewels."

The boys returned three days later, this time with twenty pesos, and the following day, and the day after. Frank was thrilled the first few times but what really brought him back after that was the fact that he didn't feel at ease anywhere else and because at Herminia's he at least entered into a state of lethargy, of stupor, of sinking deeper and deeper into senselessness, of fleetingly being somebody and then nobody, surfeited with flesh-make-believe-mirrors-Carmen Isabel, lies, and constantly recurring boredom, sexual replay and glut. This went on until the night Don Fortunato, a flaming torch, a swinging scythe, appeared, found the lad, his skin impregnated with the smell of patchouli, his breath a blast out of a sugar-refinery boiler, his neck marked with scarlet rosettes, set him on his feet and propelled him to his car.

"No cops, no faggots, no pimps in my house, dammit! You're going to be a priest. Get used to the idea."

Meekly, Frank accepted his father's decision as a liberation and went to visit his Aunt Amelia that same night; he hadn't seen her in three weeks. He felt strange when he came to the Colonial Zone, as though he were returning from a blurry world to one where order ruled, where everything was exactly, beautifully in its place. He felt as if he had been let out of jail that day, that the last three weeks had made an ugly dent in his life.

Sitting in Colón Park out of the broiling sun and in the shade of Columbus's statue, having his shoes shined, Frank leafed apathetically through *El Caribe* until he stopped short at a photo of Dr. Mario Ramos and Tirano chatting at a reception in the National Palace with the Apostolic Nuncio, the bishop and other important personages around them. A few months before it would scarcely have attracted his attention, but now he felt a surge of disgust, of dismay. He recalled his grandmother on his father's side four years ago waving a photograph of Pope Pius XII surrounded by Tirano, Dr. Mario Ramos, and other figures radiant in uniforms and frock coats at the Vatican. The Concordat had just been signed and she was foreseeing an end to all the island's problems. That was the first time Frank had heard Dr. Ramos referred to. Subsequently, he was mentioned in the literature class at the Seminary, a field in which he was considered an authority, and by Arturo who repeated what Antonio had said about him. The bootblack knocked his brush against the shoeshine box, and Frank changed feet as he tossed the newspaper into a nearby trash basket. The cathedral clock was striking eight, the bronze notes wafted over the tree tops by the soft December breeze. Another bang from the bootblack's brush signaling the end of his work roused the young man from his thoughts of Arturo, Antonio, and Amelia whom he would be visiting in just a few minutes.

He had left the Seminary before seven o'clock for the purpose of paying his Aunt Amelia a visit to settle the details for Antonio's escape and his hiding place. Despite the tension engendered by its inherent dangers, this enterprise was not central to his thoughts when he mounted the double-decker bus on Cordell Hull Avenue. Parapeted on the open upper level, he had enjoyed the cool seasonal breeze, the early morning sunshine, and the quiet of Bolivar Avenue, still drowsy at that hour. As he passed the zoo, however, memory of Carmen Isabel surfaced and with it anticipation of quick, satisfactory revenge. This happened whenever he passed that neighborhood, and he soon accepted its consummation as inevitable, fated. At other times he was able to repress the sharp pangs of remembrance, but that day he was not disposed to do so but instead blew on the hot coals of memory. He had gotten off the bus at the Independencia Park stop with the intention of strolling by familiar haunts and had gone to the Malecón where he sat on the wall for a while, his back to the avenue, watching the waves. The city was quiet, the silence broken by the occasional traffic or a hawker's cry. These were new experiences; he had never before been to the Malecón that early in the morning. When the streets became more active, he had strolled over to the Colón Park where he bought a newspaper, had his shoes shined, tried to clear his mind of memories, and surprised the bootblack by dropping the appreciable sum of 50 centavos into his hand.

Amelia was expecting him. When he had called the day before and said that he wanted to come over the next morning, she thrilled with anticipation. Shopping in the afternoon, she bought him a couple of shirts and socks to match and then the ingredients for preparing his favorite coconut-cream dessert. On the way home, she stopped at a store window with the thought of getting him a pair of shoes as well, but decided that he had best try them on first. She continued strolling in the cool of the afternoon, lighthearted, light-footed, her long hair floating loose over her shoulders, its ends over her breast insinuating themselves into the loose neck of her gauzy white dress. Back at home, she was tempted to break her promise to Frank not to let his parents know that he had taken the day off from the Seminary, but resisted because it would be a special delight to have him all to herself. Besides, there was the secret she and Frank shared, her sympathetic collaboration in the proposed adventure, her desire to please him, to make him happy, all those things that meant a regression to the morning of her life, at the awakening of sexuality when they engaged in voluptuous childish play, she, her pearly buds not yet flowering beneath her transparent blouse and, he, his head, heavy with drowsiness, resting on her bare thighs; and, then, at night and the next day, both unmindful of their secret, as though nothing had transpired; and then, once again, nestling together on a rainy afternoon, he feigning sleep, she caressing his genitals with silken fingers; and she feigning sleep, his small hand trembling upon her unripe pubis, upon her seething breast; until they grew older and began to live in their separate worlds, shutting away in a vault with a thousand locks their thrilling juvenile games never shared with word or vow but as something asleep in the secret garden of a chimera, and which had to remain so always at the threshold of their lives, never to be reawakened.

Amelia awoke with the birds that Saturday, she had so much to do. Living alone in a world all her own, it was organized at her whim. She never had servants because she considered it degrading to subject people as poor as they to an environment of abundance. She prepared her own meals and took care of her household. Her home was not in a fashionable section as might be expected. That was her decision when she married a man almost twice her age but who was much more interesting than any of the bevy of hot-breathed, empty-headed, vain young men who pursued her, their conversation devoid of charm or intelligence, leaving her with an impression that they were nothing but pretentious puppets. Bernardo Alcornoz was not favorably looked upon by her family because of his age and meager material assets. A violinist, concertmaster of the National

Symphony Orchestra, he touched her heart with his artistry, his serene personality, and old-world manner. And in their time together she knew him to be a sincere, kind person. He had come to the Dominican Republic from Spain on summer vacation at the invitation of Amelia's brother who had been studying medicine there and never returned. He bought a small apartment near the Cathedral, frequented Amelia's family circle in the exclusive Gazcue section, and gradually sent out effective roots from there. All had gone well until his intentions became evident. Amelia's parents misread Bernardo as just another Spanish fortune-hunter and flatly rejected him. The Spanish immigrants in Santo Domingo concentrated for the most part on acquiring dowries, but this was not true in his case. Bernardo Alcornoz was a gentle soul whose inclinations were in quite the opposite direction. Amelia knew this from the start and soon convinced her parents of it; they gave the couple their blessing and an apartment in the Colonial Zone picked out by Amelia that had balconies giving on the street and a huge terrace in the rear facing the river. She felt more at ease there with her husband in that middle-class environment. Her joie de vivre never flagged, and now as she bustled about the kitchen preparing Frank's sweet, she began to feel nostalgia for the past summer when she had been in mourning. It had been her favorite time of the year during her marriage. Her brother Claudio Alberto, who seemed more cut out to be a flamenco guitarist than a doctor, would come home from Spain on vacation from medical school and spend the dog days entirely on the roof of his house, in a pair of shorts, drinking wine, taking bullfighter stances, and strumming his guitar, inspired by the flow of the Ozama River. In the warm evenings, Amelia would give parties on her wonderful terrace where she and Bernardo sang endless duos, carried away by the enchantment of the ceiba at which Columbus tied up his frigates when he entered the mouth of the Ozama with the idea of setting up the Primada.

When the sweet was ready, she ladled it carefully into a crystal serving dish, set it on the dining-room table, and returned to the kitchen. Noting that it wasn't even seven o'clock, which gave her ample time to prepare other things for Frank, she set about confecting a pineapple and cherry upside-down cake and biscuits for him to enjoy and bring back to the Seminary to share with his friends. It was about eight-thirty when there was a sudden, thunderous banging on the door.

"But my dear boy," she said, laughing out loud, as she opened the door, "that sounded more like a roughneck from the slaughterhouse district announcing himself than a student of a divinity school."

"Don't believe that those Jesuits teach anything better," replied Frank.

They embraced and skipped toward the kitchen like a couple of children, he, nose in the air, sniffing, drawn by the confluence of odors of prunes, cherries, vanilla, cinnamon, and marmalade that floated temptingly from the oven; she, with the freshness of a maiden, her beautiful eyes open like wildflowers, her arm around Frank's waist, holding herself pressed tight against him, looking, looking at him, devouring him with her eyes. Then, in the kitchen, picking a biscuit out of the hot pan in the oven, she tested it first against her lips before bringing it to Frank's lips, which parted to receive the sweetmeat as though it were the sacred host.

Her face pink with the heat of the stove, her loose black hair caught up with a purple ribbon at the nape of her neck, its strands spreading to the sides like a butterfly's wings, her delicate, golden slippers, and yellow nylon robe almost like her own skin, all made an irresistibly attractive picture. This was her everyday self, her lifelong guise, an image Frank could never have enough of, that stirred passions that lay muffled deep inside him. When she embraced him in the kitchen after popping the biscuit into his mouth, drawing him to her, he felt the firmness of her taut breasts against his chest and trembled as he once did on dark, rainy afternoons of his youth.

Frank, thirteen years old, elegantly attired in a white suit, present at Amelia's wedding ceremony in the church, nobody noticing that his eyes were brimming over with tears as the priest pronounced the couple man and wife until death did them part. The guests were too aloof to be aware that the lad with the lavender bow tie was suffering through an agonizing farewell, an incomprehensible dismissal impossible for him to cope with, a kind of wrenching away of a phantasmal allegory; nor could they know—nobody was party to the secret—that the kiss Amelia implanted on his cheek was a mute entreaty, a tender, exquisitely tender plea for comprehension. The myth had lain dormant within them for years, like luminous silt, until the nuptial flare revived expiring embers to remind them, at the same time, that they were condemned to keep the veil of mystery drawn forever over their hearts. A sultry peace would reign again, with memories muted and sufficient to confide the day's turn of events to one another, guilelessly taking refuge in each other, as though readying themselves for the last judgment. And, now—it would be wrong to say unheralded—the spark leaped anew from innermost recesses to bridge the gap between those bodies embraced in magical communion in the kitchen.

Without a word they went, holding hands, to the dining room where, at her initiative, they took seats on opposite sides of the table. Their eyes held one another across the chasm of the prolonged silence until finally it was broken by Amelia's voice, saying, "Here, these are yours. I bought them for you yesterday." She had unwrapped the package that was on the table and, holding them up one by one and passing them to him, she asked. "Like them? I picked those colors. Yellow and green look best on you. What do you think of the one with the thin green stripes?"

"They're beautiful, Amelia, just beautiful. Thank you."

"And, look, these go with them," she said handing him the socks. "And, now, wait a moment for me, I'm going to change my clothes. I'll only be a second. I want us to go to El Conde. I saw some lovely shoes there yesterday and I want you to try them on. But, oh, my goodness, we must have some breakfast first. You must be starved. What would you like me to fix for you?"

"Anything at all, Amelia. Whatever you make is delicious." And they smiled at one another.

"I shall fix you...now, let me see...a Spanish omelet. That's the ticket! Come to the kitchen and after breakfast we'll go the shop and get you your shoes. We have loads of time."

As she was peeling the potatoes, she said, "Let's talk about your friend Antonio. Antonio Bell, right? Don't think I've neglected the mission you gave me. You must think the world of that boy to be doing what you're doing for him."

"Yes, I do," said Frank. Actually, he knew Antonio only by sight and though he felt admiration combined with concern for him, there were no ties of friendship between them as he had intimated to Amelia in order to motivate her more strongly. "He's going through a terrible ordeal and is in serious danger. He must be gotten out of the Seminary or he could die there, and in the worst possible way, under slow torture."

"This is a wild story. Now, tell me the truth Frank. You wouldn't be making any of this up, would you?" Amelia swept back and forth in her kitchen, hunting for the scallions, beating the eggs, heating the oil in the frying pan.

"It's the absolute, Amelia. When you see him with your own eyes, you'll know I didn't exaggerate."

"But it's incredible...incredible," said Amelia biting her lips as she shook her head. "Poor little fellow. You said he was only fifteen years old, didn't you?"

Yes...fifteen and practically a wreck. Say, Amelia, do you happen to know Dr. Mario Ramos?"

"No, not personally. He's such an important figure and a fine person, they say. I understand he doesn't care about money, just books, and that he's never involved in shady business. Is there anything that goes on in this country of ours that everybody doesn't know? What makes you ask me about him?"

"Just wondering, Amelia. I've heard other say the same thing. He's held up as a model, even in the oratory class."

"Do you have doubts about him?"

"No, not any more. Not even about this being a screwed-up world." It's hard to believe but this same Dr. Mario Ramos is the person put in charge of Antonio by Tirano. Do you follow me? And it seems like he's doing a good job of it."

"How do you know that?"

"It's the truth, Amelia, believe me. He and the priests are working together to torture that poor boy. He's a perfect example of split personality."

"Or one that keeps on cracking, maybe. I believe you. Well, that's not our problem. Let's get down to the business at hand. How and when are you proposing to get him out of the Seminary?"

"It all depends on you, now."

"Don't worry your head about that. I have it all figured out," she said pinching his cheek.

"You mean you've arranged where to hide him?"

"Of course, my darling. And where do you think? Here in my house. Yessir! Right here. I'll show you in a little while," she said, pinching his cheek once more. "For the time being, let us sit down to a royal breakfast."

After they had eaten, Amelia went to her bedroom to change, and before leaving for the shoe shop, with an air of great mystery she led him up to the roof where she unveiled a room she was having built there.

"I was holding back this surprise for the last. As you can see, I waste no time. It will be all finished next week, Thursday or Friday, at the latest. How do you like the new observatory? Your friend can stay here as long as he has to."

"Wonderful. Amelia, you're fabulous. But what about friends and the family, and whoever else comes to the house?"

"Naturally, I've taken that into consideration. I'll think up some excuse to sleep at *mamá's* house. I'll say that I can't bear being alone at night. Nothing to it, I'll spend my days here and evenings there and I'll cancel all social obligations in the house for the time being. At least, we won't have anything to worry about until June when Claudio Alberto comes from Spain."

"Amelia, what makes you so wonderful? You're unbelievable. By, the way, could you visit me at the Seminary on Sunday."

"Tomorrow?"

"No, I mean the following Sunday. Most likely, we'll have something planned by then and I'll have to consult with you personally."

"Yes, sir, *comandante!*" she answered, saluting smartly, "and, now, let's be on our way, it's getting late."

Trees, *maestrillos*, seminarians: shadows moving in the dimness of the yard. Some light came through the three doors and venetian blinds of the recreation hall projecting pale patterns on the dark ground. What illumination entered from the adjacent avenue was reflected in the East from the distant center of the city faintly highlighting branches and leaves and figures.

Leaning against the trunk of a pine, Arturo waited uneasily for Frank who had hinted at arrangements to be made in the city. He was anxious for details, to talk it through and clear up doubts though he was sure that everything would fall into place at the end. He was not specially concerned about Frank having been ordered to report to the Prefect after supper. He had complete faith in his friend's shrewdness. What really worried him, however, particularly after three o'clock in the afternoon, was the long delay in Frank's return from the city. By six o'clock, he had been preparing himself for the worst. He knew of boys who were gone one day never to return, even having left their suitcases behind. But all at once, at around seven, he spied Frank as the boys were lining up to go into the dining hall, and his heart slipped back into place. The rest didn't matter. It was like when somebody believed dead turns out to be only wounded or in prison. "Never mind Father Sáez and his threats. Frank would have thought of a good excuse. Let the priests check with his Aunt Amelia and stop bugging him." There was one thought, however, that his mind refused to entertain for even a moment, though it was well within the realm of possibility, that they were calling Frank in to expel him. "No, preposterous! Too remote." If such a thing should happen, he knew he would never see him again. "Out, out, evil thoughts, tempt me not!"

The night, unseasonably dark for tropical December, held out further temptation, a dense darkness appropriate for burrowing in as though it were a tunnel to hide, curl up, and think in, to give wing to one's thoughts. But Frank was on his way, at last. "Of course, he was coming." He stopped to get his bearings, letting his eyes accommodate to the darkness of the yard; then, he stepped out firmly on familiar terrain.

"Hurry it up, Frank, everybody's hopes are pinned on you. Don't worry about Antonio, he knows you went to the city today to see your Aunt Amelia and go over the plan for his escape. And now that he's convinced it's for real, he's on pins and needles to get out of here. It's like he's been so bitten by the bug of freedom, that he assures me he'll go it on his own, if he has to. His life is really in danger, dammit. He's so desperate that he could be risking death, maybe asking for it. And you and I, Frank, or you alone with the news you're bringing today, are all that stands between Antonio and death. And, it looks like his last hope is your aunt, who's being so kind and helpful. So hurry it up, Frank, hurry it up. Shit, I'm suffering what Antonio is suffering myself!"

In giving Arturo the rundown on his errand, Frank guarded each word that came out of his mouth. It all emerged, syllable by cautious syllable, barely audible, as though ears were cocked behind every bush, tree, and niche. He was making sure that his whispering reached only Arturo's ears.

"I didn't get the last thing you said," Arturo complained.

"That starting next Sunday, Antonio should be ready at any time."

"He's ready right now. Why wait that long?"

"Just for a week. I'll explain it to you."

"Another thing, Frank. I'd like to figure out between us how to deal with something that's bothering Antonio. It has to do with his mother. She must be told."

"Right...but after the escape, not before. And she mustn't ever know where he's hiding or who helped him. That has to be made absolutely clear."

"It goes without saying. What we have to figure out is how to get the message to her. Antonio agrees not to use the mail. It would be intercepted."

"I think I know what to do. All I have to get settled is when and who. Actually, it all boils down to two things. One: everything is up to you, me, and Amelia; two: it can't be before nor after the breakout. The thing is, it's going to be impossible to go near that house there in Jarabacoa. It'll be swarming with cops. So either of us is out for the job and, as far as Amelia is concerned, we're counting on her for the getaway. She doesn't know it yet. I'll tell her next Sunday. So, it's not so easy. I'll put my mind to it when I have a quiet moment."

"Hey, you didn't tell me what the Prefect wanted to see you for."

"That's another problem. He was pissed off at me because I got back late and he withdrew my pass privileges indefinitely. Can you beat that? Makes me feel like breaking out, just like Antonio. But don't worry, I'll get it taken care of."

Frank recognized her, or thought he did, and as she went by he whispered something to Amelia who glanced at her furtively, as the Prefect led her down the hall to his office. From the woman's heartbroken expression and exhausted gait he knew without having to be told that she must be Antonio's mother. He said to himself, "You won't be able to see him next Sunday, but don't let it worry you, dear lady, it's just because he'll be out of the priests' clutches." The entrance hall, quiet until then gradually turned into a beehive.

"Keep every detail in mind, Amelia, and listen to me, don't let yourself get distracted," Frank said to her. He was unable to hold her full attention which was wandering because of the constantly changing spectacle of the visitors, the comical behavior of a grandmother practically smothering a seminarian with kisses, and her newly critical eye fixing on the priests, who strolled back and forth giving an impression of detachment that was far from being the case. "Come on, let's leave," he insisted. We can talk more peacefully outside."

Frank couldn't help laughing at the sight of Amelia's automatically obsequious reaction before one of the priests, like that of an army guard snapping to attention at the approach of an officer, as she forced her face into an expression of bland innocence while gingerly dropping Frank's arm that she had instinctively reached out to take. They walked to the stairs at the entrance and were obliged by the press of people surrounding the portal and little rotunda in front to continue on to the street.

The sidewalk was about fifty feet from the Seminary grounds. The area was enclosed by a low brick wall crowned by ironwork arabesques. It sloped downward from the northernmost point of the Seminary, where a rocky outcropping continued the boundary as far as the main gate, leaving one opening approximately the width of two cars and continuing on from there to the extreme south of the area where it made a right angle that sloped upward to a somewhat higher plane for the entire length of the yard and then turned again to form the huge wall that had once closed off Arturo's vision.

"Tell me again, but slow down. You sound like an avalanche," Amelia told him.

"We've prepared the flight for Thursday at 4:45 in the afternoon. I was just telling you that you would have to come and pick him up, but you weren't listening. There's nothing complicated about it and the only thing is that it has to be timed with absolute precision, to the second. See that street there? César Nicolás Penson is its name. Okay. You'll have to meet Antonio on that corner exactly at the time agreed. Let me explain it to you in more detail. You're not going to have to wait for him on the corner. Nothing of the kind. You're going to drive slowly down Cordell Hull in your car and when you turn left to go into César Nicolás Penson, the hands on your watch must be exactly on 4:45. While we're at it, before I forget, let's you and I synchronize our watches. I'm going to give mine to Antonio, so there won't be any slip up. At the exact moment that you are approaching, Antonio will be crossing the street to meet you exactly as you are making your turn. He mustn't have to wait and neither should you. When you leave here today, rehearse what I just told you. Figure your time exactly and do several practice runs. And listen to this other thing which is the key. Antonio will be disguised as an old man. His clothing will be torn and dirty and he'll be wearing a hat to match and walking with a stick. Now you have the whole story: He will be crossing the street at 4:45, and you'll recognize him from the description I just gave you.

Amelia repeated Frank's instructions to the letter, her eyes sparkling with excitement, and then asked, "Why did you pick Thursday at that hour? Wouldn't it have been better to do it at night?"

"It would be more of a problem at night. Poor people come to be fed on Thursdays at that time. The nuns who work in the kitchen take them into the Upper Seminary yard. Antonio will pass as one of them without attracting attention. Besides, it's recess hour. There won't be any problem. They consider the boy destroyed, so he isn't being closely watched any longer. Anyway, having this happen is the furthest thing from their minds. What we can't foresee is how the priests are going to react when they find out. It'll be a great Christmas present that they'll receive around seven or eight o'clock and by then Antonio will be far away." And turning to Amelia, he asked, "How's the room? Did you get it finished?"

"Yes, of course, and it looks just great. Don't you worry, he'll be very comfortable there."

"It's almost eleven right now. Will you have time to get me a little jar of rouge? There should be a drugstore open somewhere. What do you think?"

"Rouge? What for?"

"And a little annatto, if possible. For Antonio. He uses that stuff for his disguise. He has other makeup, too. Also, get me three boxes of matches, four cigarettes, a deodorant spray for tobacco odor and a bottle of gasoline. Here, it's all written down on this slip of paper."

"That better be it. If I'm to have time to get all this stuff I must go right now."

Amelia was back before twelve with Frank's things and they spent another ten minutes going over details of the Thursday action. Before leaving she took a pair of wrist watches from her purse which she handed over to Frank, saying, "Here, you might need these."

It was definitely decided not to notify Antonio's mother of his flight from the Seminary, at least for the time being. However, they lied to Antonio to spare him additional pain. They told him that his mother would be told the same afternoon. It was Frank's coldly calculated solution to the problem, and with misgivings Arturo concurred. He wanted to avoid causing the poor woman the anguish of uncertainty. She would be quite justified in anticipating the worst and with nobody to turn to for information, she would have every reason to assume that her son was dead or back in prison. Frank's logic was airtight. He had outlined everything carefully to Arturo on Tuesday night, on Wednesday afternoon, and still again on Thursday. After lunch he went over it once more with the calm conviction that getting Antonio's letter to her could expose her to the danger of being arrested. Although cruel, it was the only possible solution. He had told Arturo that if Antonio's mother read his letter, it would put her mind at rest, but in case of a Secret Service interrogation that very serenity could certainly be interpreted as a sign of collusion. It would be quite a different matter if she were obviously suffering pain, grief, and despair. And so, their decision would leave her in relative peace and, at worst, under possible surveillance. It was a measure of security for Antonio's escape, for everybody else, and his mother would be recompensed for her suffering within a few days or, at the outside, a couple of weeks.

Arturo waited anxiously for the class to end, assailed by the most disparate thoughts. It would soon be four o'clock, soon four forty-five. One important thing still remained to be done at four thirty-five...four thirty-five on the dot, part of the plan ticked off by Frank's clockwork brain. He pondered the contradiction between the passionate spirit with which the undertaking had been conceived and the cold, meticulous intelligence with which it had been set up and coordinated. He didn't understand Frank's psychology, deeper feelings or motivations. He found it thoroughly admirable that without ever even having exchanged a word with Antonio, he should nevertheless have risen to his defense as though he were his brother. He thanked his lucky stars for having gotten to know this generous person without whom it would have been impossible to set the boy free, to save his life. He wondered whether he himself would be capable of running such a risk for somebody with whom he had no strong ties, though he had not the slightest doubt that he would take any risk for Antonio. He understood his own motivations only too well but Frank's not at all. From the very beginning, Frank had begun to behave as though a jigsaw puzzle—which he had to put together—had been placed in his hands, as though his intelligence were being put to the test. He recalled the first time he told him about Antonio's predicament and how his body tightened and his expression sharpened, wolf-like. Perhaps that was where the explanation lay, that his was a nature that sought adventure, adventure of any kind, that he had a need for intense emotions, to gamble with the dice of death. That would explain the change in his voice whenever he discussed Antonio's breakout, as though his ego, deep-seated and complex, was betraying its eagerness to satisfy his appetite for danger.

In the yard, Frank studied the best angle from which to keep simultaneously in view Antonio's exit and the point where Amelia was to pick him up. Then, he walked through the corridor that cut through the pine grove and across to the basketball court where a group of students was practicing. He checked his wrist watch: 4:20. Arturo was nowhere in sight but he knew he would find him in Our Lady of Mount Carmel's grotto marking time till the moment when he had to go into the wooded area to put a match to the heap of dry twigs and branches he had made two days before.

At 4:25, Antonio left his dormitory, his footsteps re-echoing in the empty hallway. He was wearing his regular clothing on top of the costume he would be using on the street. He went down the last stairway of the east zone building where the Upper and Lower Seminaries met, entered the toilets at the end of the first floor and quickly stepped into one of the compartments. On the toilet tank cover he lined up rouge, annatto, a coarse, ash-colored pomade, a narrow bottle containing a liquid, a white rag, a small aluminum dish in which he prepared a smooth paste. He checked the watch Frank had given him. He had only twelve minutes for the job but that didn't worry him for he knew that once he got started he could finish in less than seven. Taking a small mirror from his pocket, he held it up to his face and with the other hand began to touch up around the eyes, cheeks, neck, over the cheekbones, on the chin.

Amelia arrived a half an hour early and parked her car two minutes away from the intersection of César Nicolás Penson and Cordell Hull where she waited. She was calm, listening to soft music on the radio and observing the scanty movement on the street through her dark glasses as she waited for the moment to launch her heady adventure.

The moment for Arturo to go into action had come. He slunk off like a cat toward the scrub and a few seconds later reached the pile of dry branches that would soon be turning into a pyre. He lit a cigarette, coughing as he drew on it till the tip was glowing brightly. Opening the match box, he pulled out several of the matchsticks making them protrude slightly. He then tied the lighted cigarette to the top of the box with a bit of thread so that it would burn down and come into contact with the heads of the matches which would then burst into flame and set off the rest of the box. He prepared two more match boxes in the same way after which he retrieved the bottle of gasoline he had previously hidden among the branches, opened it, and sprayed the contents over them. His task completed, he made off and would be far away when the flames began leaping into the air.

It was 4:38 when Frank saw Arturo emerge from the scrub. He walked from the basketball court to the place where he would watch for Antonio to come out.

Antonio, satisfied with his handiwork, wrapped the mirror and the rest of the makeup in the shirt and trousers he had taken off and made a bundle tied up by the sleeves. He then pulled a cloth out of a pocket of his new costume which he tied over his forehead knotting the ends tightly in back. With a hat jammed down over it, wisps of gray hair poking out underneath, he looked for all the world like an old man with a bad headache. His watch told him it was 4:41 and time to leave the toilet. Opening the door a crack to peer down the hall, he didn't see a soul on the left but on the right just where he had to pass to get out stood the Prefect and *maestrillo* Garmídez. Antonio was not aware that the *maestrillo* had noticed him from the second-floor hallway as he headed down the stairs. However, losing sight of him and not knowing that he had gone into the toilet, he went to report his concern to the Prefect. Both were now looking for him. Antonio, trusting his disguise, was about to venture out when he heard shouts and people running. The fire had caught. After waiting a few seconds he started out. The Prefect and Garmídez were gazing out into the courtyard to see what the commotion was about and paid no attention to the old man walking by them.

Arturo joined Frank, smiling with strange satisfaction at the sight of the flames spreading farther than planned. Priests, *maestrillos*, students from the lower school, and then students from the upper school, came running with hoses and buckets to put out the fire.

Antonio did not stop to pick up the stick that was to serve him as a cane; he had left it leaning the day before against a bush in the garden. Instead, he walked straight on, through the rotunda and out to the sidewalk. What Arturo and Frank saw was a poor old man crossing the street to get into a car that had stopped for a few seconds at the corner. Frank glanced at his watch. It was 4:45.

Ignorant of what Antonio had done, Doña Alfonsina arrived at the Seminary on the Sunday three days after his escape and waited for the Prefect to come out to meet her as he invariably did each week. The priest had seen her get out of the taxi and now watched from his office window as she waited uneasily with the bundle in her arms. As usual, the lobby was jammed with visitors. Doña Alfonsina waited a long time for the Prefect to come for her and finally went to the main entrance to find him, her head shaking, eyes wide with anxiety. Timidly, she pushed her way through the crowd to the corridor where she saw that his office door was open. Hesitating for several minutes, she gathered courage to make her way towards it, feeling with each step that she was violating Seminary rules. The Prefect, still standing at the window, observed the woman who stood at the threshold, unsure of herself, as though waiting for an order, a greeting. "What are you doing here?" yelled the priest. "You'd better go find your son and tell him to come back to the Seminary before the Intelligence Service hears about it and kills him. Go and tell him so you'll have nothing to regret."

The expression on the priest's face was even more vicious than his tone of voice.

The usually tranquil, timorous woman suddenly turned into a wild creature. The worst of her forebodings had come to pass. As in a horror film, the memory came back to her of the warnings so often repeated by Antonio. The entire transformation took no more than seconds, and a moment later she flew across the room like a ball of fire to where the Prefect stood at the window, seized him, her hands like a pair of grappling hooks, and hurled him against the glass smashing it to bits. Then, with the strength of one possessed, she dragged the priest about the room upsetting and breaking lamps, books, and furniture with the impact of his body.

The hall was so jammed with students and their families who had come running upon hearing the disturbance that the *maestrillos* found it impossible to force their way through the door until after the woman had finished her devastating assault, leaving the cassocked form lying face up on the floor like a disjointed puppet. The onlookers then approached silently, astounded to contemplate the priest, eyes popping out, grabbing at the ankles of those surrounding him as he struggled to rise.

The woman, huddled meanwhile in a broken, monastic chair, kept repeating in a voice that gradually faded out, "What have you done with my son? What have you done with my son?"

As the *maestrillos* picked up the Prefect to rush him to the infirmary, Frank and Arturo, who had watched the scene, took advantage of the confusion to get the woman out to the street and to walk her, still in a state of shock, almost as far as the Church. They spoke soothingly to her on the way, telling her that Antonio had run away because the priests were going to kill him, but that he was now in a safe place with kind people, and that they, his friends, guaranteed he would be well cared for. They advised her to go back to her village and wait for a letter from her son that would explain everything. She had gradually calmed down when the boys said to her, "...and please, Señora, don't tell anybody that you discussed this with us."

Doña Alfonsina left quietly. Two weeks later she was reading a letter from her son. It had appeared mysteriously under the door, a letter in Antonio's own hand.

On the terrace of the hotel on the outskirts of Jarabacoa, Amelia contemplated the imposing view from the mountain of the Vega Real Valley. The sun was just beginning to come out. From there, the entire plain was enveloped in fog that was lifting little by little. It has been said that on the hill in the distance wrapped in blue mist which the morning was beginning to reveal, tens of thousands of Indians were skewered by Spanish steel. It was supposed that the "deed" was brought on by an appearance of Our Lady of Mercy. Perhaps—thought Amelia—it was after the apparition, when the wineskins were passing from one bloody hand to another in celebration of the memorable event that the Admiral of the Ocean Sea spoke those words that were repeated with pride for generations after: "This is the most beautiful land ever beheld by human eyes." The hill is crowned by a sanctuary for worship of the Virgin and close by it is the pit where her image appeared. Amelia kept looking towards the "Sacred Hill" and thinking of the hundreds of thousands of believers who had come there seeking miracles to assuage their anguish. She herself had made many pilgrimages to that holy place.

A little over two years and five months had elapsed between the time of Antonio's escape and Tirano's death.

Relations between Doña Alfonsina and the grandfather had grown warmer since that ill-fated Sunday when she vented her fury upon the Prefect. As soon as she arrived home that afternoon she sought out the old man with the anxiety of a daughter returned to grace, to throw herself into his arms seeking refuge from her distress. She told him everything that had happened, begged his pardon for not having informed him of Antonio's constantly repeated fears and the anguish of the living death she could see him helplessly undergoing when she visited him each Sunday. Only then did it seem to Alfonsina that she was discovering reality, her eyes opening to the world of horror. She had suffered through her husband's death, and it had ruined her life, as with so many other women under similar circumstances all over the country, but there simply had been no place in her wildest imagination for the truth she had learned at the Seminary. Her faith, so interwoven all her life with her physical being, had been pulverized at a single blow. Unable to sleep and exhausted by so many tears, later that night she took out the letters Antonio had been sending to his grandfather every Sunday, which she had never delivered, and laid them in the old man's lap as he sat in his rocking chair. He stood up, embraced her tenderly and, smoothing his hand over her hair, said, "Let us accept that Antonio's companions told you the truth. We can wait calmly now; there's nothing we can do for the moment, anyway. So, from now on, we're going to have to pull in our belts real tight. I see bad days ahead for us."

And that's how it was. They had nothing but trouble since Antonio was imprisoned. The townspeople turned their backs on them; customers abandoned the carpentry shop; lifelong friends crossed the street to avoid them; Auramaria's suitor left for parts unknown; and when the household savings had been exhausted to pay for the last pound of rice, the only remaining pigeon flew out of the yard. "There were many," said the grandfather as he watched the bird beating its wings in apparent desperation on neighbors' roofs, "and one by one, they've all gone off."

By April, there was relief. At certain intervals, a mysterious envelope began to appear under the door, in it a letter from Antonio along with enough money for their needs.

Very early one morning, when everyone was asleep, Amelia woke Antonio to break the incredible news that a friend had just come by to tell her, with discreetly controlled jubilation. She informed him that Tirano had been killed. He had been ambushed on the outskirts of the city, his body riddled with bullets. Long hours of apprehensive waiting and fear followed as the city buzzed with rumors until it was verified that those involved in the assassination were, for the most part, old comrades of his. One of the most closely guarded secrets eventually came out. A leader of the coup had met in private with Dr. Mario Ramos four or five months earlier to notify him of the plot and to invite him to take over the government as soon as Tirano was out of the way. Acting incredulous, Dr. Ramos covered his eyes with both hands and in a voice of anguish, said, "Why do you approach me with such a thing? Who do think I am? Kindly leave my house and go about your business at once." As the man started out, Dr. Ramos rose from his seat and said, "In exchange for my keeping this conversation confidential, I will expect you not to tell anybody that you had made me such a preposterous proposal." As he accompanied him to the door, he thought: *"I shall carry Tirano's glowing ashes upon my shoulder to sprinkle them there like volcanic dust upon the air so that his deadly presence will forever be breathed."*

While Tirano's body lay in the Government Palace before the incredulous eyes of an endless line of people, Dr. Ramos, to whom he had entrusted the reins of government some time before, devoted himself to putting the final touches on his eulogy of the great deceased.

The poorest of the poor suddenly orphaned, bereft of the protective hands of their Beloved Father, shed copious tears. There was now a great vacuum where once a solid national homeland had existed.

"That's our people for you," said Amelia to Antonio with some sadness as they watched the spectacle on the television screen of the packed, inconsolable masses wearing black ribbons on their arms.

"It's nothing but ignorance and fear, Amelia," commented Antonio.

"The same reasons that drive them in hordes on their pilgrimages to the 'Sacred Hill.'"

The funeral services were conducted with strictest religious solemnity, the bishops in their finest miters and most elaborate rain capes, reverently providing a beautiful rendition of the chants for the body that lay in state, the generals in full-dress uniform, the society ladies in elegant deep mourning, the barefooted crowd in whatever they had, bordering on hysteria, arms stretching towards the heavens.

Then, in the presence of the "glorious departed," Doctor Mario Ramos made the vaults of the temple ring with his eloquence, the mourners spellbound by his panegyric talents displayed to their fullest in a long eulogy that gave the impression of having been prepared years in advance.

"Behold, Señores, the mighty oak that withstood for more than thirty years every lightning bolt and sailed victorious

through all tempests, now laid low by a treacherous blast. The dreadful deed has left our spirit aghast and the nation's soul shaken by the thunderous shock of catastrophe.

"Never has a man's death produced such a sense of consternation in a people nor weighed with greater anguish upon a collective conscience. For we all know that in this glorious departed we have lost the best guardian of public peace and the best defender of the security and repose of the Dominican home. So devastating has been the event that we are unable yet to accept that it has happened. The earth still hesitates beneath us and it seems that the world has come down upon our heads!

"Who would have imagined that this extraordinary man whom we saw smiling in his office at the National Palace no more than two days ago would return to it a few hours later having been immolated in so dastardly a form! But here we have the overwhelming reality in all its terrifying eloquence. The voice that issued so many commands of leadership is now mute. Motionless upon his breast, wherein the heart has ceased to beat, the hands that held aloft the sword that for forty years symbolized all the nation's physical power. Lifeless and vilely pierced by bullets, the heroic breast upon which the tricolor sash proudly blazed as though floating on its staff. The tears that becloud our eyes and the emotion that chokes our voice do not allow us to discharge this righteous duty with equanimity. But great men truly become part of history when they leave life's stage with its conflicts and contradictions.

"The fateful moment has now come for the great chieftain, whose mortal remains we are now preparing to deliver over to the earth, to be received as by a mother. Whatever attitude posterity may take towards his achievement and towards his memory, Señores, we may now assert that his name is forever engraved upon material that time respects and that is susceptible to transformation but not to disintegration in the generations to come. The legacy he leaves us is vast and

*imperishable. His works shall endure as long as the Republic
endures and there lives one single Dominican in it who is aware
of what the border treaty signified, the retirement of public
indebtedness, financial independence, the accomplishments
realized in the field of public works, agriculture, health, and
of all the good that has been done over three decades of a lasting
peace which has assured progress, widespread well-being, and
tranquillity for the Dominican family.*

"*...He was human, all too human, often, but his very errors
are worthy of our respect, for they were the outpouring of his
unflagging passion for order and the messianic concept he held
of his mission as a man of the people and leader of the State.
His stern character and unbreakable will never wavered even
in the fiercest struggles that constantly confronted him, nor in
the inevitable drain signified by his forty years of intense
participation in public life and in the debates that divided his
fellow countrymen over the last three decades.*

"*His religious faith, for example, remained unshakable
despite all appearances and the last of his thoughts—they were
inscribed by his own hand and delivered personally the very
day of his death to one of his private secretaries for the
preparation of a speech he was to deliver at the inaugural
ceremony of a Seventh Day Adventist temple—gives proof of
a stalwart character that was faithful to his profoundest
sentiments. I remember that he told me on one unforgettable
occasion, a note of emotion in his voice: 'The dead are much
in my thoughts, always.' He would often say, thinking of his
children, 'Work is what brings man closest to God.'*

"*His pleasure in receiving decorations and his fondness
for titles and all theatrical pomp in his implacable power
struggles were not prompted by simple vanity, as many
believed, but represented one of the devices employed by this
artist of politics, profound connoisseur of popular psychology,
to influence the masses and to impinge upon the imagination*

of men with the full prestige of his powerful and disconcerting personality.

"Beneath that breast of steel there beat a heart of boundless generosity. Only a will of granite such as his could have withstood, without stooping to unpardonable excesses and vain acts of vengeance, the multitude of unwonted snares, of infamous treacheries, and perverse insinuations laid daily by certain of his collaborators upon the table already heaped with problems of this conqueror of fate. Many debts were charged to his account that he never contracted and those responsible for so doing were masters of sycophancy and intrigue who played upon his good faith and the natural passions of a man whose love of life's sensualities was boundless."

"...The moment has come, then, for us to take an oath before these beloved remains that we will defend his memory and that we will remain faithful to his principles and maintain unity, joining with all Dominicans in an embrace of conciliation and harmony.

"Beloved Leader, good-bye. Your spiritual children, veterans of the campaigns you fought during more than thirty years for the aggrandizement of the Republic and the stabilization of the State, shall look to your sepulcher as to an upraised banner and we shall spare no measures to keep the flame from being extinguished that you lit upon the altars of the Republic and in the soul of all Dominicans."

Tirano's remains did not repose in the crypt of the church for long; they were surreptitiously removed a few months later to save them from the fury of the same masses which were called upon to honor them in a contrite posthumous tribute.

The people's spirit was imbued with a secret hope after the funeral. Antonio, however, was unable to conceal his pessimism with regard to the nation's future. Though the circumstances seemed to belie it, he remarked in a firm but gloomy tone, "The devil was buried but the false gods are coming out of their graves to replace him."

This opinion was not well received by Don Fortunato and Doña Kiki who were unceasing in their praise of Doctor Mario Ramos's funeral oration for Tirano. Antonio did not modify his judgment nor, obeying a sign from Amelia, did he elaborate on it. He opted for respectful silence. The post mortem discussion continued in which the couple insisted on arguing that a government headed by Doctor Ramos could guarantee the health of the country.

Antonio would be turning eighteen in July. He was still the same taciturn youth, but now more self-assured than he had been at the Seminary. Although he had managed to recover considerably from his nervous breakdown, he still betrayed the symptoms of a persecution complex. Following the flight from the Seminary, his first nights in Amelia's apartment were an inferno of strange noises punctuating the silence and a return of the torture of unending nightmares that had beset him in the Seminary. He confided his nocturnal anxieties to Amelia who lost no time in leaving her mother's house to return home to keep him company. Amelia found him a doctor who saw Antonio through this dangerous initial period. Later on, she shared her secret with Don Fortunato and Doña Kiki, as well as with Claudio Alberto when he returned from Spain. Antonio's condition improved steadily, and he soon became obsessed with books. He devoured them in an effort to learn truths about the world, a pursuit that transformed him into a fervent idealist. As in a dream blurred by time, his thoughts were often with Father Paula. The revolution had succeeded in Cuba, and he relished the imagined possibility that his former teacher was happy and achieving his goals there.

Frank left the Seminary the summer after Antonio's flight and was now studying dentistry at the University. By then, he had overcome his infatuation with Carmen Isabel. The fact that he had once suffered for the sake of that wretched girl who now seemed to him hollow and graceless with her duck walk and tastelessness in dress, represented an embarrassment that he preferred to forget. He now felt quite above what he termed "adolescent stupidity." Amelia and he kept up the same affectionate relationship with the difference that their mutual erotic attraction had waned.

Frank was the opposite of Antonio. He disliked reading since a certain amount of concentration was necessary and because he shunned all ideological involvement. His was a world of show: elegant tailoring, fine cars, and trendy deluxe restaurants. And now he was gazing with sickly ambition upon the pinnacles of power. He had acquired the ways of the upper crust and though he continued to hold Antonio in high esteem, albeit with a somewhat paternalistic attitude, he maintained a certain reserve towards this boy possessed with the idea of social redemption and pursuing chimeras that Frank neither understood nor was concerned about. On occasions when he discussed politics with Antonio, he heartily agreed with his friend's bitter view of Doctor Mario Ramos for whom Frank still felt some repugnance. However, he did enjoy poking into the dark recesses of the man's character, the craftiness of which held for him a certain fascination.

Nonetheless, years later, Frank Bolaño became a notorious spy exclusively at President Ramos's service and one of the most feared figures in the government. He would spend hours in the privacy of the President's bedroom, delighting him with recently tapped telephone conversations that cast an almost lyrical spell over him. Under those conditions, wondering at the vagaries of chance, he would recall the time when Doctor Ramos's very name turned his stomach.

Several months after Tirano's death, Arturo decided to leave the Seminary. On a Tuesday in March, moments after the two-o'clock class, without consulting anybody, he took a deep breath and rushed to the street in a fit of despair. First he walked rapidly, then jogged nervously, and when finally a distance away, after looking back for a last fleeting glimpse, began to race along the avenue as though running for his life until he reached Independence Park where he stopped at a bench to catch his breath and determine the course his joy of freedom should take.

Not having seen Antonio since August, he was anxious to talk to him before leaving for his hometown. First, he looked for Frank at his parents' house without success, then he tried Amelia's, but she was out and he wandered the streets until he finally caught her at home. She, as well as Antonio, was delighted to see him, and they all had a warm reunion over a splendid supper of butterfly shrimp that she prepared. Frank arrived later in the evening in answer to a message left with Doña Kiki and stayed toasting Arturo's liberty, chatting, and reminiscing for hours. At Amelia's and Antonio's urging, Arturo spent that night there and the next.

Arturo returned to his town two days later to bad news. Laly had a new boyfriend. He pretended not to care but it was a cruel blow. She had seemed more mature and her beauty was now that of an adolescent who has the appearance of a woman. His mother, however, to his surprise received him with evident pleasure...the man of the house had come home...and after a few days he was back in the routine of daily life.

At the time of Antonio's flight, Arturo and Frank had not appreciated the impact of the event on the Seminary authorities. Since there was a chance that the seminarian had been kidnapped or killed by government agents, they delayed a week before informing Doctor Ramos. He dismissed that possibility and prompted by his customary astute political vision warned the authorities at the Seminary that the only possible chance of avoiding Tirano's reprisals was to hush up Antonio's disappearance. A kind of secret entente between him and the Church was thereby established, an obligation he was to cash in on later. After Tirano's death, his effort to retain power, which he had hung onto like a tick, failed and, pressed by the people's wrath vented even on the privacy of his home, he climbed over the fence one night that separated him from the Papal Nunciature's mansion next door where he was received and given the protection accorded a Prince of the Church.

Note: The people raised the banners of revolt in 1962 but Dr. Ramos was back in power five years later.

PART TWO

And with a bow to Aristotle,
the author remarks that it is not the
poet's job (or, the novelist's, let us say)
to "tell how things happen but how they
should have happened."

Alejo Carpentier

Librado Santos is a poet inspired, like Juan Luis Guerra, by the stars and by goblins. Now, however, his inspiration derives from a different source and it obsesses and overwhelms him. He is a young man who aspired to glory, but for somebody else, coveted evidently as eagerly as if for himself. Librado considered Dr. Mario Ramos's star to be in the ascendancy and that the time had come for him to take his place in history. He was devoting endless hours to the enhancement of Dr. Ramos's image, a mirage displaced by successively more tenuous ones. Lacking even remotely valid arguments with which to defend his idol's public conduct, the poet withdrew from the usual circles hoping for a miracle to restore luster to his idol's name but with little faith in his possibilities for the coming election. He realized that, much as he might wish it, the leader was unable to provide the kind of government he claimed he had dreamt of since he was a boy, particularly since the voters now rejected him, and he had only the well-oiled machinery for an obviously fraudulent count to give him a dubious victory.

In his lonely room, the young man lay in bed pondering the dichotomy between the literary persona of the Dr. Ramos that had so captivated him and that of the politician transformed by power. He knew that rightly they should have complemented and reinforced one another but was unable to comprehend the turns of fate that had contributed to preventing such a conjunction. He realized that the President's past performance would contribute nothing to achieving that state of glory. Eyes glued to the ceiling, he concluded that there was one last hope of consecration: In a selfless act unprecedented in the nation's history, Dr.

Ramos would renounce his shady victory and deliver a speech the likes of which had not been and will never again be heard from the lips of a Dominican statesman. After all, how much longer did he have to live? He would be bending history to his will, become invulnerable to enemy barbs, and turn into a living myth, a guiding light for the spirit of his people during the rest of his days. As he dozed beside the radio waiting for the crucial moment, the poet foresaw such a miracle. Closing his eyes, he cradled his head in his hands, and slipping away into a magical world, imagined or dreamed this mesmerizing oration:

"Mr. President of the National Assembly, members of Congress, distinguished guests and representatives of foreign governments, people of the Dominican Republic:

"I have often been unjustly accused of being power-mad. For years, I have been slandered, called the vilest of names. Allow me to repeat to you here what I said a long time ago—almost as an unburdening—something I am not accustomed to doing to a small group of high-ranking churchmen. I said to them: 'During more than thirty years of tyranny, I remained in the shadows, acting with anxious courage, casting the beam of a searchlight placed in my hands by a mysterious act of fate. Like a Jonah, many times over I have remained for eleven hundred days and eleven hundred nights in the belly of the whale, my spirit imprisoned within such a grim dungeon. But I have walked through the mire and emerged unsullied, brushed against sword blades and not been wounded.

"Thirty years have gone by since that meeting, and today I can proudly repeat those same dramatic words.

"*What I most desired throughout my life was to approach its close with the necessary peace and independence to be able to devote my leisure time to the only things that I truly enjoy.*

"*I always cherished the idea of settling down somewhere on the earth 'far from the madding crowd' to write and think to my heart's content, to travel as often as I could, and to be, in short, my own master.*

"I believe, ladies and gentlemen, that today I have come to that point, unsullied in spirit as a new-blown rose in a garden under a dryad's tender care. Yet, with my body worn by the ravages of time and strenuous work, I must declare before you and the world that, of my own free will, I decline to take upon myself the duty that is the be-all and end-all of human ambition: the Presidency of the Republic.

"You will be asking why I waited until this day and this solemn occasion to make so dramatic an announcement. I must respond that had I done so sooner, I would have lost the courage I wanted to bring to this moment, because I would then have acted under the duress of what I most hate: pressure and threats.

"There would have been nothing to impede my way to the presidential seat for the sixth time except the staggering burden of doubt that plagues me as to whether my victory at the polls was legitimate or not. In view of this, I, a man incapable of trickery, wish to clear my conscience and leave quietly for the peace of my house, to enjoy the respect of my people and to contribute my humble experience, if it be considered worthy, to assure the success of whoever takes my place on the rocky road to power."

The young poet emerged from the magical mists and in a burst of joyousness rushed out to the street to confirm what was for him already a certainty. But he found no echo in the people's glum faces. He hurried to the Legislative Palace and losing himself in the crowd waited for the inaugural ceremony.

In view of the fact that Dr. Ramos was deaf in the left ear, his two aides, military and civilian, stationed themselves on his right side and the Judge, who had been rushed there by an army patrol to administer the oath of office to him as President of the Republic, stood at his left side.

Dr. Ramos was very old and in addition to being quite deaf, was nearly blind. His spirit, however, remained indomitable. His inert, hard-lined face, like a plaster cast, seemed to belong to a person embalmed while still alive. The man's roaring voice remained his only outward sign of life. It retained all its power as in the days when it so thundered praise of Tirano from the rostrum that it raised goose pimples in the listeners.

"Put the sash on him anyplace," said the military aide in a loud whisper to the Judge, "it doesn't have to go across his chest, throw it over his shoulders and forget it! We've got to get this over with, for godsake, Your Honor!"

Far from the Palace, the men of the city, were leaning against window frames, frowning faces against clenched fists, eyes fixed on an indefinite point in space.

"I didn't come here to hang the sacred tricolor any which way. What do you think I am, General? As if it were a pot holder! Let's lift his arm up! Not that much, General, lower it a little so I can pass the band over it. That way is fine. You see, General, there's nothing in this life that can't be fixed."

Unconcerned with national events, naked children played in the streets with sticks they used to stir up the stains they made by peeing on the ash-colored ground.

"Now, tell him to raise his right hand. I'm about to administer the oath of office," mumbled the Magistrate to the General, as the two of them stretched their necks over Dr. Ramos's head.

Women kneeling or standing beside their basins and tubs, waited anxiously in the backyards for a miraculous rainstorm that would make it possible for them to wash their sweaty clothes and take care of other urgent needs. Their hands, menacing talons, crowns in a jungle of arms, reached rigidly toward the sky as in a magic ritual of the Furies, on the edge of violence, seeking to penetrate the atmosphere, to rip open the belly of a black cloud. As they watched with impotent eyes, it floated away. "A downpour of the wet shits is what we'll get!" yelled a desperate toothless old woman as she pulled her empty can away furiously after hours of waiting under the tank that had grown drier and drier every day, more and more caked with the excrement of vermin.

The Judge changed places with the military aide so that Dr. Ramos could hear the list of duties he was pledged to carry out as head of state.

"Mr. President of the National Assembly, I swear! I swear! I swear! I swear! I swear! I swear! and will go swearing century after century..."

"Your Excellency, I am not the President of the National Assembly. I am Judge Celestino Collado, your old friend and classmate. The National Assembly was unable to come to an agreement on electing officers so they sent for me and that's why I came."

"Ah, are you the Judge?" Good...it makes no difference." And Dr. Ramos proceeded to raise his right hand again so awkwardly that he banged the microphone a couple of times. Finally, his hand in place and steady, he said, "I reaffirm my oath by the ashes of Alfonso the Wise, by the tears of Beatriz the Unfortunate; I swear by the heroic breast upon which the tricolor band so proudly blazes; by Ruggieri's gnawed brain; by the sacred memory of Pittini, the Archbishop and Primate; I swear by..."

"Get your oath over with, please, Your Excellency!" interrupted the Judge.

Terror-stricken, the women foresaw death for the people and announced it with sad and prophetic voices. They envisaged the septic tanks backing up through the holes in the toilets, saw a pack of mangy dogs and starving rats taking over the city, fighting over garbage that lay heaped for weeks on the street corners. They were horrified at the swift onset of night that would come to plunge homes and streets into darkness and with it, their last hopes.

The city's old men and women knew that these were much, much harder and more anguishing times than at the beginning of the past century. They knew that today's poverty was direr and more unbearable than any in memory.

"I swear! I swear! I swear!"

The civilian aide, a rather ridiculous-looking little man with a long nose and extremely long arms, wiggled a finger over his ear as he stood up, provoking a chorus of hurrahs, the enthusiasm of which was less surprising than the fact that it was being voiced by people who had maintained such an awesome silence for so long.

The echoes from the Legislative Palace reverberated along the dusty streets, swelling over the identical patios drenched with pain, through the windows crowded with scowling faces, blending with the stench that permeated the atmosphere permanently and which seemed particularly offensive that sultry month of August.

At eighty-three, Dr. Mario Ramos's ways had changed little. His life was governed as though by a timer, every minute of the day and night accounted for. In contrast to the unvarying routine to which his physical being was subject, his spirit floated freely in a nebula of vagaries amenable to extremist speculations. Frugal and abstemious in his habits, for some mysterious reason—often misinterpreted with slanderous malice—he was a confirmed bachelor, a status that permitted him "to get up on either side of the bed." Although his sexual encounters had dwindled to solemn geriatric simulacra, Dr. Ramos maintained his long-standing ritual of receiving a favorite bed partner on Sunday afternoons at five. In consonance with his advanced age, he had adopted the biblical practice of clasping to his wizened body the ardent flesh of young women, tremulous before the godhead of power, from whose inexhaustible springs he sought to tap the elixir of rejuvenation. In the enlistment of these fresh and nubile recruits he was assisted by a former private of the guard whose devotion to duty won him rapid advancement to the rank of general.

These companions were unfailingly accorded kind and affectionate treatment and when special efforts to please were put forth, they would be met with poetic expressions during moments of abandon, though none were ever led on to expect the possibility of more substantial expressions of favor. It is also true that many of the women who shared his bed felt a certain pity for him, especially those in whom he had implanted his seed. No less than a dozen offspring, male and female, of varying ages, shepherded by despairing mothers in urgent pursuit of official support of some kind, would be making the rounds of the government offices to show off the patent authenticity of inherited features to ministers and department heads. Finally, though he avowed paternity in no case, government officials, well aware of the truth of the claims, had doubts only as to how many more were waiting in the wings. Those in the know have suggested fifteen, others eighteen, and some as many as twenty, at least. To add to the confusion, there appeared women by the dozen, now for the most part fat and/or wrinkled, who proclaimed themselves to have been the inspiration of *Mencía*, the romantic poem most frequently recited by Dr. Ramos.

Strange as it may seem, he appeared to have permanently won the hearts of those transient amours, for they bore him no ill-will whatsoever. "He has his secrets, no doubt, and will take them along with lots of others to the grave," Such were the comments about him where people gathered in homes and bars, on the Malecón, street corners and squares of the city. The man's personality was so complex, so bifurcated the pathways of his soul, that by the end of his second term he had become the quintessence of incomprehensibility. Experts specializing in certain areas of his behavior had arisen from among the ranks of government functionaries, former bureaucrats seeking reappointment, aspirants to public office, public works contractors, military officers of all grades, and even opposition politicians, all seeking the keys to the conundrum, interpreters of what it signified if he waved good-bye with his hand up or down as he left the meeting the night before, what his tone of voice meant as he escorted a visitor to the door the night before last...

Moreover, the practice of voodoo became one of the most lucrative of professions during Dr. Ramos's incumbency. Never before had this sector, once monopolized by the desperately needy, made such inroads. Many wizards and witches grew rich and wielded influence over a clientele that moved in the highest spheres of government and the military. People avidly sought in voodoo a trail that might lead them to the answers they sought on how to interpret what was happening or was going to happen...

Dr. Ramos's secret dwellings beyond the sightlines of ordinary mortals, those mysterious lairs, the distant, funereal background sounds of beastly growling, undoubtedly constituted the lure that attracted Frank Bolaño. Rashly savoring the dangers from afar, he approached by the stormiest route, that of conspiracy. Grudges, though old and quiescent, were not lacking, but he set about stirring them up the better to motivate himself. He had graduated from dental school with honors, driven by pride rather than vocational devotion, his voracious spirit finding little satisfaction in the practice of the profession. He did, however, set up the best-equipped and most elegantly appointed dental office in the country. But he found that dealing on a daily basis with saliva, cavities, and teeth repelled him, and he turned the work over to assistants. Exceptions were made, to be sure, for certain favored patients (he was known to have hands like silk) highly placed in the government who could further his career. He who seeks shall find and Frank Bolaño, moreover, was well equipped to handle whatever came along. Accordingly, one Monday early in June soon after Dr. Mario Ramos had won the first of his many re-elections, he received a telephone call at his office from a man who needed dental work. The caller was a person of considerable notoriety who had suffered reverses in his military and political careers and seemed to have reached a dead end. This caused Frank to hesitate at first about taking care of him personally. Curiosity, however, won out and it was curiosity that drew him to the former general who happened to have been involved in a attempted coup, few details of which had reached the public other than that it was a fiasco. The officer was exiled after being cross-examined, without disavowal, and before the television cameras (with a pistol barrel jabbing his spine, it was said) by Dr. Ramos himself. In the course of the investigation, one of the confidential associates of the conspirator, Frank Bolaño, became a confidential associate of the one conspired against.

Frank Bolaño enjoyed sailing in treacherous waters, was held in high esteem, and abhorred failure. The former seminary student who, at the age of seventeen, already showed a marked talent for handling contentious situations, was now taking his first sure steps as a high-powered operator in terrain where he was to become a legend of sophisticated terror among his high-placed victims.

Now, at the age of twenty-eight, a voracious bald patch was eating its way to the nape of his neck. He dressed impeccably, selecting masterfully from among a collection of beautifully custom-tailored suits in accordance with the importance of the occasion. One of the things that rankled the most after having plotted for eleven months along with the former General was that several secret service louts yanked him out of bed at dawn one day in May and without letting him get dressed dragged him into the street in his pajamas and shoved him into a patrol car. He was brought to the luxurious office of General Nataniel Piro Cristóbal, the Chief of Police, who did not leave important matters in the hands of subordinates and induced his prisoners to talk by the discriminate use of reason, threat, or torture.

"I must say, General, your officers have very bad manners. They wouldn't even let me get dressed," Frank told him, as he stood at the desk passing his hands over his shoulders and chest as though smoothing the wrinkles in his shirt. "It's very unbecoming to appear before an important man in this disreputable condition."

"And you're lucky at that," roared the General," they bring others in bare-assed and not here to my office, but down to the dungeons." Lowering his voice, as he stared at the spiral that rose from his cigarette, he said, "I assume you know why I sent for you. Is that right?"

"I beg your pardon, General, but I have no idea why I'm here. If you would be good enough to..."

"I'm going to hang you up by the balls, if you don't come clean right now," the General interrupted, laying his pistol on the desk.

"Honestly, I have no idea what this is about, General. All I know is that your officers were disrespectful to me," Frank said in an offended tone.

"Look here, Doctorcito, I'm going to begin with the Our Father and then you can chime in with the Ave María. We know that you are mixed up in a plot to overthrow the legally elected government and if you refuse to confess what you know in a civilized manner, I will be obliged to send you down to the dungeon where, I warn you, the boys are really heavy-handed and have practically no compunctions."

"Oh, so that's what it's all about. Then, why didn't you say so from the beginning. We would have saved time," Frank replied making a conciliatory gesture as he smiled beatifically.

Frank was well aware of what it was all about from the moment he heard his front door being smashed open though he had no idea what had gone wrong. He was prepared for this situation and believed that he had strong counter measures available which would, however, have to be used with consummate skill against this bloodthirsty villain into whose hands he had fallen.

"General," said Frank, speaking in a slow, steady tone, "don't take offense at what I'm about to tell you, but it's common knowledge that Doctor Ramos's security is poor. Very, very poor, General! Does he know, do you know, that he's on the verge of being overthrown?"

"What do you mean?" The General had come all the way around his desk and now sat face to face with Frank.

"The coup you mentioned is ready to break out and the only one who won't be firing a shot is me. But, in any case, General, let me congratulate you for your shrewdness in bringing me in. It was a real coup on your part."

"And...?" said the General, growing impatient, as he lit a fresh cigarette from the butt of the previous one still burning in the ashtray.

"I am party to certain details, certain evidence with respect to the pending coup... Naturally, as you can see, things have changed, my position is reversed... I'm on your side, now, and will be investigating the enemies of the government."

"Yes...yes...alright. Sure, of course, you can work with me. Why the hell not? But that's not what's on the table, right here." The General's eyes gleamed.

"I know. Proof of the plot. As I told you, I have solid evidence. If you will be good enough to allow me to go home, I'll get it for you. You can accompany me if you wish, General."

The General roared into the intercom and an officer instantly appeared.

"See this man home. Take along four officers and don't let him out of your sight...not even for a second. No phone calls. Got it, officer? Follow him even into the toilet. Got it, officer?" He raised his left arm to look at his wrist watch. "It's almost three. Be back here in one hour at the latest." And to Frank in a sharp and menacing tone, "As for you, I don't have to tell you, you'd better be back here with the evidence."

In less than an hour Frank Bolaño was there, a leather attaché case in hand with the initials F B C in Gothic letters. He was wearing an elegant dark-brown suit, a red necktie with white polka dots, and an expensive wristwatch with a wide gold band. In Frank's house, the policemen, while keeping a sharp eye on their charge, gradually relaxed their angry-gorilla expressions in view of his calm and polite behavior towards them, to say nothing of his generosity, as he went about, handing out, first a fine shirt in its original wrapper, next, a ring in a velvet case, then, a suit fresh from the shop...and so, here and there picking up and distributing valuable articles with such an air of distinction that Frank Bolaño gradually evolved from a prisoner into a monarch bestowing treasure.

The General was hard put to hide his eagerness when Frank returned. His imagination had run riot while he waited. He desperately needed a coup of his own, and perhaps this would be it! His arch enemy, General Pedro Prieto, was shoring up his foothold in the General Staff while he languished in a rat hole without military prestige where the President had flung him to hunt down petty criminals. (Shit! how could he do such a thing when he knows that I, General Piro Cristóbal, am not just his best but his only guarantor!) Now, the intuition of a devoted professional (not often duly rewarded) was telling him that he was on the point of turning up the most dangerous plot against the government (through an investigation entirely of his own with absolutely no input from any other intelligence agency) pieces of which he would soon set before the President like the parts of a dismantled bomb. And as he sucked on his overgrown mustache which he had neglected too long to trim, the General rubbed the tips of his thumb and forefinger in a dumb show of crushing the conspiracy.

Shrewd Frank had learned how to handle the General. He would play on the man's impatience as part of his strategy, the success of which he now had no doubt. He sat down, placed his attaché case on the desk, slowly opened it, and went about hunting for a small tape recorder which he finally found and set out before the General with the air of a priest presenting a chalice during the Offertory at Mass.

"General, I'd like you to listen to this first," he said as he introduced a cassette into the apparatus with extreme deliberateness.

After a moment, a voice came on that caused him to instinctively raise his hand to his belt as though to grasp his pistol. He had recognized his own voice, personal and intimate, as though stolen and coming from an enemy camp.

"What the hell is this?" he roared.

"Listen, General, don't be impatient."

The General's initial reaction of surprise dissolved into one of utter horror as he sat hypnotized by the sound of his voice, his mouth open, cigarette dangling from his lower lip.

The two men had changed roles, the prisoner was now in control of his captor.

"Hold on, now. What in hell has this got to do with the conspiracy?"

"Nothing, General, nothing. I only wanted to show that the tape you just heard could put you in a very compromising position. For example, you'll recall the detail—

very significant—where you refer to the country being in chaos and you say, 'What's lacking here is an iron hand. Another Tirano is what we need.' Couldn't that statement be interpreted as meaning that you would like to take the President's place? It could be very dangerous if the President interpreted it in such a light. You know that better than I. I tell you this for your own sake, General, so that you'll watch your step. I have no intention of doing you harm, but somebody else might act differently. You have very powerful enemies. If this tape were to fall into General Pedro Prieto's hand, he could use it against you, wouldn't you think?"

"Right. Of course...of course... I appreciate it." The general's face was a picture of distress. "But let's get back to what we came here for. Tell me about the conspiracy."

"Yes. As I was telling you, I have the proof. The reason I began by playing your own tapes was to show you that in my role as an enemy of the government, my work was to investigate high officials, beginning with you, as would be logical. Naturally, as I already explained, everything has changed. From now on, I will be at your service and my mission will be to investigate the President's enemies."

"Agreed... I told you that you could work on my staff. But let's get down to business." The General mustered no more then a weak thread of voice.

"Yes, I know, the conspiracy. That's where I'm heading. Listen, General, I repeat...I have conclusive evidence, but I can't give it to anybody but Dr. Mario Ramos. As far as the tapes that involve you are concerned... Listen, you can have them, I have no interest in keeping them. And the same thing goes for these other two." Frank rummaged in his attaché case for a moment and brought out two cassettes. You might like to have these. They are of General Pedro Prieto and *Licenciado* Filiberto Alvarado, and you can hear some very interesting things. I offer you my friendship, but you'll have to take me to Dr. Ramos. I must bring him up to date on a number of details. You will, of course, attend and, in any case, be the one to get the credit."

His captive had beaten him, and he recognized that he had no alternative. "We'll see about it," he said. "I have to consult with the President, first. It all depends on what he thinks. Meanwhile, you're under arrest, and will have to stay here. I'll leave orders with the Captain to let you have whatever you need. I should be back here in a couple of hours."

His bland face revealing nothing of the emotions he was feeling to the soldiers around him preparing for the changing of the guard, Major Estanislao Elermoso discreetly thanked the Lord that he should find himself this day the envy of highranking officers who had once trampled on him, as well as of many other comrades in arms, career soldiers, who despite having the seniority and merits had not yet made even captain. Seated on a bench in the patio of Dr. Ramos's house, he was admiring the gleaming insignia on his cap that lay beside him, as he sipped a cup of coffee just brought to him still steaming by a servant. The promotion had come just three days before, and he still found it hard to believe that he, a man who had barely learned to read and write until adulthood, should have risen to such a high station.

Major Elermoso was President Mario Ramos's adjutant, and the one member of his entire staff who was privy to the Doctor's most intimate secrets. His official duties were limited entirely to household matters, which included arranging appointments usually to be held in the Rear House before the President left in the morning for the Government Palace or, in the afternoons on his return, after his siesta. He was also responsible for internal security within the perimeter of the presidential residence. A short and paunchy family man, his figure was a far cry from the military bearing of the young officers with whom the President preferred to surround himself, but he had served his master, now in his second official term, with doglike devotion.

He had finished neither drinking his coffee nor congratulating himself when he saw General Piro Cristóbal coming through the main entrance. He immediately set his cup down, put on his cap, and stepped out to meet the Police Chief. Standing beside Major Elermoso, the figure of the General, a tall, olive-skinned, well-setup soldier, took on added dimensions. However, the Police Chief didn't make the mistake of belittling the man, for he was well aware that there was considerable power wielded behind that humble, illiterate-flunky facade. Elermoso's goodwill was essential if business of any kind at the house was to prosper. With his expression of benevolence and his unfailing politeness, he was able to set up impenetrable barriers between the President and even his most important functionaries, the worst of it being that he accomplished this almost as though a favor was being done the interested party. He defended Dr. Ramos's private preserves with a sweetness that was yet zealous and steadfast: a tiger with velvet claws.

When the General outlined the reason for his visit at such an unseasonable hour, the Major evinced surprise, extreme concern, and spoke words of admiration that inflated the General's ego, but did not accede to his request that the President be awakened. With extreme courtesy he ushered him into the little anteroom to Dr. Ramos's private library and suggested the advisability of waiting until seven o'clock. The General reformulated his case with strongest arguments and for a moment even considered pulling rank, but the Major, almost reverently begged him to have a seat and wait until he could fetch him a cup of coffee.

"Wait just a little, General, we don't want the President waking up in a bad mood. When he doesn't get his proper hours of sleep that's what happens," the Major told him impassively as he left the room.

No one but Major Elermoso was permitted to make the rules in his domain. He shared power only with Dr. Ramos's two sisters. Their only brother had not lived in the Big House with them for a number of years since he decided to build a place for himself at the rear of the yard. He was thus spared the indignity of a house that received visits from morning till night of loudmouthed women who screamed gossip and obscenities at the top of their lungs, often ending up pulling each other's hair out. Though he did find this amusing, he considered it prudent to put some distance between himself and an environment that had grown increasingly intolerable. His own was now a haven of quietness presided over by his faithful watchdog.

Discomfited, but convinced that it would be useless to protest, The General waited until the Major deigned to enter the presidential bedchamber.

When he reappeared, he said, "The President will be with you shortly, General."

"Major, did you tell him why I came?" Though subdued, the General's voice held an edge of reproach.

"Sure, General, sure," he answered, not granting the question great importance.

He then had to wait longer than expected. Finally, Dr. Ramos appeared. He wore a handsome scarlet dressing gown and held a kitten in his arms with the tenderness of a mother bearing a newborn infant.

"Good morning, Mr. President," said the General as he clicked his heels and saluted rapidly. "I apologize for coming to your home at such an hour, but it was urgent that I talk to you."

"What's happened, General?" asked Dr. Ramos, his eyes half-closed, his expression that of one who tolerates no nonsense.

"Since three o'clock this morning, I have had a person detained in my office who is involved in a conspiracy to overthrow the government, Mr. President. He is Dr. Frank Bolaño. I assume he is an important piece in the game, but he would give no information no matter how I interrogated him. He confessed that he knows the plan in detail but will inform nobody but you, personally. It is an urgent case, Mr. President, and should not be put off."

"Who did you say it was, General?" he inquired with greater curiosity than concern.

"Dr. Frank Bolaño, Mr. President, a young dentist. I've had him under investigation for some days. I received confidential information that he was conspiring against the government. I thought immediately it might involve the plot of retired and active military officers which we suspected but couldn't prove. It is important to get everything this Dr. Bolaño knows out of him before the day is out. His family will start moving pretty soon. They'll get to the newspapers, the broadcasters, the priests, and everywhere else and that won't do."

"Why don't you persuade him, General? I don't know how to cope with those things."

"I tried, Mr. President, but wasn't able to get anywhere with him. He insisted it was you he had to talk to. That's as far as it went, Mr. President. The doctor belongs to the Bolaño-Caprino family, and you know how those millionaires are, raising the roof over anything at all.

"Very good, General, if you see no other alternative, bring him here."

Frank Bolaño removed his jacket, necktie, and shoes and stretched out on the cot. The Captain brought him coffee for which Frank thanked him with a smile. He was the same officer who had arrested him, later took him home, and now treated him with discreet indulgence.

The captive had remained alone in a room next to General Piro Cristóbal's office, flat on his back for some three hours, listening to the sounds that entered from the hallway and the esplanade in front of the building, this new train of events whirling round and round in his thoughts. He wondered whether Dr. Ramos would receive him. Or would they throw him in the dungeon at police head-quarters? Were they going to torture him? He knew that the prisons were worse nowadays than in Tirano's time when Antonio Bell had been interrogated. He was quite convinced of his incapacity to resist torture. He knew even before Antonio described what they did to him at "Number Forty": the electric chair; the cigarettes slowly extinguished against his skin; the "bull's cock" whip that whistled mercilessly over his back. He knew that the tortures had gotten crueler. It gave him goose flesh just to think of needles pushed under the skin and finger nails, and the ones heated red hot in a candle flame. Who are those who devote themselves to devising new and better ways to torment? Are they in-novative thinkers who go to the chief and say proudly to him, "Boss, how do you like this idea?" And the boss will call in other officers to celebrate the underling's cruel notion amidst howls of laughter. Sotico Paredes? The reputation of this monster was well-known and Frank remembered having seen him swooping through the halls that same morning like a vulture.

When Amelia telephones him (would she already have done so?) and gets no answer, will she suspect something wrong? She would keep trying and when she got to his house and saw the condition of the door and the disorder inside would she set out running around like crazy looking for me? His parents would start a hue and cry. Would they already be at police headquarters demanding to know where I was being held? And when it has blown over, will they be saying, "After this happened to him, do you think he'll lead a more orderly life?" and, "Will he pay more attention to his practice, now?" He imagines himself married, with children, and then scoffs at the idea. He couldn't possibly live through that, either. Will Lieutenant Leoncio de la Rosa, known as "The Alligator" because of his short, stubby and powerful arms, notorious for dealing such a tremendous blow with his huge, horny, stone mason's right hand to the ear of his torture victims that they were knocked stone deaf to the ground. And what about Colonel Rolando Pardo? His hands, on the contrary, were small and soft as a schoolgirl's but few were ignorant of the fact that this effeminate-looking man was the cruelest and coldest officer, the angel of death, in the Police. God save me, he prayed, from falling into the hands of those hyenas.

"Let's go, we're leaving"! shouted General Piro Cristóbal from the doorway, abruptly shutting off Frank's apprehensions.

He got to his feet, stretched, slowly put on his shoes, and with the same deliberation walked to the clothes tree for his jacket and tie. The General watched every movement without moving from where he stood.

It was 8:45 a.m. when Major Elermoso escorted the two men to the library-living room of the Rear House. His aide-de-camp took up a position at the door leading to Dr. Ramos's bedroom, while the Chief of Police and Dr. Bolaño sat at the opposite ends of a couch. They waited half an hour for the President to complete his ablutions. There was total silence during this lapse, Major Elermoso staring into the pages of a manual as though deciphering the secret of life, the General's eyes fixed on the doorway through which the President was to emerge, Frank, scanning, radar-like, the room's decor. A woman's touch was evident in every detail. All was symmetry, neatness, and order, distilling an aura of seemliness, of repose. Six chairs were set around a table-desk upon which there stood a crystal vase with an exquisite arrangement of white roses and red lilies. At one side four rockers turned towards one another, ready for dialogue. Mahogany shelves covered the walls completely, with three, four thousand volumes, many bound in dark leather. A beautiful goose-feather duster hung at one side constituting another decorative accent. Frank wondered if Dr. Ramos had read all those books. Was this fastidious room not inconsistent with the image of the writer, poet, and thinker as a free spirit conceded a certain degree of disorderliness? Or was this meticulousness actually in tune with Dr. Ramos personality? Frank's keen intelligence probed for answers to such disturbing questions. In a few minutes he would be face to face with Dr. Ramos, and he intended to extract every possible scrap of information from the encounter. Meanwhile, thoughts of the distant past—actually only from eleven years before—welled up recalling the role he had played in the Antonio Bell case, crisscrossing with others so recent, so vivid that they seemed to be hovering constantly in the forefront of his consciousness; of the blood spilled, the atrocious crimes committed, and the unfailing indifference, the duplicity of Doctor Ramos, envisioned as one with an aura of mildness, of benevolence, about him, yet with the stench of death upon his hands.

The General instantly snapped to his feet and saluted when the President entered and remained standing stiffly at attention, arms pressed to his sides. Major Elermoso, however, fell in before the President without saluting, and then stood immediately behind him. Frank, who had stood up together with the General, fixed his eyes on the man's face, ghastly pale, as usual, while he whispered into his aide-de-camp's ear. General Piro Cristóbal's exaggerated posture might have been dictated by the presence of an outsider, but Frank was not convinced that such was the case. It was in response (Frank's painstaking investigations told him) to the barriers that Dr. Ramos set up between himself and everybody around him. Although such behavior might well be interpreted as political, merely a measure for eliciting respect by keeping the world at arm's length, Frank was sure that it was not a question of tactics but a manner of being, of intrinsic and mysterious pettiness that spread throughout his spirit like a poisonous fungus.

Then, extending a limply courteous hand in greeting, he indicated that he wanted them to sit in the rocking chairs. At that moment, Frank caught a fleeting glimpse of a skinny, humbly dressed, gray-haired little woman of unknown age who slipped out of the President's bedroom and through a side door at the other end of the room onto the patio. Later, after they had left, General Elermoso identified her as one of Dr. Ramos's sisters.

After the three men had settled into their seats, the President looked at the Chief of Police who understood it as a signal that he should take the floor. They had worked together many years. The General proceeded tactfully and with a certain practiced eloquence to introduce Frank as a young man anxious to collaborate with His Excellency in maintaining the existing order and, to that end, was offering to provide him with the details of a conspiracy by traitors plotting to overthrow the government.

The General's peroration concluded, Frank heard the words "Pleased to meet you, young man," escaping from between Dr. Ramos's lips without breath to expel them, as he reached down to pick up the kitten on the floor that was stretching its legs to claw at his trouser cuff.

Frank's studied and masterful presentation, his handling of the description of the evidence for the conspiracy, exaggerating its importance, suggesting how to deal with future plots which would be made to dissolve like magic under his hands, would be the starting point of a strange rapprochement with Dr. Ramos. As a result of it, Frank would pull the secret strings in reckless investigations of possible acts of treason in the highest reaches of civil and military power.

"Your Excellency," Frank explained, "My friend General Piro Cristóbal had the courtesy and good judgment to invite me to his office where I informed him that the constitutional government, as well as your own inestimable life are in danger. The fact that the person heading the conspiracy happens to be the retired General Califa Adad is in itself an extremely telling sign. I'm sure you are aware that he is not only an ambitious man, Your Excellency, but also one of great prestige with many fanatical followers among the active and retired military, as well as important and wealthy civilian elements. This is not a matter to be taken lightly. It is my personal opinion that the case should be approached with professional criteria, in other words, to proceed methodically, then to move fast at the precise moment. Nothing will be gained by taking him in prematurely. He could still pull the trigger from prison. Keep him under surveillance, close in on him, yes, but the important thing is to tear this conspiracy apart at the root. I believe that the situation has not yet clarified itself sufficiently to warrant immediate action. But, for my part, I am placing my services at your disposal from this moment on, together with some of the information I have available for you to see. It is not as abundant as I would like, but it will be in a few days, and serve as a measure of my loyalty to you, Your Excellency. If I may, I will now play for you a tape of the speech that General Califa Adad has already prepared to deliver if the coup succeeds. Though not definitive proof, it will, at least, give you a sense of the scope of the conspiracy. I was, unfortunately, taken by surprise. Give me three or four days, and I will be able to put the full story in your hands...into your very hands!"

Without waiting for approval, he turned on the tape recorder, his eyes fixed on the man's face, studying his reactions as he listened. He was let down, however, when after about a minute, the President waved his hand in dismissal, ordering the apparatus turned off, his lip curled cynically as he said, "A blunder on the part of the poor devil. He's an habitual conspirator of not much intelligence." With an expression of disdain, he turned to the Chief of Police, "You hold that tape General, and act accordingly, but I want no commotion. See that Dr. Bolaño gets home, his family will be getting worried."

The sidewalk in front of the presidential residence swarmed with people, many jamming the entrance, pushing their way towards the guards, waving their IDs. The "doorway regulars" congregated just outside, constituting a lottery of hope. Outstanding among such groups were the one known as "The Sisters" who made a daily ritual of shouting and cheering for the President at the top of their lungs, each recognizable to the crowd by their nicknames and special signature voices: "The Tigress," for her hoarse, long-drawn-out tones developed by years of hawking newspapers; "Poster Girl," booming out a variety of slogans like, "We want forty years more just like before," in an alcoholized baritone; "Fatty Puchula," who cheered everybody from the President down to "The Shrimp," a former doorway companion who was taken into the Big House to be dressed up as a kewpie doll; and "The Warbler" who rendered Mexican *rancheras* with such syrupy feeling that before she finished one the crowd was calling for another. It was a circus that reached its highest pitch of excitement whenever the presidential caravan of sleek black limousines and showy, open, armored jeeps fitted with heavy machine guns in the rear, was getting ready to move out.

Frank remained in the library with General Piro Cristóbal waiting for the crowd to disperse so they could leave without running the risk of being recognized. As soon as the huzzahs and shouts of "Viva Ramos...! Viva Ramos ...dammit!" were heard, he moved to the window to peer through the venetian blinds as the last vehicle slid into the street.

The excitement over, General Piro Cristóbal's car moved into the rear of the yard now emptied of the presidential Cadillac and its escort, and he and Frank Bolaño climbed in. No sooner had Major Elemeroso seen them off than Frank asked, "General, who was that woman who came out of Dr. Ramos's room?"

"Señorita Albricia Ramos, one of his sisters."

As they rolled down Bolivar Avenue, the General had no reason to be curious or to take any interest in what reaction his answer might have produced. It came as an unpleasant surprise to Frank that a person so obviously linked to the President's personal life should have been unknown to him. It was not until now, and by chance, that he became aware of her existence. Was it possible? Señorita Albricia Ramos! What part could such an unprepossessing creature, that poor wisp of woman, be playing in Dr. Ramos's mysterious world? Frank had been made aware that day of the power wielded on the domestic scene by Major Elermoso with his dark, square face a mask of serene discretion, who had confirmed to his satisfaction the rumors of his role as guardian of the doctor's love bower. Frank was aware that the sister who lived in the house was a well-mannered woman, not given to scenes, and that another sister, a woman of no particular distinction, occupied a mansion of her own in the center of the city. A fourth who also lived outside her brother's home, Ana Altagracia Ramos, called "Tatica" by everyone, was the best-known of the sisters. A sharp-tongued, impulsive woman, she was the only one who led a public political life of any sort, criss-crossing the city plugging her brother's party. Until then, Frank had been under the impression that his file on Dr. Ramos's family was complete. Now this wraith of a woman who had slipped by him in the library would be number one on his agenda after he closed the books on the case of retired General Califa Adad.

The Chief of Police dropped Frank a discreet three blocks from home. There was no sign that anybody in the neighborhood was aware of what happened. He went into his house, made some phone calls to his family and found that nobody suspected anything. That was the way he wanted it and, of course, nothing was said.

Frank devoted all his energy for the rest of the month of May to the matter of General Adad. It was not a difficult assignment. He collected routine information, tapped telephones, and tied up loose ends. Accompanied by General Pino Cristóbal, he turned over the tapes personally to Dr. Ramos, together with compromising photographs of several high-ranking army officers and a detailed written report. One of his most valuable contributions was a psychological profile of ex-General Adad that he presented orally to the President in which he provided convincing evidence of the conspirator's wavering under medium- and high-risk conditions. Frank's exposition was so effective that Dr. Ramos saw fit to bring the former General to public trial early in June before the television cameras. After confronting him in the most humbling manner with the evidence linking him to the plot, he accused him of being an "habitual conspirator" and invited him, then and there, to answer to the Dominican people for what he had done. A few moments of high suspense went by as the camera held on the man. To the amazement of the five million viewers he never lifted his head, hanging in humiliation. It was a master stroke that added to the President's prestige and, at the same time, opened the way for Frank Bolaño to be on an intimate footing with him.

Two days later, to his surprise, Frank received a visit at home from General Prio Cristóbal. His purpose was to place in the young dentist's hands a decree appointing him "Aide to the President of the Republic for Civil Affairs."

Frank did not possess the necessary political know-how and was far from having penetrated the inner reaches of the President's persona. At the outset he anticipated no great difficulties in acquiring the skills necessary for the business of power. He was deceived by his initial success and the reward of his appointment. The year 1971 was drawing to a close, and his contacts with President Ramos were no more than fleeting.

It was then that he made the acquaintance of an Argentine who, despite being very comfortably off, drove about the country in a Volkswagen. "You must never give a person the feeling that you're trying to be superior," he told Frank, partly to justify his use of such a modest vehicle and partly to convey a truth taught him by experience. As was to be expected, such advice coming from a former member of Perón's cabinet, now a confidential adviser to the President on international financial manipulation, did not fit in with Frank's own agenda. Driving back and forth in Mirador del Norte Park in his humble Volkswagen on cool December nights, the ex-Peronista would instruct him on the subject of Dr. Mario Ramos: "While the man is incapable of showing love or gratitude, he does harbor hatreds of the most vicious kind deep within him where they have become encapsulated and seep venom into his soul. He doesn't, however, let that interfere with his political objectives. If you want to get close to him do so strictly on the basis of Dr. Ramos's self-interest, his convenience. He can be convinced of anything only if your formulation sounds useful, politically useful, to him."

Meanwhile, he was finding it impossible to gain a foothold on the slippery slope of Dr. Ramos's terrain. Since it was going to be so difficult to get close to him, he opted for foraging at the fringes in search of better opportunities to run down his prey.

His starting point would be the Big House, where the President's sisters lived. Their influence in official circles was considerable, and it was the place from which to observe movements at closer range.

The days that followed were to bring Frank two surprises. The first was the discovery that yet another sister lived in the house. This one was almost constantly accompanied by a midget whom she had seen many times outside the main door dancing merengues with swaying hips. In her more lucid moments she invited the midget into the house where they played Parcheesi, put-and-take, jacks, and all sorts of other games, and when they weren't doing that she would take up a position near the door and stare out of her enormous, clear eyes at all who entered. Another of her pastimes was to lean all the way down to whisper impish remarks about them in the ear of her little lady-in-waiting. People trooped in starting early in the morning waiting to see the President for a variety of reasons, or no reason at all, and she considered everyone an intruder. It was part of his daily routine to go from the Rear House to the main hall of the Big House where he paused briefly to greet supporters and hear petitions before proceeding to the Presidential Palace.

The other surprise came on a Sunday in January when he noticed a man whom he thought he recognized in a far corner of the room set aside for private meetings where he was deep in conversation with Doña Cándida, Dr. Ramos's clever, fastidious sister. "Unbelievable," said Frank to himself, "unbelievable." He was almost certain it was Arturo and of all things, talking so intimately to that important lady.

Standing with Frank waiting to talk to her was a young Spaniard who was losing patience as the conversation dragged on. However, influential though he was, he did not dare break in.

"That fellow is Arturo Gonzalo," he confirmed with a grimace of distaste. "Do you know him?"

"Yes, but I haven't seen him in a long time," replied Frank as he continued to stare in surprise in his former friend's direction.

The Spaniard continued to fill him in. "He's Doña Cándida's advisor. They're organizing a Peace Crusade, a charitable organization for aid to the poor. It's scheduled to open next month and that's all she has on her mind now."

Carlos, the young Spaniard, was the main contact he had developed for gaining entrée to the President's sisters, that is, to the two who concerned him. The most difficult to approach, as his investigations indicated, was Albricia, the sister through whom negotiations related to juicy contracts were routed, as well as other matters of a similar financial nature. Doña Cándida had evidently become the political power behind the throne, according to the former Perón cabinet minister's educated opinion. "In less than a year, the officers and generals will be kneeling down before her as if she were a goddess," he predicted, thereby drawing a parallel, considering the limitations, between her and his beloved Evita.

The young Spaniard, with less than a year in the country, had a picaresque turn of fortune. His first six months were spent without a penny in his pocket, dreaming of millions, until one day in August he was approached by Frank with sound counsel through a mutual friend. "Get yourself a wife. But, at once! That is, if it's real money you're interested in." By October he was married to the President's niece.

He had come from the motherland, a six-footer with a shock of blond hair and the face of an angel, dressed outlandishly, trousers nearly to the armpits, shirts pasted tight to the body, eyes fixed on the keys to the treasure chest belonging to the niece of a president of a Caribbean island who had been vacationing in Spain and who had been smitten by this spectacularly handsome young Malagueñan. One fine day he hopped on a plane and, with less than fifty dollars in his pocket, landed on the young lady's doorstep. But he did have a lot of class. The young lady, an only child unprepossessing to more than an average degree, began to salivate, and when her parents expressed doubts about the acceptability of this fellow with trousers up to his chest, she would pout and stamp her little foot until, finally, her father threw up his hands and said to her mother, "Enough of this, dammit, Carolina, let's see the upshot of it...whatever God wills." And so, on the basis of such a humanitarian concept, the young Spaniard was installed in a suite at a government hotel with a government car and army-corporal chauffeur at his service. So that he should lack for nothing, he was also appointed to a post in one of the government enterprises at which his presence was not required but which paid him a handsome salary beginning immediately. "Hooray for the government!" yelled the young Spaniard, a Tarzan look-alike on the high board at the hotel pool. He dove into the water and came up at the other end with the elegance of a dolphin where his corporal was waiting, martini in hand. The martini dispatched, he poised himself again on the high board to dive once more into the golden image of his future shimmering brightly in the depths of the lukewarm blue water. However, his was not a nature to be satisfied for long with well-being of such a passive character. He had an urgent need to lay hands on a fortune in large bills he could count with his own dampened fingers. That was what he had come for, not to be listening to the banalities of a homely, skinny wench with a face full of pimples. "If only I could get my hands on, say, five million without having to be married and smell the stink of acne salve every night."

"No," Frank advised him one afternoon when the young Spaniard had laid out his plans before him. "They won't let loose of a peso until you're married to her."

"Okay...so be it. To the altar, then, and well worth the sacrifice!"

Enjoying the young Spaniard's impatience, Frank waited patiently for the interminable dialogue between Doña Cándida and his former Seminary companion to end. Not until they had gotten to their feet to say good-bye did he approach to embrace his old friend. "Brother, this is a pleasure I was not expecting!" he said, noting out of the corner of his eye Doña Candida's expression of surprise at the warmth of the encounter.

They met outside the President's house that same evening and had supper together at the pleasant Vesuvius Restaurant on the Malecón with a view of the sea.

Arturo was not very different from the youth he had known and had none of the biliousness of the politician he had evidently become.

As they reminisced happily, Arturo interrupted to call his companion's attention to a couple who had just entered the room. "Take a look at that fellow. He's the congressman for my town and the boss of the whole district. He resents it that an upstart like me should have influence at the President's house, and he seems to have it in for me." After the couple was seated at a nearby table, Arturo and the man crossed glances, nodding glumly to each other.

The two young men resumed their conversation and Frank suddenly opened a subject they seemed tacitly to have been avoiding. "Have you heard anything of Antonio?"

"The last time I saw Antonio was just before I left the country about five years ago. He was studying law at the university and seemed to be an important student leader.

But, I have no idea what he's doing now. I imagine he must have gotten his degree and is still an activist on the left."

As they ate, Frank eyed the congressman's table as the stout little man ordered dinner. All at once, he stood up and excused himself, saying he would be back in a few minutes. When he returned, he asked Arturo to introduce him to the congressman but not to do so until the couple was about to leave and to lead them to his table at that point.

Frank returned to the subject of Arturo. "You know, I wasn't even aware that you left the country. Five years! How's that possible? Actually, you never looked me up again. I had an idea you were making yourself scarce in these parts."

Arturo noted a hint of reproach in Frank's tone but was at a loss to interpret it. "Frustration, idealism. Brother, that's out of tune with the times. Occasionally, it occurred to me that, being such a romantic, you might have gone off on a tangent of that kind. You can't imagine what a surprise it was for me to see you in Dr. Ramos's house. If somebody had told me I wouldn't have believed it. I had to see it with my own eyes. How in the world did that happen?"

"I guess there comes a time in a man's life, Frank, when he begins to be concerned about his future. Each of us was trying to find his way. I ended up in exile and that's one of the worst solutions to the problem. Now, I'm back, older in spirit, more conservative because of things that I often don't understand but which I let influence me."

Arturo cut himself short when he saw the congressman paying the check. He approached, greeted the couple as they were about to leave and inviting them to meet Frank, he escorted them to his table.

"Mr. Congressman, Señora, I would like you to meet my friend, Dr. Frank Bolaño, Aide to the President for Civil Affairs."

The congressman was mumbling the usual formulas with a somewhat defensive air when Corporal Ignacio strode up to the table, clicked his heels, and stood at attention. "Excuse me for interrupting, sir, but I just left the Palace to bring you a message from the secretary that you and Don Arturo have an appointment with the President this evening at 8 o'clock."

Corporal Ignacio was a tall, young, athletically built mulatto at Frank's service, elegantly dressed in an officer's uniform, thanks to his employer's generosity, with a .45 pistol on his hip.

He stood in place, stiff as a ramrod, until Frank told him, "Thank you. Dismissed," at which he did an abrupt about-face and strode off with military precision.

"What appointment is he talking about?" asked Arturo when the congressman and his wife had left.

"None, brother, none. It's all part of a charade you're going to have to learn to put on. That little congressman is in your pocket, now. Remember, nobody in this country figures he can be suckered, especially peasants like that."

"And Corporal Ignacio...what gives?"

Frank stretched out his arms on both sides and without moving his head, rolled his eyes heavenward as he spoke, looking for all the world like St. Ambrose of the chromo in Arturo's mind's eye.

"I've trained him for such occasions. When I left the table I explained the situation to him. You saw how well he took care of it. Very often, he doesn't even need a suggestion from me. There have been times when I wasn't sure myself whether what he said was true or an invention. Pretty soon, Arturo, you're going to have to arrange for a Corporal Ignacio of your own. They are an essential power tool but more important than having one is knowing how to make proper use of them."

As he listened to Frank's engaging, ceremonious discourse, with which he was generally in agreement, Arturo nevertheless felt certain that no corporal would ever fall to his lot. He could not imagine having a soldier or bodyguard always on hand to complicate the simple routine of his life. However, he did suspect that he was venturing out on a stormy but seductive sea where mirages replaced reality. In any case, it was an amusing way of life from which he would separate himself in due time. Easier said than done! Would the mere intention be sufficient to give one the strength to abandon a world in which the senses were gradually befuddled in a drunkenness of power? He did not think it possible to repeat the involvement of his younger days in the Seminary, but he was able to imagine himself entangled once again, through a fatal attraction, in a web of dissemblance.

It was after eleven when they left the restaurant in Frank's sumptuous Continental Mark IV, one of the finest cars in the city. Arturo had left his car parked outside the President's house. Frank asked Arturo to drive him home, and Corporal Ignacio parked the Mark IV in the vacated space. The two young men followed the Malecón slowly to a point just past the spot where Tirano was assassinated, then turned into the Avenue and continued along at the same slow pace. Frank made use of the time to launch a cool, reasoned exposition to persuade Arturo of the advantages that could accrue from an alliance between them. There were many dangers to be faced, he told him, and working as a team would be the best defense against elements already conspiring or beginning to. "We would have to be ready to fight many small wars," he warned. They pulled up at the Capri sidewalk cafe where they took seats and ordered ice cream. That part of the Malecón and the cafe brought back many memories for Frank. Arturo was bewitched by the moonlit evening in combination with the strange and fascinating panorama his friend had been opening for him and the two forgot about home and lingered on until twelve-thirty when Frank asked to be driven back to the President's house. Corporal Ignacio was asleep in the driver's seat of the Mark IV. The maneuver was explained by Frank.

"Anybody who passes on the Avenue will think I am with the President or, at least, one of the sisters. Since it's nothing that can be confirmed, when in doubt it's always easier to believe. Corporal Ignacio will be leaving before one. Well, I hope you've taken these introductory lessons to heart, Arturo. In a short while, you're going to be dealing with one of the most powerful men in the country."

Towards morning, Arturo was still wide awake on the balcony of his apartment drinking coffee as his wife lay sound asleep in the bedroom. He sat gazing at the starry sky with the same intensity as in his Seminary days at the window of the dormitory. Now, smoking one cigarette after another, he was sensing the steady, throbbing pulse of the city just as he did then. One thought kept going round and round uncomfortably in his mind, of the young blonde girl with the sweet face and guileless eyes, Dr. Ramos's mother's nurse and companion whom Frank had told him was part of his team. He found it hard to imagine her as one of Frank's spies in the President's house. In her white uniform, she was constantly at the ninety-year-old woman's side whether in the dining room or bathroom, or sitting next to her as she waited in a rocking chair for her son to come from the Palace. He would sit with her for a bit after supper while his stomach settled and pay her his last attentions of the evening. The President also used the occasion to hold one or two interviews with persons only his sisters had the right to seat in the adjoining rockers. Frank had no scruples about telling Arturo, "The girl spills everything to me that she overhears in those conversations." He also shared matters of such a highly confidential nature that, as Arturo mulled them over in the course of his night-long vigil, things jelled for him by the time morning neared. The road would be rough, he had no doubt, but the decision to set out on it was not irreversible. He would agree, then, with appropriate reservations, to throw his lot in with his friend.

Pistón was kneeling on the volcanic ground alongside the square, ten or so naked little boys around him eagerly waiting to be hypnotized by his tales. The lad, holding a string of dead quails newly collected and still warm from the snares he had laid on the plain, was not in the mood for storytelling. The boys, however, continued to wait patiently for him to relent as he sat silent, eyes fixed on Arturo who, contrary to his habit since he had commenced his project in this forgotten barrio, sat apart on the steps of the old monument. It was a rough cement obelisk that had been erected in that desolate spot to commemorate one of the numerous shadowy engagements with Haitian invaders in which the principal weapons of war commonly utilized by both sides were knives and river stones by the thousands. The battleground was nearby: the hill, the stony plain, and the river itself that ran red with the blood of the barefoot troops. In the absence of a school, Pistón, like many of his neighbors, enriched history with invention as they re-enacted the ancient battles, running about the area, filling the air with warlike shrieks and wails of the wounded.

Imaginative as he was, Pistón was capable of appreciating that Arturo, like ordinary mortals, was subject to periods of sadness, discouragement, and ill humor, such as he appeared to be going through since the day before. Yet that behavior confused and pained him in a man whom he held to be all-powerful, who had been coming regularly for three months to this shithouse for goats, involving himself in the poverty of so many poor devils, advising them, solving their problems, with a smile on his lips and words of encouragement, always. Pistón was thirteen years old but he looked a lot younger. Thin and very short for his age, he had a pair of small sharp eyes that sparkled against his black skin. His kinky hair had been clipped short by his father to save time and the centavos that would have gone to the itinerant barber. He became Arturo's favorite from the time he first arrived at the town. That fact and his lively imagination established his influence over the other boys. Before, Pistón sold his quails by waving them at the passing cars on the highway. Now, Arturo took them off his hands, bought beans, oil and salt which he had the boy bring to his mother who prepared tasty meals which Arturo, seated in one of the hut's three rattan chairs, would share with the family—Pistón's parents and four brothers and sisters— happy to have this largess to fall back on.

Considering Arturo's dark mood, the boy understood that it was rooted not in bad temper but in worry. In any case, sadness, ill humor, and worry, according to his reasoning, were characteristic properties of the poor not the rich. And Arturo knew that words could not uncloud the glass through which he was regarded, nor was it his intention to try. Preferable that he should be looked upon as wealthy, happy, and powerful, and not a man entrapped.

Arturo was making up his mind to spend the night in the village, to have a quail supper with Pistón's family and sleep in one of the twenty cement block houses under construction which, in groups of five, enclosed the weeded undergrowth of the town square with the obelisk at its center. Across from it on one side was an empty lot on which it was planned to build a church. This project would fulfill the most ardent desires of the women of the village but Arturo had left it for last. Priority was being given to finishing the houses, a water main, a soccer field and, with luck, the installation of power lines. The original plan, as presented to Doña Cándida Ramos, President of the Peace Crusade, had been more modest, for ten dwellings, which she accepted with alacrity principally because it was to be financed by Don Piro Taranzo, a contractor whose political fortunes were at a low ebb and who would be opening the door to the President's house with an outlay of only fifteen thousand pesos. Overwhelmed by the degree of misery he was seeking to alleviate, Arturo fought for double the number of dwellings, a water supply, and the soccer field and, three months later, was on the point of obtaining authorization for the electric lines. It was impossible to meet all the needs and difficult to pick 20 out of the 138 families of whom 130 were living in the most abject poverty. Finally, he narrowed it down to those with the most children and even then there were more heads than hats and a lottery had to be held. Promises had to be made to the losers which Arturo knew would not be kept. The people were placated, and it was not difficult to convince the men to organize in volunteer work brigades and the women to cook great basins of rice and beans to feed them. Arturo brought in architects and engineers from the city to oversee the project, construction crews from the police department, as well as stocks of food, and the solitary and eager hamlet began to buzz with activity and hope.

Progress was being made but Arturo continued to be downcast and worried and Pistón couldn't understand why his God-figure should have been sitting there on the steps of the obelisk not wanting to talk to anybody. It was nearly five o'clock but the sun was still quite high and the sounds of construction and voices could be heard. Pistón watched as Arturo stood up and headed for the soccer field. He followed at a distance like a timid small animal, saw him sit down again in the shadow of a locust tree, prowled around keeping an eye on him, and finally went home to give his quails to his mother to prepare for supper.

The previous day at the same twilight hour when the accumulated heat of the day made it feel as though the town was inside a great bubbling double boiler, Pistón went bustling around looking for Arturo until he found him in one of the outlying huts at the edge of the plain. A white man had arrived in a station wagon, asking for him. Pistón saw them greet each warmly and then move away to talk privately. The man left half an hour later. Pistón immediately noted a difference in Arturo's demeanor for he went straight to his car and drove off without his supper or a word to anybody and did not return until late the next day. It was the end of April and one year, two months, and thirteen days had elapsed since the founding of the Peace Crusade. At first, Arturo had illusions that the organization was truly embarked on the social crusade for which it had allegedly been created. Little by little, however, it had changed course and turned into a large-scale political and financial operation that revolved around Doña Cándida Ramos. Arturo had roused her out of the doldrums of a bureaucratic rocking chair by convincing her to take up the cause of the downtrodden with the result that the simple little lady turned into a shrewd, manipulative businesswoman who possessed the same cold-blooded capacity to dissimulate as her brother. She seemed incapable of emotion, had divested herself of all ties of affection, and turned the house into a hotbed of intrigue.

What Arturo had so dreaded was happening to him again. Just as in the Seminary, he was creating a secret world for himself. He was running away from the city to the country and spending weeks there without returning to the President's house. The atmosphere of ritual genuflection that now prevailed there had become repugnant. He would go traveling and use funds for the most trivial pursuits. On one occasion, he sought candor and innocence in the heart of a farm girl, magnificent as the moon that replicated itself in the wavelets of the brook, only to discover that she had big-city finger nails. A friend told him a short time later, after seeing him with her in an expensive restaurant in town, "You'd best leave that kind on the mountain because when they're brought to the city they turn on you like cats." Spent, he returned to the habitual warmth of his marriage in which he rediscovered true candor and the subtlest innocence. Soon again, however, he felt the goad of intense emotion, as though life, following a scenario of war and peace in tumultuous alternation, was seeking a balanced synthesis.

Pistón could see that his idol was worried and downcast now but had no idea why. He had had a visitor the evening before, Father Rey, the parish priest of his town. They had been friends since his childhood, from the time the stout young man, recently ordained, arrived from abroad to be Father Santiago's assistant. A sociable, dynamic person, he was more concerned with the human drama than theological intricacies. He and Arturo hit it off well despite being on opposite sides of the political fence. Father Rey, a man of forty-five whose deliberate, almost gloomy tone of voice hardly reflected his intensity of spirit, had come to tell Arturo of a problem he was facing and ask his help. Two political leaders accused of involvement in the introduction of a guerrilla group into the region were being pursued by the Army and Police. The priest had been hiding them for the last ten days in the attic of an old people's home and was afraid that they might be discovered at any moment. Father Rey had good reason to expect that they would be killed if they were taken prisoner and that he, if he was lucky, would be expelled from the country.

Their nerves in shambles, urinating and defecating in their rat's quarters, they were hardly able to get food down anymore, and Father Rey wanted Arturo to help smuggle them into the city.

It was a difficult, risky task, but Arturo took it on gratefully; he needed a noble mission to counteract his current emptiness of spirit. The guerrilla leader was holed up in the mountains fighting a lost cause, and many of Arturo's old and estranged friends, stoking themselves with self-serving fanaticism, traveled a leftward path leading nowhere, while he himself was trapped in a course of applying social cosmetics to the vast scars of poverty, his deep and unassailable decency offended by the unceasing horrors of the President's house, the Peace Crusade, and the vice and lewdness that surrounded him. And just as in the Seminary, he again saw no way out of the maze. Life seemed one great mistake.

The light had faded when Arturo made his way, slowly, meditatively to Pistón's house. It was a Tuesday and he was planning the rescue for the following Friday using the same type of stopwatch procedure that he had learned from Frank when Antonio's escape was engineered.

The village was some twenty miles from where Arturo was overseeing his community project, It lay in the mountainous heart of the island on an ancient, narrow, dirt road, hacked out with pick and shovel, that snaked dizzily around the peaks up to the bluish crests where the guerrilla operated. The entire southern part of the country was occupied by literally thousands of troops and between the village and the capital there were five congested checkpoints manned by guards with jittery trigger fingers and orders to kill exercising fine-tooth vigilance over all traffic.

Pistón was pleased to see Arturo back at the hut for supper. Arturo drew him aside, poked a five-peso bill into his shirt pocket with one hand as he rubbed the stubble on his skull with the other. After eating, Arturo disappeared from the village. Pistón, the tale spinner, surrounded by small boys in the darkness on the steps of the obelisk, waited until well past eight for Arturo to return. It was about ten o'clock when he finally heard the motor and saw the lights of his car through the cracks of the wall next to which he slept.

Like the night before, he had made the trip to his village to study the itinerary and the behavior of the soldiers at the checkpoints after nine o'clock. They were less aggressive towards him this time at the three posts between the village and El Cruce where the road dipped on the way to the southern zone and the capital. The night before, his car had been closely searched despite his having identified himself as a government official and director of the Peace Crusade who was also interested in observing how the surveillance operated. He particularly cultivated personal contact with the guards on the two trips, chatting with the officers in charge and the soldiers, passing out cigarettes and rum, and encouraging them to carry on their good work, letting them know he would inform the President's sister, Doña Cándida Ramos, whose assistant and close adviser he was, as well as the President himself.

By Thursday he was convinced that he had won the guards' confidence sufficiently for them to let him pass without a search. As insurance, on Friday morning he obtained an official license plate and convinced Doña Cándida to give him her card with a handwritten note because of the heavily militarized conditions of the zone in which the community project was located. He devoted less attention to the last two checkpoints, in the city of Bani and San Cristóbal, than to the other three between his village and El Cruce because they represented less danger.

He left the capital at three o'clock on Friday afternoon and drove the seventy miles to his village, stopping on the way at San Cristóbal and Bani to pass the time of day with the guards, and at each successive checkpoint, as though they were stations of the cross, until he reached his village at around seven o'clock.

The plan was as follows. The first checkpoint was on the way out of the village. The old people's home was on the highway a hundred yards beyond. Arturo had suggested to Father Rey that, starting on that Monday when he had come to see Arturo until the Friday scheduled for the rescue, he should go out on the highway shortly before nine o'clock at night, driving a dump truck belonging to the Parish Development Organization and return to the village in half an hour so that the soldiers' visual inspection of those exits and entrances would become routine. On Friday, however, after having placed the escapees in the truck covered by a tarpaulin, he called the parish house from the asylum to notify the assistant priest, the only other person in on the rescue, that he was now ready to go. The assistant would then notify Arturo who was to be waiting in his car outside the parish house. As soon as Father Rey had left, headed towards the highway, Arturo would take off in the same direction for a point a mile further, the agreed-upon spot for the transfer of the two refugees to his car. Father Rey would then return to the village just as he had been doing all week. The rest would be up to Arturo.

Arturo checked his wristwatch and glanced at the window of the parish house where a light was to go on as soon as Father Rey had departed with his truckload of fugitives. It was two minutes to nine when he got the signal. He started out expecting to catch up with Father Rey in eight to nine minutes but on arriving at the guard booth he was informed that no vehicle could leave the village after nine without a pass from the chief of police. This took him by surprise and even though he presented all his credentials to the guards they insisted very courteously that he must have the pass. In desperation at the thought of Father Rey out on the highway with his load of dynamite and the prospect of having to wait for an officer who had probably stepped out, he arrived at the station, his heart pounding. However, the corporal on duty pointed next door where the captain was playing dominoes in a neighbor's patio.

The officer interrupted his game to return to the office, typed out the pass, signed and handed it over to Arturo. It was past nine-fifteen by the time he had cleared the checkpoint and was racing down the pitch-dark road when about a mile ahead he slowed down at the sight of approaching headlights. It was Father Rey's truck. Both stopped and Father Rey explained through the window that he had to drop the two men a short distance back on the top of the hill at a point known as Vuelta de la Paloma where they would be hiding until they saw Arturo signal by blinking his lights three times. Father Rey wished him luck, they waved good-bye, and the two vehicles continued on their way.

As he approached the indicated spot, Arturo slowed to a crawl, his eyes glued to the side of the road where there was a ditch, beyond it a field overgrown with weeds, and down below the legendary river said to have run red with the blood of Dominicans and Haitians in battle on more than one occasion. He gave the signal but there was no response. Worried about the possibility of a patrol car passing while he was parked, he continued on his way for a short distance, turned and went back to the same point where, slowing to a crawl, he gave the signal again. This time to his relief it was answered by two disheveled figures scrambling out of the ditch and racing towards the car. He waved them into the back seat. Smelly, filthy, and frightened, they seemed on the verge of nervous prostration.

As Arturo turned again, they apologized for not having come out the first time around. They explained that seeing the official license plate had made them wary. After driving for five minutes during which he outlined his plan for getting them through, he stopped at a convenient spot in the road told them to get out and proceeded to open the trunk, but they were reluctant to get in. He assured them that the next checkpoint was a fairly rigorous one and that there was no other way for them to get through to the capital. They argued that they would rather take their chances going down the ravine and climbing up on the other side of the checkpoint where Arturo could pick them up. He would have none of it, however, and threatened to abandon them then and there if they didn't get in the trunk. Finally, they had no choice but to accept and get into what they referred to as their coffin.

If there were anything Arturo could have wished for at that juncture it would have been a cloudburst, for the skies to open. Actually, he didn't really think it would substantially ease his predicament, that it would loosen surveillance, but he wished for it, anyway, a heavy rain would be a companion for him or a blanket under which he might hide. The clouds were dark and there had been a hint of rain earlier in the city but they had dispersed later over the mountains to the north. He had wished for it then as he was doing now without any logical basis. His brain raced as they neared the checkpoint, the second of the four they had to pass, surprising him with its capacity for conjuring up phantoms. He had covered the same stretch of road for the last four days, more or less at the same hour, without seeing a single military vehicle or foot patrol.

Nevertheless, he was now convincing himself that at any moment he was going to meet up with one or the other or both, that he was going to be stopped by guards he had not previously met, and that it was only logical to expect the car to be searched. In that case he would be up against the same fate as the fugitives. Analyzing further, he reasoned that if there was no red tape at the next station the same would hold true for the rest since military orders are issued in series.

He drew up to where five guards armed with rifles blockaded the road, got out, greeted them, noting with satisfaction that their demeanor did not seem to deviate in the slightest from that of the previous days, reached into the back seat to retrieve a bag of sandwiches and bottles of rum which he handed to the sergeant who smiled his thanks and waved him on. The same routine was repeated at El Cruce, the next point.

It was ten-thirty as he was approaching the city of Ban. If all went well, he would be entering the capital in an hour and a half. The mountain road with its steep and dangerous curves was now behind him and he was relieved to be driving on level ground. Ban was deserted as he came through, but when he came to the checkpoint on the way out he was surprised to see a dozen vehicles ahead of him, mainly small pickup trucks carrying agricultural products which were apparently being gone over by the soldiers like vultures tearing apart carrion. Even worse, there was an ambulance at one side where a patient on a stretcher had been pulled out onto the pavement and was being subjected to a search over the objections of the driver and a weeping woman. Arturo realized that under no circumstances could he risk a search.

He pulled out of line, drove slowly by the guards as he pointed to his official license plate, and shouted, "Special mission of the Presidency. Very urgent, have to get through immediately!" There was no answer so he accelerated, his heart in his mouth, waiting for whistles or shots, but nothing happened and he sped on.

From there on his mind was a blank, his eyes simply concentrated on the highway. There were no options, now. San Cristóbal was the last checkpoint and if they suspected anything at Ban and raised the alarm ahead, he was done for. When he reached the station, he glided up to the barrier where a guard approached, peered at the driver, and poked his nose in through the window to look in the back of the car. Arturo handed the soldier his credentials which he glanced at briefly, handed them back, and waved him on.

When he had left the city lights far behind he stopped at a curve in the road to piss, then opened the trunk to let the two fugitives out. He reassured them that they were safe now and could stretch their legs and sit in the back of the car for the rest of the drive to the capital.

The two men were relieved, relatively calm, and with a need to unburden themselves. Arturo let them do all the talking. The one who seemed to be in charge spoke in a tone that Arturo found overbearing and patronizing. He seemed to be telling him that he should feel proud and even grateful that he had done something that would elevate him in the opinion of the people who would soon be deposing Dr. Mario Ramos. He hinted at some vague recompense and even insinuated that he continue to collaborate in the cause after this. Rather than becoming angry, Arturo felt pity for the man who was incapable of seeing his action in a proper light. He remembered how the man now making high-flown declarations had been trembling like a leaf only a few hours before. However, he held his peace and took them home with him where he let them bathe, gave them a change of underwear, and asked his wife to prepare food for them. In the early morning he woke them up, gave them some money and drove them to where they wanted to go in the city, where he took leave of them, saying, "Don't consider what I did for you an act of political partisanship or solidarity on my part. Take it simply as a humanitarian act for which you can thank Father Rey, and I'll thank you to keep your mouths shut about it and forget you ever saw me."

Before me is the handsome stone house with the elegant iron fence and fragrant garden where Laly Pradera's tender lips trembled against mine one moonlit, starry night. Invariably present were all those things that had been a regular part of my life, that my eyes sought out anew so eagerly each time, for the perfumed traces of her presence clung to every element: the broad treads of the gently sloping stairway, the rectangular terrace, the tall, majestic palm tree at the end of the patio; the varicolored roses, the echo of a far-away guitar, the church bells again ringing out the hour of the rosary. After the rain, in the warm sunshine before afternoon faded, I would stroll the town calling up memories, still feeling them all the way to the marrow of my bones. After so many years! The paths in the park covered with the pale blue blossoms of the jacaranda trees; the sad absence of chessboards on the benches, with no Giol, no Claudio, no Fremio, no Pilico, no Negro, nor anyone else leaning over them, battling it out; Colón Street without Patricia or the group of girls who so beautified it (for most of us had fled the town sooner or later, and it angered me to see all those houses which had held something precious to me, now profaned by strangers); Chile, looking out on the river, now a trickle, where friends gathered on the balcony exchanged verses that reached out to the ends of the world: Dolores Peralta, turned into an old woman sitting on her throne at her Magnate palace waiting for night to fall and the porgies to swim to the water's edge to eat the bits of flesh from the hides of her workshop; the Tres Rosas, the tavern where lone and rebellious Chavo still sat getting drunk, as he had done all his life, because he couldn't look at the world unless his eyes were clouded by unreality; the lower town and the cemetery where Maceo once saw the Marimanta, the evil specter.

All these irrecoverable things, however, perceptible only as a vapor of shadows hanging over the hollow of this town, serve only to depress my spirits, to confound it with a yesterday that was not even remotely as I want to imagine it, since I know it was really more a place of tears and unhappiness than of pleasure. Yet, I stubbornly persist in looking back over a false past, trying to retie the loose strands of the lash, as though I could then recreate the spontaneity of my young years, the time when each drop of pain was an intense spasm, now that I apparently possess all the things that don't fit into even a tiny corner of my heart, now that I think and think as I wait at the wheel of my car on this corner till it's time for the meeting of the government party heads to plan the election strategy...all a damn tissue of lies, arrogance, and emptiness.

Before joining this meeting at the home of a highly placed gentleman across the street from the house where Laly once lived, I see two of the leading politicians. Drugged as I am with my old memories, the story of Maceo's ghost comes to mind, the recollection of which will be much more interesting than this dull meeting. Still, I am curious to see the reaction of these snobs when they see me walk in with Lame Luisito, their former bootblack and errand boy. I have no interest beyond that in being there, nor is there anything else of concern worth mentioning that might happen.

(Hostile and in bad humor, the people watched from windows, doorways, and patios as Maceo's funeral procession went by. Led by Father Simón and three altar boys, no more than a dozen friends and family followed to bid a last goodbye to that uncompromising, incorruptible man who had been practically a legend. Many years later, I learned that among the onlookers there had been a beautiful woman, bathed in tears, standing on a high balcony. That afternoon, I couldn't go hunting partridges with Leonel Castillo, though I had promised to. My eyes dazed and damp, something of me went along in that rough coffin that I followed from the alley of my house. Years have gone by and I feel that it's time for me to defend Maceo's good name against all the misunderstandings and slander.

One day, his wife Inocencia, my godmother, confided the details to me of that nebulous Marimanta incident, and I have not been at peace with myself since. It was then that I fully understood why Maceo was so careful not to divulge the secret of what happened on that unfortunate night. His silence so irked the townspeople, so piqued their unhealthy curiosity, that they never forgave him.

Maceo turned fifty-two two days before the incident. This last celebration of his life was associated with a series of outlandish, reckless events. As could be expected, popular imagination exaggerated everything. However, it was true that he and his old friend Bolo had gone up into the hills surrounding the town to look for buried treasure. A popular story was that while they were in the midst of their digging, a little dog ran between their legs and immediately took off into the darkness. The two men were not frightened off by this nor by the chorus of growls that accompanied each blow of their pickaxes nor the sinister gleam of a pair of eyes like red-hot coals that moved threateningly in the adjoining woods. With curses for the Bird of Evil and a prayer to the saints they continued the working and soon came upon a great clay vessel filled with gold pieces. Stumbling under its heavy weight, they arrived uneventfully at the outskirts of town. When they reached the first streets, they were suddenly set upon by a ferocious dog that looked very much like the one on the mountain except that it was much larger. After getting bitten in several places, they succeeded in driving it off. They continued on their way thinking they were now out of danger. However, when they came to Maceo's house they found their way blocked by the same dog, only now very much larger and fiercer, frothing at the mouth, and terrifying to see. This beast refused to be driven off and so Maceo attacked and killed it. The next day, his neighbors cleaned up the blood while pigs up from the ravine fought over the carcass.

True or not, the fact is that this is how the story was told, repeated, and believed and the myth grew like the mountain that overshadowed Maceo.

He was a contradictory person. Though professing disbelief in life after death, he was not beyond having faith in disembodied voices of the dead that would guide him to buried treasures like the one he dug up with his friend Bolo. Though he considered the Catholic Church a "perverse anachronism" (a term lifted from a pamphlet he had found that attacked the nation's tyrannical government) guilty of unspeakable evils throughout history, whose priests were puppets obligated to act out of hypocrisy, he did not interfere with his wife and three daughters attending services; the approach to his sons was different, he educated them for what he called "a man's life."

Fair-haired, tall and lanky, his image in my memory is associated with boots clasped at the ankle by heavy buckles, britches, birds, the smell of gunpowder, fatigues and a soldier's stride. Despite his age, he had strong, agile legs which he kept in trim by walking the fields hunting partridges and pigeons. There were two loves in his life: his family and the village where he was born and grew up, which he glorified always by magnifying its beauties and exaggerating its virtues. The tolling of the church bells, the sunrise rosary attended by half the population during the missionary seasons of the Jesuits, the processions of Holy Week and the month of May with its wealth of flowers and canticles to the Virgin were aspects of the faith that attracted him passionately, not for their religious content but for their folkloric wholesomeness and the resonance of innocence and unity palpable among the villagers.

A nonbeliever more by intuition than reason, Maceo accepted with dissatisfaction what in his judgment was "the community's state of innocence." He would expound to his circle of close friends: "This is a childlike and good society, and as with children, they must be allowed to evolve in their goodness. Let them have their illusions if it makes them happy. I don't want the burden on my conscience of exposing the realities of life's harshness to them." And, because of the great value he placed on social integration, he respected

Father Simón and helped him in various good works. The priest was aware of how Maceo thought and on more than one occasion they met in sharp-edged dispute on the subject of religion. There was no love lost between them but they coexisted on a basis of mutual respect.

The people of Maceo's village were a relatively tranquil lot among whom outbursts of passion and scandalous behavior were practically nonexistent or, at least, kept in leash. The last dramatic incident had taken place many years before. A doctor, an outsider, had fallen madly in love with the beautiful daughter of a wealthy family which, with equal fervor, found him unsuitable. As a result, one December night while they were at supper he burst into their dining room waving a revolver. They fled to the street, escaping death while he searched the mansion for his beloved. Not finding her, he turned the gun on himself and blew his brains out. Stamped in the people's memories is his epitaph on the cemetery cross: "Here lies Doctor Jorge Castaños who died for love." Then came the Marimanta incident, a blend of scandal and mystery which never having been completely clarified gave rise to the oddest, most hysterical reactions and rumors.

Maniel was a peaceful community until its nerves were suddenly set on edge. A strange creature began to appear late at night in different parts of town. It was draped in a huge white mantle and wore a red kerchief, one corner of which hung over its forehead. It drifted like a ghost through the streets, alleys, and passageways of the town. The monster's hands—it was said—had fingers that ended in purple claws as thick as a parrot's beak. These sightings were real as were some of its alleged characteristics, but you could discount the exaggerations as the superstitions of a rural community.

The people have changed considerably since then, but at that time they were too terrified to venture out after ten o'clock, the hour at which the generator closed down and the town was left eerily in darkness.

The first to raise the alarm was a group of drunks returning from a visit to a brothel in Magante at the upper reaches of the town. They exploded the bomb the following day in the circle in the middle of the plaza. I was a kid of about seven at the time and one of the first to be taken in by the uproar that ensued. A lot of years have gone by since then but I can still hear the echoes of Chavo, the spokesman's great booming voice and the laughter of the crowd at his gesticulations.

"It must have been eleven or so when we decided to get out of Magante," he said loud enough for everyone to hear. "There were four of us. See, they're all standing right here ready to back me up in case you think I'm lying! With two bottles of rum and a guitar we headed to Lower Town to serenade a couple of ladies. We'd had our eye on a duck since the day before and at that hour of the night it was going to be a cinch to grab it. What better windup, my friends, for a good night's binge? Well, we had the bird in hand in no time and dropped it off at Dionisio's for him to roast it for us. We left his place with our mouths watering in expectation and as we turned the corner we saw the bushes shaking in the field next to the church and something moving through them. It looked like a giant bird, was making a strange noise like a cat in heat or a goat bleating, or something of the kind, and had wings like a bat except that they were white. They kept fluttering till the creature floated in the air. We hid behind Don Perico's fence but that huge monster saw us. It had a head brighter and redder than the fires of hell and was coming right at us. In one second flat we were cold sober and on our way. Feet do your stuff! What can I tell you except that we took off so fast and so far that we forgot our binge and haven't been to bed yet. All I can say is: there must be some good reason why we're still alive."

Chavo enjoyed being the center of attraction, answering questions from the crowd and exchanging banter with them after the pall of fear had lifted. Maceo was there, too, and people looked to him to comment but he chose to keep silent and soon left. It was not until some days had passed that the people began to give credit to the tale when similar weird reports started to circulate. I remember being scared, very scared, but it wasn't a feeling of actual terror. Deep down, I really wanted those episodes to keep happening that brought us together around the benches in the square every day and had us sleeping in shifts at night. As a rule, life in town shuffled between boredom and routine and, as I think back, it seems to me that then the adults felt more or less as we children did, that fear was slowly mounting into panic. At the same time, however, we all derived the same morbid pleasure from it.

Anything new was a fiesta for the people of Maniel, including tragedy. It was under such conditions that the Marimanta affair became a kind of fiesta in celebration of the patron saint and chance, in its mysterious way, chose Maceo to provide the key to the riddle.

One Wednesday in August, not long after midnight when normally it should have been cool, the unbearable heat had not yet abated. There had been no letup since early in June. Maceo, sleepless, finally left the oven of his bed to take his cigarette first in the yard and then out by August 16th Street. His sharp hunter's eye caught a slight movement at the corner of the Post Office which would not have attracted his attention had it not been accompanied by green flashing of wild animal eyes. A knife appeared like magic in Maceo's left fist as he advanced toward the building, flattening his body against its fence and slowly, calmly sliding himself to the corner where he had seen the movement. There was an empty lot along which there grew a corn patch and a number of trees, all of whose leaves were motionless against the black curtain of night. Maceo stood tense, surveying the area foot by foot.

Suddenly, his eyes widened as he saw the cornstalks swaying as it neared. His muscles tensed and he gripped the blade, waiting, ready to spring. "The Marimanta! It's the Marimanta!" he gasped, as the weird figure burst out of the foliage, making a hideous and unearthly sound. It jumped forward and rose, raising its right arm from its chest, the hand a metallic hook that glittered sinisterly in the night. The body was a shroud crowned with a cadaver's face in which two eyes burned like fire. Thinking that the specter did not want to attack but rather to scare him, Maceo, as though possessed, leaped at it. Just as the blade was about to penetrate its eye, the Marimanta dodged the blow and disappeared into the corn patch with Maceo in pursuit. He combed every corner of the lot but the creature was nowhere to be found. Then, all at once, something happened for which there is no explanation. The heat which until then had been stifling was suddenly relieved by a soft cool breeze blowing from El Rancho hill. Maceo, skirting the edge of the cornfield on the side bordering the square, looked towards the church steeple and was horrified. Dense shadows flickered rhythmically on the grove of trees in the square. The image of a gigantic Christ upon his cross hanging from the church facade, dominated the entire panorama. Maceo looked about sensing that he was being watched in the Argus-eyed, tranquil and mysterious little town. He hesitated for a moment that lasted an eternity. He was deciding to leave the place, when something in the square drew his attention. Lying in one of the flower beds, was what appeared to be a large strange looking shape. As he approached, ready for anything, the mass began to edge away, slowly at first, then more rapidly as it rose and straightened up, until finally it was running away with Maceo in pursuit, his footsteps echoing in the silent night. The once aggressive Marimanta, was now running for dear life and stubborn Maceo, not knowing exactly why, gave chase.

Leaving the square behind, the Marimanta went flying down the center of Altagracia Street on its way to the cemetery kicking up stones and dust as it went. Gathering enormous strength (he had no idea from where), he kept gaining on the creature until he was almost able to touch it, shouting at it all the while. The street ended at a ball field where the mysterious figure began to pull away again until it jumped the wall into the cemetery with Maceo not far behind. He followed and there among the gravestones where he slowed down, Maceo was able to tackle it. On the ground he realized that whatever it was, it had a mask on. Despite it's struggles, he pulled off the mask and revealed its identity.

The townspeople had followed the chase of the Marimanta from behind their shutters. They knew only what they could see from their windows and so, for them, the story ended with Maceo trudging back from the cemetery. The next morning, he told the neighbors that there was nothing for them to be afraid of any longer, that there was no more Marimanta. This answer, on which he would not elaborate, instead of clarifying the incident served only to further mystify it.

Stubborn as he was, Maceo would offer no further explanations and answered all questions simply by turning a deaf ear. And so matters stood, in a fog of silence, until his death four years and seven months later.

Courageously, he had ignored insult and spiteful gossip prompted by the townspeople's most fevered and pernicious imaginations regarding the events of that night. All Maniel censured Maceo, whom they were sure was concealing something frightful. His body was a ruin when he died, but signs of peace and satisfaction could be read between the lines of his devastated face.

Some years later, my godmother decided to reveal the secret of the phantom to me—but only after making me swear by Almighty God that as long as I lived I would not reveal the name of the woman involved in the secret of the Marimanta. She left me free, however, to reveal the rest of the secret on condition that I would do so only after she, my godmother, was dead. It is now eight months since she died and I have decided to tell the story. When she was on her deathbed, I did not leave her side for days on end during which, from time to time, she would wink an eye at me, and smile.

The vow of celibacy among priests is too much for the nature of men to cope with. Father Simón and a beautiful, elegant lady of the town fell hopelessly in love and, unfortunately, became involved in an uncontrollable sexual madness and she would go to visit him at night in disguise. Maceo, to whom the woman with the golden ringlets betrayed her identity in the cemetery, understood that ungovernable passion in all its terrible and tragic dimensions and so concealed it. And he did so because his silence shielded the ingenuousness of his town and the good name of two persons without sin.)

Invisible inside his parked car, Arturo watched the last of the invited guests straggle in, and it was not until then that he decided to pick up Lame Luisito at the town hotel. He was already waiting, bathed and shaved, elegantly dressed in a handsome brand-new, long-sleeved white shirt and navy blue trousers of British cloth, and perfumed with Vetiver lotion. They had been friends since childhood, since the days when Luisito, a happy-go-lucky black kid, was shining shoes under the laurel tree in the square. They had set out for the capital city thirteen years before and no matter where each happened to be, they never lost contact and kept their friendship alive. Arturo's ties of affection with Luisito were so close that once he had entered the charmed circle of the President's house, he lost no time introducing him to Doña Cándida Ramos and having her take him into her confidence. Despite the disadvantages of being born black, poor, and with a birth defect, his innate good humor, intelligence, and ambitious energy made it possible for him to adapt to the environment of the Peace Crusade. He was more readily accepted in the capital than he would have been in the more straight-laced circles of Maniel where memory of his condition of bootblack and dues collector for the upper-crust social club had not been forgotten.

However, fate picks its moments to put its wry whims into play and it was at one of those times that Lame Luisito returned to his home town with his inseparable chum, a respected figure and now head of Dr. Mario Ramos's re-election campaign in Maniel.

It had been difficult and fraught with danger for Arturo to displace the boss who had handled the President's political affairs in the region. He was a dangerous character and it was a knock-down, drag-out battle. He had obsessively undertaken the task of cleansing the town of corruption and was now well on the way to achieving it. He was particularly concerned with the case of Father Rey. The priest had fallen into disfavor with the local authorities and on more than one occasion the bishop in connivance with the government had tried to get him transferred and so nullify his support for the underprivileged of the area and to remove him from the pulpit where he made the church ring every Sunday with sermons on the subject of Christian justice. An agitator, Communist, heretic, who didn't even charge a fee for baptisms or funerals—third-class always and without street-corner stops—who spent more time out in the country than in the House of God, who disregarded salvation and neglected his congregation, concerning himself with earthly matters—what about the poor and the hungry, what about this and what about that—going about in ordinary dress, his sleeves rolled up, always busy at something and...well, why go on?

However, Father Rey, tempered by the plight of Maniel's downtrodden, stubbornly went his way, resisting the pressures. And now, after so much struggle, Arturo had finally succeeded in getting two independents who respected the priest's social concerns nominated for congress and for mayor, men committed to defending the priest against the dangerous intrigues of the Ramos clique and the treacherous Army guns.

Arturo arrived half an hour late at the meeting where ten puffed-up village notables waited, smarting silently with offended provincial dignity. The lady of the house, an alumna of the distinguished Santa Teresita Catholic School for Girls opened the door personally. Extending an amiable hand to him, she glanced in surprise at his companion whom she neither greeted nor spoke to as she led them into the dining room. The gentlemen were seated there around the table which held glasses and a bottle of wine. They all regarded Arturo with perplexed annoyance. Besides coming late he had brought along an outsider whom they considered had no business being there, and the host let him know as much in a barely veiled aside. There was one vacant chair at the table where Arturo was invited to sit while the polite Señora motioned his companion to wait in an adjoining room. Arturo pressed his lips into a tight smile, put his arm around Luisito and led him to the chair. After nudging him into it, he opened the meeting, standing. First he reached into his pocket and took out a check for the campaign that he had picked up in the morning at the National Palace. It was for a substantial amount, a symbol of power that he waved in the air. The Señora hastened to fetch him a chair.

Though the atmosphere was tense, the meeting would have proceeded smoothly had Arturo not given Luisito the floor to convey the instructions for the campaign in accordance with the wishes of Dr. Ramos himself. Luisito was prepared and proceeded not only to make an excellent presentation of the leader's strategies but added his own suggestions (which sounded more like orders) for maximum effectiveness in accomplishing the re-election of the President of the Republic. The gentlemen listened, squirming in their seats as though there were fleas in their pants. Arturo corroborated and amplified Luis's ideas and lost no time in pointing out that his friend was a trusted collaborator of the President and also worked closely with his distinguished sister Doña Cándida. He was applying Frank Bolaño's tried and true method for making an impression. In this one situation, however, the gentlemen neither appreciated nor were interested in understanding the buzz words of political influence. Accordingly, when Luisito, turned to the treasurer, a short-tempered man of sour disposition, to announce that he had purchased a mule that same afternoon for 100 pesos to give to an individual in the upper part of town who could help in the campaign, and that he had obtained it on credit, against Party funds, the treasurer, who had been ready to explode for some time, jumped up, bumping against the table and knocking over a half-filled wine glass. Glowering at the upstart, he said: "Señor Cundito, since when and with what right do you donate mules in the name of the Party or determine which persons are useful or not useful for this or that purpose?" Except for the two candidates who owed Arturo favors, the rest of the arrogant and aggressive gentlemen got to their feet shouting and waving their arms in support of their colleague who continued to raise his voice above the din: "Just because, out of decency, we permit you to sit down with us does not mean that we will accept your giving us orders and telling us what we should or should not do. What is the meaning of this, anyway! Begging your pardon, Arturo, but this is going too far!"

Poor Luisito sank deeper and deeper into his chair. He felt inferior to these mostly middle-aged, gray-haired men, so sure of their white selves, big wheels in a small town who had been running things their way, with nobody to challenge them. They accepted Arturo Gonzalo's interference in their politics because they considered it a passing phase and because the so-and-so had it made up there where it mattered. There was no question about his pull, judging from the way he was able to drive the drunken, degenerate, womanizing, excommunicate honcho out of town and to position his own candidates.... And there sat Lame Luisito waiting for a look from his friend who had gotten him into this inferno of yelling and glaring who should have come to his defense but who stood with his arms folded, almost laughing.

Resentful peasants nursing grudges, no reason to pay them any attention. Arturo Gonzalo, the campaign chief, stayed put impassively accepting this blowing off of steam. It was actually a death rattle, for their political power was over, and they were taking it out on the most defenseless one, thereby exposing their own weakness. They were bleeding, now, and Lame Luisito, their former errand boy, was the dagger that had stabbed them, the boss who was bossing them, a bit fearfully still, but he would get used to it and thumb his nose at them. After all, Lame Luisito was no coward.

The campaign was over two months later and Dr. Ramos, consummate manipulator, the politician with gum on his ass, remained stuck to the Chair. Tireless air traveler during the campaign, his retinas grown as foggy as the clouds through which he flew, Dr. Ramos was in once more, with the secret support of the great Dodó Sol, international *ogún* of voodoo in the guise of the Archangel Saint Michael, always faithful and effective, and of the Virgencita de Altagracia, mantle of light and protectress against helicopter accidents.

Arturo left town and so did Luisito. Father Rey remained behind enjoying the peace that was so firmly established. The notables finally accepted Lame Luis's existence. No one was infected, but the treasurer refused to make good the 100 pesos for the mule. That was Luisito's main concern, money being the one thing he lost sleep over, so Arturo paid the bill and he breathed easily once again.

Corporal Ignacio's words took Arturo more by surprise than his sudden appearance at the Sugar Agency Office. He sounded as though he had come with an order to put him under arrest.

"Don Arturo," he said, "with all due respect, the Doctor wants to see you immediately. He ordered me not to come back without you..."

He had not seen Frank in a long time. Arturo hardly frequented the President's house anymore during the three years since the '74 campaign and had practically nothing to do with the Peace Crusade. Its atmosphere had become distasteful to him, polluted as it was by the likes of such creatures as Luisa, the most treacherous tongue in town, den mother of the capital's political caverns, and Aníbal Llanero, the guru of shady business deals, Doña Cándida Ramos's confidential companion, in command, each with a knife between the teeth. An unruly crew of freebooters and sycophants, among whom she walked, head high, a corrupted goddess of pride and civic virtue. There were sexual inverts and experts with high-placed functionaries in tow, procurers and procuresses, bodyguards and blackguards, dangerous types, gunmen and intriguers, under the wing of Colonel Demetrio, chief of Candida's escort, being counseled in good manners and proper pronunciation—getting the esses out of where he had them and in where he should have—being groomed for general, the ultimate desire of an illiterate black, giddied by the attention of those advisers in tactics and strategy eager to see him replace General Elermoso, absolute chief of the Rear House where there was money by the bushel and power without end. And there were others, more modest, like Piro Taranzo, recovering from bankruptcy, builder of public works like the housing projects Arturo used to direct, who moved into another area of the President's household, dominating the lower echelon of the forces of President Ramos's mysterious sister, Albricia.

This was a mine field in which one had to have the equilibrium of a tightrope walker to move about without getting blown up.

"That's it, Don Arturo. All I know... Just to bring you to the house. The Doctor is waiting for you." Corporal Ignacio, not moving a muscle, standing at attention in his elegant uniform.

He was no longer the big kid with the athletic build he had met five years ago. He was now, what?...twenty-seven or eight...fat and doughy-faced. Strange that he should still be at the same rank when he could easily have become an officer, a lieutenant, at the very least.

When he first started driving for him, Frank didn't have the clout to get him promoted, and then when he was very close to President Ramos and with the country's fate partially in his hands, the generals had him arrested and exiled.

Those were years when Frank was able to indulge his passion for spying to the hilt. He would arrive at the President's house at about ten-thirty, pass unchallenged through the main entrance, stride through the Big House living room, nodding loftily at the late hangers-on who were silently waiting until Doña Cándida deigned to emerge and notice them, go out through the door to the rear patio of polished tiles, squares of lawn, and trees that hid other shadows armed with rifles, and take a seat among others on one of the benches there until General Elermoso came out to escort him to President Ramos's private chambers. At no time in this trajectory did Frank avoid drawing attention to the portfolio he carried. Everybody knew what was inside: his tape recorder. Here, he bestowed a half-smile on the housing developer who would soon be making his way into Albricia's bedroom to settle accounts in dollars and other more intimate media of exchange; a nod to the others and a salute with the portfolio which (who knows?) might be holding the indiscreet voice of any one of them.

It was a sinister weapon and Frank held it affectionately in his hands.

He had not arrived at the pinnacle of his career as master spy overnight. Two long years had gone by since General Piro Cristóbal had brought him the decree appointing him a civilian aide to the President and giving him a secure foothold in the President's inner sanctum. At the outset, he had prowled around Doña Cándida, but the Peace Crusade then was no more than a group of deprived ladies to whom Dr. Ramos paid little mind for he did not grasp their political significance. Nor did Frank have any faith in Doña Candida's pilgrimage with Arturo from village to village with a scanty escort of idealistic women, preaching redemption for the poor. From time to time, he would accompany the straggly caravan but soon had his fill of the sterile dust of the road and began to cast about for clearer trails to the seat of power. He had also drawn apart from the little Spaniard, a self-centered individual, who tired of the pursuit of millions, concentrated on squirreling away every peso he could lay hands on, cheating his partners in small business deals. He was generous only toward the native mulattas whom he bedded with a sailor's passion and toward a golden-haired little Italian, in a class by herself, with whom he set up housekeeping near Boca Chica beach. When this was discovered, the poor fellow begged and wept but his wife and her parents were adamant. He was dumped at the airport without a céntimo in his pocket and deported.

Those were stirring times with horizons opening in one direction and clouding over in others. Arturo pursued the chimera while the more practical Frank remained in the capital lying in ambush, knife in hand, waiting for opportunity to present itself.

The offer he had made Arturo at the Malecón to team up with him the day they were reunited at the President's house never jelled. At least not to the degree Frank would have wanted. Their purposes and their life styles did not jibe. Frank would have liked him as a companion in his up-scale round of deluxe restaurants, hotels, and beauty queens, but Arturo rarely accepted his invitations. He could not afford to share the expense, which was of little concern to Frank but, more important, it was a vacuous way of life that didn't interest him at all. His feeling was that "to come away from the Peace Crusade setting to that of the beauty queens was like going through life floating in chloroform." That and, particularly, what happened later on when Frank, with that time bomb in his pocket, began spying for the President on a group of the most dangerous of the generals estranged them to some degree. They kept in touch, but Arturo elected to keep out of range of that wolf pack which could only lead to disaster.

"Sit down, Ignacio, I'll be ready very soon. I have to organize a couple of things," Arturo told him with a smile.

He had no idea why, but he was pleased at the corporal's unexpected visit. Frank had never been one to give him disagreeable surprises. In any case, this probably concerned some favor he needed, perhaps to intercede with Doña Cándida, who still held Arturo in high regard despite his detachment and received him like the prodigal son whenever she summoned him. But, on second thought, Arturo discarded that possibility. Frank was at the peak of his power and influence right now. What favor could he need from him? He had been back from exile for only six months and was already in a much stronger position than when he left.

He had been able to return from abroad where he had languished for five months because the Army clique that had driven him out no longer held positions of command. The affair with the generals was very strange, familiar though he was with the way Dr. Ramos did things.

When he was getting started, Frank had difficulty finding the right avenue for getting into President Ramos's good graces. He tried via Doña Cándida but soon abandoned that possibility for at the early stages of the Crusade she had little political clout with her brother. Next came Señorita Albricia, skittish as a goat, so difficult to get to that he quickly gave up. However, with frustration setting in, during a casual conversation with Don Piro Taranzo, a new approach came to light. The developer outlined a plan in which Arturo would have to play a part. Frank had become aware of certain vagaries of Albricia's intimate life. The blonde nurse to whom he was ministering exciting, if unorthodox, sexual attentions had fed him the information.

"The old maid wants it, all right. The problem is that nobody dares come close enough to give it to her."

Don Piro was made to order for the job. He would certainly dare.

Frank and Don Piro made a pact. He, Frank, agreed to pull wires to get him admitted to the house. Once inside, the developer would know the proper approach for worming his way into Albricia's confidence, The maiden lady had a weakness for U.S. currency and Japanese dolls. In her demureness, she hoped she would not be obliged to go to the next world before finding out what it felt like to have a man. She was very capable when it came to arranging big, lucrative contracts in top secret collusion with her brother at ten percent, cash on the barrelhead, in dollars. It was she who made it possible for Dr. Ramos to amass his huge fortune. Nobody could ever claim to have done business of any kind with the President, a man whose zeal in protecting the national interest and whose attention to minutiae in discussing contracts with builders—introduced to him by Albricia—was exemplary. This strange unnoticed woman, no more than a shadowy presence, was busily stashing away trunkfuls of dollars.

Arturo did his part and Frank was appreciative. Fifteen thousand pesos—in a lottery of calculated risks—and a well-considered introduction opened the door of the house to Don Piro Taranzo. Arturo broke ground for his housing project with that money. A month later the developer was having coffee in the kitchen with Albricia and petting her collies—another of the lady's weaknesses—and little by little the old wolf won her heart and stimulated her senses. However, the closer he came to this powerful woman, the further away he drew from Frank. He did not carry out his end of the bargain. Actually, Albricia had much to do with it. "We mustn't let that man with the antennae come close to us." she advised Don Piro. That was enough for him to avoid Frank for good. He turned out to be much more astute than anybody thought. He recouped financially, got a foothold politically, and built himself an indestructible bunker in the depths of Albricia's twilit psyche.

For Frank, this all added up to a waste of energy which, although having left a bitter aftertaste, did not weaken his will to seek other expedients. He then approached the recently promoted General Elermoso and, having slipped a substantial sum into his hand with a minimum of preambles, convinced him of the importance of having the President listen to tapes proving that a sector of the army around

General Pedro Prieto was beginning to take on importance beyond limits acceptable to the Commander-in-Chief. This was a step in the right direction. Dr. Ramos received him one midnight and from then on, his was a daily presence at the same hour when the Big House was aswarm with impatiently waiting visitors. Some would see Doña Cándida off to bed, others the President, and the fewest of them, Señorita Albricia. They would then go home secure in the thought that the next day would not find them with the buzzsaw of intrigue at their throats. The saying was, "If you say goodnight at the boss's door you're safe for one day more."

However, nobody in the government was safe from unpleasant surprises after Frank began to ply his midnight tape recorder. Particularly not the figures at the top. There came a time when President Ramos's private spy had the Army Chief, General Pedro Prieto, and the other Chiefs of Staff all in his bag.

President Ramos had a weakness for gossip and Frank exploited it to the hilt in their late-night sessions. Most exciting to him were the tapes in which sex was involved. Of these Frank had a rich assortment of conversations and performances recorded at varying levels of intensity. Elated at his success, Frank observed how Dr. Ramos began to squirm, trying to control his heavy breathing, as he listened, always in absolute silence. When a more charged segment would come up on a tape, Frank would roll it back and run it over and over again without having to be told. His crowning achievement in this regard was the recording of an exciting tape that progressed from the initial approaches to the act, its foreplay, and final consummation between a distinguished government official and a beautiful congresswoman. This was the star piece in his repertoire.

That is, except for the one he never played for him which was of a man poeticizing in a state of sublimity: the

President, himself, with one of his little girlfriends.

Before long, Frank became the man most feared by those in high places in the government and among the military in General Pedro Prieto's band. General Prio Cristóbal and his followers, not in important posts at the time, provided him tactical support. They watched with satisfaction as the spy harassed their enemies who would soon be out of the General Staff.

But Frank Bolaño was out first himself.

One morning at daybreak, troops arrived at Frank's house, immobilized the seven soldiers of the bodyguard platoon ordered by the President and hand-picked by General Elermoso, dragged Frank off to the Ministry of the Armed Forces where they stripped him naked, slapped him around, then beat him to within an inch of his life with a "bull's cock" whip, and after expressing their enjoyment at the sight of his deplorable condition, dumped him into solitary confinement.

Frank was surprised at the violence of his reaction and the dignity with which he faced off those "fucking gorillas" as they beat and interrogated him.

It was morning when the high command discussed the advisability of doing away with him altogether. Finally, it was decided that immediate execution was in order and as they were preparing to carry it out, the President called. "General Prieto," said the lethargic, effeminate voice, "I have been notified that Dr. Bolaño is under detention at the Ministry of the Armed Forces. I believe that the most advisable course of action would be to have that poor madman expelled from the country. See to it that the most suitable place and time are selected."

The nurse of the President's house who was warming Frank's bed when the soldiers burst in had managed to hide in time and was able to notify General Elermoso who, in turn, let the President know. This opportune intervention saved Frank's life.

For the time being, the generals had had their way. They had, at least, put their worst enemy out of circulation and the President had yielded to them. Several months later, however, Dr. Ramos had relieved them of their command in one of his surprise maneuvers.

"Good to see you, brother," Arturo was warmly welcomed by Frank with a broad smile, his hand outstretched. He had kept him waiting for a few minutes. Both were 34 years old, but Frank, almost totally bald, seemed much older. Clasping his hand, Frank plunged in. "You've got problems at the Sugar Agency, and you don't call me...don't let me know what's going on," he complained.

How had Frank found out?

A friend had recommended Arturo for a post in the Sugar Agency. It would be a new experience, and he was glad to accept because it would get him out of the Peace Crusade. Vetusto Santaro, the agency's Executive Director, at first welcomed the recommendation by a possible future presidential candidate and furthermore he would be gaining an employee who was close to Doña Cándida Ramos. Theoretically, Arturo's job was to coordinate the Agency's branch offices throughout the country with a view to organizing the powerful official machinery for the approaching presidential elections of 1978. However, Señor Santaro, a headstrong man and old Party boss, soon felt miffed that a subordinate should be conducting himself with a certain air of independence when he was accustomed to a submissive staff. He also received angry complaints from plantation managers regarding the interference of this upstart, giving orders as to what should and should not be done in the political and social terrain, matters which they were accustomed to handling in their own way. As a result, before long, Arturo found himself relegated to a tiny office, muzzled, disenchanted, and ready to quit.

He had had no intention of asking anybody to help bring those ruffians into line until Frank offered a solution the most attractive aspect of which was the implied interplay of forces.

The two were ensconced in the office, whiskey and soda in hand, surrounded by luxury and elegance. Frank savored the imminent defeat of an enemy, smiling—the talons of power etched in that smile—brushing his hand over his bald pate, while he reached into a desk drawer and extracted a folder. Holding it up, he announced with an air of self-satisfaction: "Vetusto Santaro's file."

"I hereby place in your hands," Frank told him, heightening the solemnity, "a magic talisman with which you will bring a corrupt and arrogant scoundrel to his knees." Frank pulled his chair around to Arturo's side and began to show him one by one the documents and photos, carefully explaining the significance of each. When he finished, he put his hand on Arturo's shoulder and told him to make an appointment with Vetusto Santaro at his home that same night. He outlined everything he should do, finally stressing the importance of holding the interview in the man's home, in absolute privacy, and the later at night the better, for he should take the shock to bed with him.

At first, Arturo accepted the proposal with tentative enthusiasm, expressing some doubt and apprehension.

"Frank," he said, "are you sure this is going to work?"

Histrionic, as always, Frank raised both arms, threw his head back, gazed up at the ceiling, and replied. "Like the fellow said in the movie, it's an offer you can't refuse."

Arturo was not entirely convinced, however. He was aware that Vetusto Santaro was an influential figure— arrogant, coarse in his behavior, and brutal in his tactics. He was in his seventies and had spent most of his life on his hacienda, raising cattle, and in the rough company of his peons. Accustomed to giving orders he was nevertheless subservient to the army and fascinated by soldiers. He dressed and behaved as though the army were in his blood. Pale complected, with regular features, he spoke with pride of Germany, the land of his forebears, about which he knew little. He also boasted of friendship with Dr. Ramos that he claimed dated back to the days of Tirano. He had taken part in and contributed to the founding of the Party that brought Dr. Ramos to power in '66. Like hundreds of others, he would bring up the many times he had sent the leader money when he was down and out in exile in Puerto Rico and New York. However, unlike many others, he did not complain of Dr. Ramos's ingratitude toward those who had helped him over hard times. Finally, towards the end of his administration, the President rewarded him with the important post of Executive Director of the Sugar Agency. He gained considerable prestige on the Atlantic coast which was his home country where he had his economic and political base and where his voice was heard and obeyed.

Arranging the appointment with Señor Santaro had been no problem. He had gone to his office at five o'clock and after a longish stretch in the waiting room was received. There were several other people around his desk who didn't bother to move when the Director motioned to him to take a seat. Arturo told him that he had a confidential matter to discuss and would like to talk to him in private.

He nodded and they moved into a small bathroom next to this office where Arturo told him, "I have a very sensitive matter to discuss that concerns you personally and your position as Executive Director, but I can't do it here. There's no telling who might be listening. It would be preferable in your house, tonight, if possible."

Warily, demandingly, Santaro asked, "What's this all about?"

"It's a rather long story and it would be preferable if we could sit down comfortably, alone, so I can get it off my chest once and for all."

"Very well, tonight at my house." Santaro's tone was distrustful and not a little irritated.

"What time would you like, so that we won't be interrupted?"

"Come after ten o'clock." It was an order.

It was after ten-thirty when Arthur sat in a rocking chair on Vetusto Santaro's porch waiting for him to finish attending to a Party leader. He knew that the man he was going to face in a few minutes was no pushover but at this late hour his nerves were well under control and he felt confident, having spent the best of the afternoon at home rehearsing the part he would play, memorizing everything down to the smallest detail.

The night was pleasantly cool and, since Santaro's meeting with his visitor was dragging on, he walked down the steps from the porch to the garden. The November sky was just right for a serenade by Los Panchos, and as he gazed up into it his thoughts turned to the current love of his life, and searching the firmament for its brightest star, he wished that he could run off with her out of this world in which he had become enmeshed to another where there were no Cándida Ramoses, Frank Bolañoses, or Vetusto Santaros. No sooner did he think the name than the old man's hoarse voice saying goodnight broke into his reverie.

The tall, bulky figure on the porch beckoned to him from the doorway above. The sight of him put the tiger back into his spirit, claws and all, and gripping his portfolio, he climbed back up the steps and followed his host into a sitting room in the rear of the mansion. It was dimly lit and cozy and there were no sounds of life anywhere. As he watched Santaro take a seat in an overstuffed easy chair opposite him, he again felt a fleeting recurrence of disgust at the farce on which he was about to raise the curtain and at himself for his inability to create the world he desired.

"You scarcely know me, Señor Santaro," he began, "but I would like to assure you that I am at your command and wish to do everything I can to be helpful to you in your work as Executive Director of the Agency. As you know, problems, obstacles, come up that it may be impossible to deal with."

Arturo had a feeling that the man was not following him. "As I was saying, Señor..."

"Go on...go on," Santaro interrupted.

"There are various intelligence services in the government, Señor Santaro. You know them, we all do. There's the DNI, a kind of overseeing agency whose functions cover everything that has to do with national security. Then, there's G2 and J2, and so on. However, there's one very sensitive aspect that none of these official organizations cover properly and that is keeping the President informed of many details that are not outside the scope of national security and, particularly, that of the President himself. J2— and this is only one example—which is Army Intelligence puts in more of its time in tracking the personal enemies of the head of the Armed Forces and on matters of concern to the American Government, than on ensuring the security of the Government and its President. It's the same story with respect to the other intelligence agencies. All these generals, you know, are independent, each with his own group, keeping an eye on one another. The DNI skips from one side to the other depending on where the authority is. Another thing that happens is that when one general is relieved of his post, the new commander lops off heads and puts his own people in. Then, the one who was displaced takes his people with him to wherever he is sent, as though they were personal property. They are elements who because of their many contradictions and their personal interests keep the President informed. And so, it is only fair to ask: What measures does the President take to defend himself? That, Señor Santaro is what I am going to explain to you right now. It is the reason I requested this interview with you and, above all, to offer you my disinterested support, with a view to making it possible for you to carry on your difficult job without problems."

Santaro had been listening with apparent disinterest but upon hearing these last words, he started as though stung by a wasp, planted his two feet on the ground, stopping his chair from rocking, raised his head and glared at Arturo who remained silent waiting for him to speak. The old man opened his mouth only to emit unintelligible sounds before closing it almost immediately, struggled out of his chair and made off to the toilet, walking with some urgency and discomfort produced most likely by an enlarged prostate. Arturo felt certain that the old bear could not run the risk of not hearing the rest.

Santaro returned, wrestling with his fly as he approached to drop his tired bulk back into his rocker, ready to hear the rest, a grim expression on his face. Arturo knew he had him in the trap and regarding him a bit ruefully, continued.

"In addition to the intelligence agencies I mentioned, there is another elite group, very small, highly trained, implicitly trusted, which works exclusively for the President. Almost nobody knows of them or their mission, and it is immune from investigation. They are the President's shield and keep him informed about what goes on throughout the country. These investigators are specially interested in the small details for they often lead to big surprises.

"Well, Señor Santaro, having explained the background, I will get down to the specifics, to what concerns you. You do not know me well, but I have connections high up. One of them is an important member of the President's intelligence group and a good friend who owes me a favor and is glad of the opportunity to do me a service. When this friend knew that I had gone to work for the Sugar Agency, he called me in to notify me that you, the Director, were undergoing an investigation and that you could be the victim of a very damaging intrigue and, as a favor to me, he offered to stop it before irreparable damage was done to you."

At this point, Arturo opened his portfolio which he had kept on his lap, and took out a folder. Holding it out to him, he said, "My friend gave me this to show you for two reasons. One, so that you will know that his offer of help is bona fide and, two, that you will see with your own eyes evidence of acts of yours that would place you in a compromising position in the eyes of the President and of public opinion."

Santaro's eyes were suddenly swimming about in a void as Arturo extracted a page from the file, saying, "Take a look at this, for example."

Santaro threw his head back and held the document a good distance from his eyes but was unable to read it. He forced himself to his feet again, went into the dining room, turned on the light, left the paper on the table, and made another trip to the toilet, looking like a corpse in motion. When he returned he was carrying eyeglasses which he put on with trembling hands as he sat at the table under the light. However, he was unable to concentrate on the document and Arturo moved to his side to read and explain it to him.

This was a copy of a document addressed to the President bearing a recent date and with the sender's name blacked out. It reported in detail the shipment of thirty-six heifers from the Livestock Department of the Sugar Agency to Santaro's hacienda. The document also referred to many other animals having been transferred to the farms of certain army officers (names omitted) and suggested that the President order an investigation.

Also attached to the document were letters going back over ten years from Santaro himself to the President in which he made accusations against fellow Party members. Among them was one in which he accused the man he had been talking to in his own house that very evening of smuggling textiles into the country.

"This file among others is up for screening by his intelligence staff before being sent to the President. Imagine if he had to look at all the complaints that come to the Palace every day! These, of course, will not reach his hands. I can promise you that. My friend also told me I could assure you that any other documents involving your name will be intercepted. And, not only that, but official communications from your agency to the President will be expedited. You are not aware, of course, that an application you made last month for a million pesos to be applied to fallowing sugarcane acreage was received and pigeon-holed. It is a complex situation but with my friend's help I can see to it that such things won't happen again."

Silently, Arturo gathered up the papers and replaced them in his portfolio, waiting for comment. When he looked at his pale, dazed, dumb companion, he realized none would be forthcoming, so he stood up and said, "Mr. Santaro, it is late and I must be leaving. I hope you will understand that I have your best interests at heart. Good night."

"Yes...yes, good night," he mumbled, as Arturo helped him out of his chair, "let me see you to the door. Thank you for everything. I appreciate it."

Arturo drove home slowly taking a long route, letting his nerves unwind but was unable to wipe Santaro from his mind. He considered the possibilities of how that arrogant man with all his wealth and power might react on second thought. It could be a different story when he got up in the morning no longer the doddering, submissive old man he had just left. Calmly, coldly, he could very well check out the alleged intelligence group. But how, through whom? He could go to his good friend General Pedro Prieto and lay out the whole affair. Actually, though—Arturo reasoned—that would not be a likely path to take. On the one hand, criminal that he was, the General was out of favor at the moment, and on the other, the military did not relish getting involved in political intrigues in official circles. They were all aware that anything was possible in President Ramos's dark, tightly sealed-off world. Then, again, to what lengths might Santaro go on his own accord? Arturo had no way of blotting out those disturbing thoughts. In any case, everything had already worked out to the letter as Frank had foreseen it would.

Bright and early the next morning, Arturo was at his friend's house listening to him repeat with his usual assurance his theory that nobody in the government was capable of getting to the bottom of certain dubious situations. Furthermore, he assured Arturo that even in the most unlikely case that Santaro should go to Dr. Ramos, the President would be quite pleased to see this official worrying over a nonexistent threat and end up scaring him even more.

Frank was not mistaken. A proud man, Santaro, opted not to risk further humiliation or expose himself to other possibly dangerous consequences, and so he accepted his submission to Arturo.

Far away, resonating in the depths of timelessness, in the boisterous days of Epiphany, was the echo of eternally frustrated innocence. Under the bed the little bundle of herbs in the glass of water, the mints, the cigarettes, and the hopes lying neatly on the paper with the list of wishes. Then, the early awakening to armfuls of nothing, that emptiness of disappointed expectation with which children of the people grew up. Outstretched hands, infinitely long, reaching wide-eyed for the toy in the hands of another, the chosen of the Magi (gods to the children of the people). However, the times are different now, and different the ignominy. On the sidewalk of the President's house and far, far beyond, to a point out of sight stretches the line of unfortunates waiting impatiently. Epiphany, Day of the Kings 1978, has come, the year of elections, and they have been up all night, pushing, insulting, fighting. The early light exposes the rags, the horror of the brood, their little bodies clutched in the arms of the women and the men who have carried them as banners of their misery. The sun rises, the security guards impose order carrying on their war of brandished clubs. Towards noon a bestial roar erupts. The crowd acclaims the arrival of Cándida Ramos, head of the Peace Crusade, the new incarnation of the Magi. She is surrounded by "Sergeant" Patita, "nobody like her to quench a female's fire"; Doña Clementina and Doña Soledad, flamboyant in their gowns and tall hairdos. General Demetrio, recently promoted, the old wart gone from his nose. Aníbal Llanero, the mathematical wizard, expert toy buyer in the Oriental markets, a profitable business, two for me, one for you. Doña Cándida is in accordance, it's a big cut in any case, and there's lots more coming in from this, that, and the other. The photographers will be coming soon, the press is very generous on these occasions. Arturo Gonzalo is there on the platform, has at least put in an appearance on the fringe of it all, but observing every detail. Doña Cándida blesses a toy, pointing her finger at it, a guard picks it up and passes it to the mother who takes it in her free arm, the other holding the child; light as a hummingbird, or heavy as only agonies can weigh. A mother cries out, shouting demands that are almost smothered before she reaches the platform; Doña Cándida answers with a smile, one hand waving rhythmically. The woman is removed from the scene by the guards, a face like a million others, who will remain nearabouts dragging herself through the desert of her life. The guards make way for another mother. Doña Cándida keeps waving her arm, she is beautiful, truly a goddess. One, two hours go by. Those towards the end of the line begin to mill around, pushing, they are afraid there will be no presents left for them. General Demetrio gives an order. A patrol goes to the rear of the crowd and threatens them. Shouts and complaints can be heard, as well as hurrahs for Doctor Ramos and Doña Cándida. Arturo fixes his attention on an old man who is holding not a child but a fighting cock. The bird is nervous in his hands and the old man tries to soothe it, running his hand over its back. Arturo watches him step out of line and approach the fence of Dr. Ramos's house where he stands, performing a ritual. He caresses the bird's beak, legs, and spurs, then lifts its wings and blows gently on its trembling thighs. After that the two look into each other's eyes and, finally, he smoothes his hand over the animal's body from the head to the tail. Arturo is some distance away and cannot hear the old man say at the moment he turns it loose, "Dammit, Juanito, lose, if you want to!" But, shaken by surprise, he is able to see how the man, with an imperious toss of his head, turns away from the cock. He has just recognized the scene and identified the old man. The cock flies to the garden and perches on a tree. Arturo then loses sight of it when it flies toward the last patio. The old man, no longer in the line, is walking up the street. Arturo approaches him. They recognize each other and smile in greeting. He is, of course, Antonio Bell. Arturo follows him with his eyes until he loses him in the distance. His disguise was perfect.

The little girl is entertaining herself in the patio under the first shower of May. Her mother, sheltered under the eave of the kitchen, is collecting the beneficent water in a pitcher as she takes pleasure keeping a watchful eye on her five-year-old. Inside the house, Arturo watches the child leap about and throw kisses with both hands at her mother, and calling out to her "*papito.*"

Elections are nine days off. Arturo knows that Dr. Ramos will lose and is delighted at the thought. He also knows that he will be out of work as a result and be reliving days of uncertainty as he had so many times before in his life. Life's gamble was meat and drink to him and he looked to the future with dark pleasure in his heart. The one thing that saddened him and made him feel guilty was the thought of how his wife and daughter would fare, both unaware of impending disaster.

He had known since Epiphany that there was a curse on President Ramos's house. Rather, it was an intuition. Conviction came at the end of April when he learned that Antonio had been murdered nine years before by President Ramos's government assassins when he had returned to the country. Frank swore to him that he did not know it had happened, and this plunged him into confusion and despair.

After Epiphany, on January 6th, on uncontrollable impulse he began visiting the President's house with some frequency. Eagerly he searched for the cock in the foliage of the trees, in the garden on the roof, among the vines of the fences, but could find no sign of him. He discreetly questioned two servant girls and one of the night guards. Although they had not seen the cock, they reported that during the night at hours when cocks are not known to crow they had heard sounds that could only have been made by a cock but which, at the same time, could have been mistaken for the wailing of a person. Since the middle of March the nocturnal cry became more insistent and notorious. Gossip spread among the household staff, and the military, and finally to the regular frequenters of the house. When General Elermoso expressed his concern to the President, his only reply was an eerie smile twitching across his mummy-like face that chilled the aide's blood. Doña Cándida and Señorita Albricia instructed General Demetrio to order a prudent investigation of the case which should under no circumstances reach the President's ears. Powerful floodlights were installed that cut through the shadows of the trees at night. Security guards on long ladders checked time and time again every branch and any other possible refuge of the enigmatic bird but to no avail. Arturo was the only one who could have cleared up the mystery. Antonio's oft repeated tale of Juanito's vengeance in the cockpit of his town was becoming grim reality. He had still to get to the bottom of this new vengeance. By the end of January, the rumor was rife that Dr. Ramos was going blind. People came in on tiptoes trying to verify the truth, taking note of the President's gait, of the assurance with which he stretched out his hand to greet the visitors who arrived at ten o'clock each morning to join the lineup of favor-seekers, the way in which he climbed into the presidential limousine... However, not even this secret could be gleaned from that enigmatic person. It was difficult to believe. He moved about as though directed by bat sonar. A sharp observer might have deduced that the silent aide, who almost never left his side, cued him like an invisible guide dog. By then, Arturo was becoming convinced, against his better judgment, that the cock must be a resurrection of Juanito who was getting ready to work on Dr. Ramos's eyes. In any case, the revenge would be slow and relentless. For the next three months, Arturo was anxiously tracking down Antonio's whereabouts until he finally learned the unhappy news of his death from his mother in Jarabacoa, now a very old woman. She also told him that before his grandfather died years ago, his last act was to get out of his deathbed, go to the patio, pick up his handsome *pinto* cock and hand him to Antonio in the same solemn ritual with which he had once tossed Juanito into the arena. A few minutes later he was dead. Arturo left the mountain town convinced that

Dr. Ramos would lose not only his sight but something else infinitely more painful without which he couldn't live: power. So he thought but, actually, it was impossible for him to have imagined the lengths to which the fury of Antonio's ghost would go.

The rain comes down in dense, heavy drops but the sky soon begins to clear and the sun to break through the clouds. The little girl's mother wraps her in a big towel and, drying her little head, carries her into the dining room. Arturo observes them sadly as he reflects on the uncertainty of the future, a question presently in the forefront of his mind.

Dr. Ramos did, in fact, lose the election. Nevertheless, the winning party had to use every means possible, every national and international resource it could summon, to pry him loose from the Government Palace. Arturo left the country eighteen months later. As in that time long ago when the President jumped the wall of his house to take refuge in the Papal Nunciature, the nation believed that Dr. Ramos had been nullified. However, eight years later, something incomprehensible occurred. Resurrected, with greater vitality than ever, the man returned to power. The tick that had fed on the host of his gigantic ambition swelled and swelled to such an enormous size that it was again capable of sucking in the Government Palace.*

Arturo, disillusioned as never before, lost faith in the revenge of Antonio and Juanito. It was then that he decided to unbosom himself in a novel, the publication of which cost him his life.

---

*Note: Doña Muñinga, a famous clairvoyant of Santiago de los Caballeros, asserts that Dr. Mario Ramos has a pact with the devil, whose presence is abundantly clear on close examination of any photograph of him or in any appearance on a television screen. The Señora also says that Dr. Ramos's constant revitalization is the result of the transfer of energy he obtains in his magical-erotic rites with adolescent girls that are supplied to him regularly by Satan himself.

The last day of the old century. In a few hours, all the church bells will be pealing together in a great bronze unison. Since early this Sunday evening, the multitudes have been pouring in, filling the churches, squares, and streets of the capital. The peasants have come down early from the hills since yesterday, since the day before. Many have taken their sick along on stretchers to find a place for them, wherever the Lord willed. Any sacrifice would be worth making for the new century would come in pregnant with miracles. The national skies will be aglow with fireworks and at the supreme moment all will have been reborn, cleansed of their wounds, redeemed from their miseries. The preacher's voice is firm and convincing. The clamor builds, rises, is lost in the infinite.

Librado Santos wanders the streets of the city, ten years older than when he dreamed of hearing Dr. Ramos's inaugural address. Gotten up in his poet's guise, bearded, unkempt, rumpled, he broods on the years of disillusion. He fuels his inebriation on every other corner with a nip of *Siglo 21* rum, the latest on the market. The poet Librado Santos has for some time been courting death, ever since he could no longer feel the thrill of poetry.

Frank Bolaño, now approaching sixty, conserves his elegance of manners and of dress. He has a wife and three children and points to the fact that he is not yet a grandfather as attesting to his youthfulness. With a sumptuous table and the choicest wines set out on the terrace, he awaits the advent of the new century. Under a moonlit, star-studded sky the guests have a splendid view of the city. His Aunt Amelia, widowed once more, is the most beautiful woman there, time seemingly frightened off by her eternally festive spirit. Having no children of her own, she lavishes her love on Frank's. There is another motive for celebration beyond the present one, the recent publication of *Las Memorias de Frank Bolaño*, which has already been selling well. As in the case of *Los que falsificaron la firma de Dios*, attributed to Arturo Gonzalo and published in 1992, it was written in collaboration with an author friend. In his book, Frank suppressed certain things and expanded others, events that appeared in his friend's novel. Page 113 for instance, is left blank except for this note at the foot: "I insert this blank page in memory of Antonio Bell, murdered in October, 1968. I am about to have the final evidence of the crime in hand and swear that the truth will not remain lost in the clouds of forgetfulness. I am sure I will have opened his grave in time for the next edition." Page 114 is in solid black and the one opposite contains a shocking revelation: "The mourning symbolized by this page is in posthumous tribute to Arturo Gonzalo, victim on March 31, 1993 of the one crime the order for which came solely and directly from the lips of Dr. Mario Ramos. The following pages are devoted to making every detail of this secret known so that their accusation will be a voice crying out to haunt the villain during every remaining day of his life." The next six pages summarize the causes and circumstances of Arturo's death. Among other things, he describes (with supporting material in another chapter) the system used by Dr. Ramos in ordering many of the crimes perpetrated in his administration. In this respect, he affirms: "Except in the specific case of Arturo Gonzalo, nobody, civilian or military, would be able to prove that Dr. Ramos ever ordered the execution of an opponent. He usually worked in a most humane manner to eliminate his enemies. At the opportune moment, taking advantage of the casual presence of one of his military commanders schooled in this procedure, in a voice tinged with emotion he would address the man in the following terms: "So-and-so is a young man of great talent and, despite his exaggerations in reference to my person and the government over which I preside, I must admit that I would be very pleased to have him with us for the good of our country. I want you to know, General, that we must be indulgent with these misguided youths, since I would not want it to be thought that there may be blood on my hands because of any punitive action on the part of the forces of law and order." Sometimes, Dr. Ramos's language was not appropriately interpreted by the military commander, in which case the individual concerned would live or perhaps go to prison. In that case, the President would not persist in his criminal intention. However, if the person were murdered, Dr. Ramos would call the top brass to a meeting in his office and severely reprimand them, an investigating committee would be appointed, and tears of emotion would be shed on television. In the end, nothing would be accomplished and later, in secret, through a third party, the perpetrator would be rewarded. It was different in the case of Arturo Gonzalo who, it is well-known, resorted to an obscure writer in New York—whose name appeared as the author—to unburden himself of a text in novel form which laid bare the always impeccable figure of the then President Ramos. This time, he had no compunctions about giving a direct order for his death.

Frank, no longer a focus of attention in the political circles of his country, perhaps sought to regain—and succeeded— his lost notoriety with the publication of his memoirs. Or, perhaps his aim was to pay tribute to two beloved friends who were murdered.

As evening fell on the day that ended the century, Dr. Ramos had performed his customary love ritual with the young girls brought him by General Elermoso, one by one, to the Rear House. He would sit them on his lap, take their hands in his, sniff the perfume in the curves of their neck and, like a blind beggar gauging the value of a coin, he would read their age by running his fingertips over their facial muscles. Then he would get to his feet and improvise verses, press them against his chest to feel the resistance of their breasts, and remain so, in ecstasy, for a long while. Finally, with paternal words, he would hand each a check for 100 pesos, and sweetly send them on their way.

General Elermoso escorted them to the inner sanctum that day as ceremoniously as he did before Dr. Ramos had been removed from power years before, serving him with the same abnegation as on the Thursdays of his endless years in office. The General had no trouble procuring the adolescents of the afternoons, nor the lady of the night, nor the choicest blossom for brightening the Sunday gloom.

On that Sunday morning, Dr. Ramos had gone to the "Palace," taken care of matters pending , issued orders. He returned from there in the afternoon and did not go out again.

"If only every day in the year were Sunday, General," Dr. Ramos sighed. The last of the adolescents had left at six o'clock and at ten Dr. Ramos was still recounting his rosary of anguish.

"You mustn't let that worry you, Your Excellency. As of tomorrow every day will be Sunday. I have transmitted the order." Dr. Ramos smiled.

He had stayed on living in the Rear House, carpeted with cats. The animals took their leisurely breakfast, lunch, and supper naps placidly ensconced on the chairs, the couches, the bookcases, the bed. He would call them, *"Misu, misu, misu,"* and they would come running to him from all sides to climb on his shoulders, his back, and his lap, wrapping around him completely. Not until the President's chuckles of delight had ceased did General Elermoso proceed to dislodge them with his baton. The collies were in the Big House. Like the cats in the Rear House they now constituted a numerous family. They lived under no law, pairing at will and giving birth in the beds of the dead. Only a few of the animals with traceable pedigree had been impregnated within the confines of the Big House. The dogs lived with

The Midget, who continued to dress in doll's clothes, and with the Poster Girl, "Forty more years, dammit!" with Fatty Puchula and with The Warbler, whose *ranchera* ballads could wring tears from a stone, and with others of the old crowd that held forth at the main door. All had moved into the Big House the day after the wake for the last of Dr. Ramos's sisters and now constituted the President's cabinet.

The Poster Girl had had a lot of work that day. After dispatching the President's office work with him, she had gone at one o'clock to Los Guandules, The Swamp, and Blue Tongue to recruit a diplomatic corps in those godforsaken spots who would pay their respects to the President at the celebration of ushering in the New Century. She appeared at seven o'clock with eighteen men, all she needed. They were ordered to strip down in the patio, and she washed them down with a high-pressure hose, strong yellow soap, and stiff bristle brushes after which Fatty Puchula, out of respect for Dr. Ramos's sensitive nose, had them wash once more with scented soap. At nine o'clock they were taken up to the second floor where they were sprayed with French cologne and each one found an assortment of clean clothes in the bulging closets that more or less fit.

At eleven-thirty, General Elermoso, in dress uniform, was helping Dr. Ramos apply his makeup, comb his hair, and straighten the knot of his necktie. Outside a cock crowed.

"He's back," complained Dr. Ramos. "I thought he was gone for good."

"He's been around since yesterday. I heard him crowing at daybreak," replied the General.

"I didn't notice," he answered, rubbing his good ear. "Will the girls be back tonight, General?"

"Yes, Your Excellency, after twelve."

At ten minutes after twelve, General Elermoso led him to the patio, helped him into the limousine, climbed in, drove ahead a few yards and stopped at the "Government Palace."

"The stairs are getting easier all the time, General. Do you know if they have lit the cross at El Faro, yet?"

"Yes, Your Excellency, and Pedrito Guzmán is going to get some fine shots of you."

The bells began to ring, the rockets to explode, and the crowds to shout, drowning out the barking of the collies.

"Hurrah, Your Excellency! The gates of a new century open to you!" calls out the man playing the role of the Ambassador of the Vatican.

"Hurrah, Your Excellency! The Archbishopric has become very small for me, now. There are many more acolytes. Would it be possible for the government to invest a couple of hundred million pesos to enlarge it all the way to the Malecón?" complains a resident of Blue Tongue, dressed as a cardinal.

"Another damn century!" shouts The Poster Girl, decked out in a colonel's uniform.

"Hurrah! Hurrah! Hurrah!"

"Your Excellency, the people wish you to greet them from the balcony," lies General Elermoso in a whisper.

"I'll come out, but first tell me, General, what time will the girls be here?"

"I've already sent for them, Your Excellency. We'll just wait until the guests have left."

"Better get rid of them, then, General."

Fatty Puchula appeared alone at around two o'clock in the morning. She had been unable to find girls. They were busy out on the reefs by the Malecón taking care of the urgent needs of the American tourists. At that hour *Siglo 21* rum had produced its peak effect: drunken crowds climbed up the bell towers to bang out the bronze notes with their own hands. Couples in the public squares, in the streets, on the rooftops, were in sexual frenzy, screwing away to the volcanic rhythms erupting from the domes of the church.

"General, stop the crowing of that cock. It's as though he was right here in this room." Dr. Ramos covered both ears with his hands. "And what is that other noise outside, General," he added.

"Church bells. They'll be ringing all night." he replied.

"No, General, I don't mean the bells. What I am hearing are strange voices, like of the dead. Go out and see if anyone's hiding in the garden. And another thing. While you're there, get rid of that cock. I can't stand him any longer."

The General had gone out to the patio half an hour earlier and Dr. Ramos, very uneasy, began to call him. His nervousness grew when there was no answer and he heard a beating of wings and bloodcurdling screams. Feeling his way to the door, he opened it and called out, "General, General!"

It was the cock that replied. His crowing seemed to be coming, tremendously amplified, from all directions. Dr. Mario Ramos spread out his arms and turned round and round. He was unable to see General Elermoso's inert body stretched out a few yards from his feet. Nor the shades of the dead. There, as in another world, the bronze bells kept tolling, the sound a distant, returning funereal echo. Day dawned with the earliest sunbeams of the Twenty-First Century.